THE ASSASSINATION MACHINE

"Throughout human history the view has always been that key individuals are the shapers of history, that they make the special decisions that shape the pattern of events. Naturally, it has always been assumed that those key people are the leaders, and therefore the assassin's trade—that by removing the key leader, that they could change the flow, divert the stream. But, despite the efforts of assassins, somehow things rarely changed according to these acts.

"This suggest an error in the view, and so we studied it and arrived at this startling idea: that there are key people, but that they never show on the surface, that they are almost never the obvious leaders. Unseen, unknown men and women, unknowingly act out the ritual mythos of an era. There has been no way to get to them or even find them . . .

"This individual has been shaped, inculcated, indoctrinated to this new theory. You may view him as a precision tool to determine the identity of the key figures, and how to remove them. We know for an undeniable fact that whatever he does, it works with a precision beyond our wildest dreams. . . ."

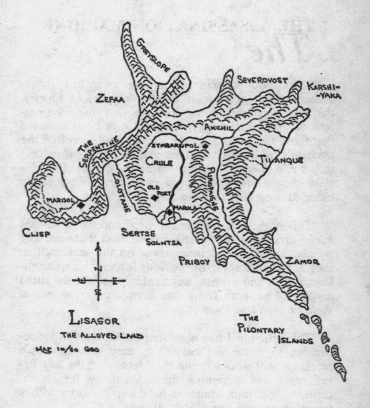

GREYSLOPE

SEVEROVOST

KARSHI
-YAKA

ZEFAA

AKCHIL

THE SERPENTINE

SYMBARUPOL

CRISLE

TILANQUE

PUGOPANZHE

ZOLOTANE

OLD
PORT

MARISOL

MARIBA

CLISP

SERTSE
SOLNTSA

N
W E
S

PRIBOY

ZAMOR

LISAGOR

THE ALLOYED LAND

MAP 10/20 GEO

THE
PILONTARY
ISLANDS

The Morphodite

M. A. Foster

DAW BOOKS, INC.

DONALD A. WOLLHEIM, PUBLISHER

1633 Broadway, New York, NY 10019

PUBLISHED BY
THE NEW AMERICAN LIBRARY
OF CANADA LIMITED

Dedicated to
Judith

FIRST PRINTING, DECEMBER 1981

2 3 4 5 6 7 8 9

DAW TRADEMARK REGISTERED
U.S. PAT. OFF. MARCA
REGISTRADA. HECHO EN U.S.A.

PRINTED IN CANADA
COVER PRINTED IN U.S.A.

~ 1 ~
Evening in Symbarupol

Symbarupol, in Lisagor, on Oerlikon: 4 Chand 22 Pavilon Cycle 7:

Two men at their ease relaxed on the terrace of one of the many bland, pastel buildings which composed the city outline, and observed the fall of night over the subtle outlines of Symbarupol. One was still, and watched the scene to the east without gesture or movement, as if completely at rest. The other, shorter and stouter, fidgeted and moved constantly, sometimes looking about the terrace, sometimes staring at the city as if it contained some vital secret. The taller and quieter of the two was silver-haired and distinguished in appearance, with long, thoughtful features which under certain circumstances might be called mournful or dolorous; the other was florid, excitable, and nervous, a worrier.

The taller man, obviously the senior of the two, seated himself in a chair and continued to muse over the soft outlines of the city, with its ranks of superimposed buildings—offices, factories, dormitories, habitats, all made in the same basic box shape, unadorned by slogans or signs or extraneous stylistic detailing. He liked it. His name was Luto Pternam, and he was the senior member of an organization which provided the guardians of public order with their raw material, and in addition disposed of the recalcitrant.

His associate was known as Elegro Avaria, and he was Pternam's confidant, executive secretary, henchman, and general man Friday. Avaria was nervous because he was expecting visitors, and he looked out over the evening-dimming cityscape as if he expected them to materialize at any moment.

Pternam said, almost idly, "Surely you don't expect them so soon, or that they'd walk right up the road as if they worked here?"

Avaria scratched his head, looked again, and shook his

head. "No. For a fact, if they come tonight, it'll be late. Still . . ."

"You're sure about the date?"

"As sure as anyone could be, dealing with people like those. I spoke with their contact-man, Thersito Burya, when the last arrangements were made. He was definite: the Triumvirate was interested in our proposal and would come in person to investigate. Today, on this very date."

Pternam mused, "Odd they wouldn't send Burya. The files suggest that he does all their contact work. Or perhaps that other fellow, Mostro Ahaltsykh."

Avaria corrected his chief respectfully, "Personally, I did not expect Ahaltsykh. What he seems to do is more in the enforcement line: muscle, you know."

Pternam answered equably, "I suppose you are right; were I to judge this, I would not wish to agree to anything like this on the judgment of anyone less than you or I, and would probably think long on a recommendation by you alone."

Avaria agreed. "Rightly so."

Pternam continued, "Still, all three? That's dangerous work, exposing the three most important heads of an underground that isn't supposed to exist, all at once, in the same place. Surely they suspect we might have treachery in mind."

"Thersito Burya suggested that our proposal was important enough to be worth the risk. They have a replacement Triumvirate in the wings, should we prove false."

Pternam thought for a moment, and then said, "Yes, important. I imagine it would be: we offered them something from the very bowels of our organization—a perfect assassin, one that can find the target, select the method, execute the assignment, and then vanish by changing its identity. They have revolutionary zeal, but they can't produce that."

Avaria nodded briskly. "Right! And when they have committed to the thing that we will give them, and he makes his stroke, which you and I know to be a sham, they'll all pop out of the woodwork, and we'll have them all, the Changemonger scum, and we. . . ."

Pternam completed the sentence, ". . . will be rewarded for the fine work we've done; I will move to the Central Group, and you will take my place here."

Avaria added, "Might put both of us in it."

Pternam smiled into the dim, soft evening light. "They might, at that. Yes, a possibility, Elegro."

The light was almost gone. Avaria looked about nervously and said, "It is about time I set out to meet them."

Pternam nodded. "Go ahead, then. We will wait for you here. Everything is ready for them."

"Including the one we've prepared?"

"Yes. Tiresio is ready. It is all ready. The moment of truth is here."

Avaria turned to go. "I suppose you know it will be late."

"How could it be otherwise? Go on—it will work out right."

Avaria nodded and set out across the terrace resolutely, turning into an alcove and disappearing.

For a long time Luto Pternam sat and looked out over the city in its evening light—surely something worth striving for. Symbarupol, a city of blocky plain buildings by day, became magic in the light of evening. What seemed by day to be impersonal and abstract became then something soft and lovely beyond words, its colors cyan, magenta, old rose, as the star Gysa sank into the Blue Ocean far to the west, beyond Clisp.

For all his relaxed manner, he felt inside himself a furious excitement building, the culmination of years of effort. The failures they had had, the making up of a suitable vehicle, even after the parts of the theory had been tested. And then, with the one specimen they had succeeded with, the long and difficult training, which had been as painful for the instructors as it had been for the trainee . . . All the arts of the assassin, and at the end of it, the loose control they had over it. And the terrifying power of Change the creature had. And the last, convincing it that what he knew to be a crackpot theory was in fact a lost science, that only he, Tiresio, could rediscover. . . . And they gave him some concepts, and turned him loose, and after a time he had said, "I can do it." Nonsense, of course, but it was of course important that Tiresio believe that he could do it.

No, this was not a trap for that pitiful Triumvirate: Merigo Lozny, Pericleo Yadom, Porfirio Charodei. Oh, no. Pternam reflected that by the time this had run its course, they would have them all, even to the farthest corners of Lisagor, the Alloyed Land.

Oerlikon was a planet with a singular history, quite unlike any other's: it had been discovered by accident, as a ship had dropped out of transitspace for minor repairs in the midst of

7

a desolate region, which, while not as empty as the famous Purlimore Canyon, or the equally well-known B'tween-The-Arms, was indeed devoid of notable features. There, to their astonishment, the crew saw displayed on their instruments a single dwarf star, one planet, and an irregular collection of asteroids and planetesimals. The star, a yellow-orange body, appeared to be exceptionally stable, and the single planet gave all the indications of being habitable. There were no nearby bright stars, and all the known O and B giants were far, far away. The region was populated solely by a thin and scattered collection of G, K and or main-sequence stars, and a few white dwarfs.

While the ship was making repairs, the crew closed on the isolated little system and took a closer look. The star was smaller than the usual for a habitable system, the single planet orbited at roughly the orbital distance of Venus from Sol. The star they named Gysa, and dutifully noted its position and coordinates. The planet they named, with a small ceremony, Oerlikon. Sometime afterwards, when someone attempted to track down the source of the names, they found that the discovering ship, the Y-42, was a small Longline ship with an under-strength crew, and that apparently "Gysa" had been a legend printed on a shirt belonging to one of the crew, supposedly a sports association somewhere, and that "Oerlikon" had been the brand name of an inexpensive pocket tape machine used to reproduce the popular music of the day. They could recall no other names they had wished to use. And of such incidents are names fixed forever to pieces of real estate such as float about tenantless.

A gig from the Y-42 landed, and reported that all was well, if a bit bland. The view of the sky was uninspiring and uninteresting: the atmosphere was thick and hazy, and at night what stars could be seen arranged themselves into random patterns which suggested nothing whatsoever even to the most imaginative.

Oerlikon was moonless, and rotated slowly with a small axial tilt, so that the effect of the seasons was small. Moreover, its orbit about Gysa was astonishingly low in eccentricity. It turned out to have the lowest orbital eccentricity ever recorded for a habitable planet. The day was long, about thirty standard hours. It was also a watery world, with deep, abysmal ocean basins. The landing party observed only two continent-sized masses, one Asia-sized, an irregular oval high up in the subarctic, and a smaller, kite-shaped mass around the curve of the planet to the west, and south, partly temperate, partly tropical. A loose association of islands arcing south from the smaller continent across the equator completed what could be seen of land masses.

The larger continent they humorously named Tartary, but they found little on it of interest. Glaciation, geologically recent, had polished it flat, and crustal measurements indicated that it was drifting slowly south. For now, and the next million years, it would be cold and barren and cruel.

The smaller continent was much more interesting. The main part of it was shaped rather like a kite in flight. It had low mountains, rivers, and a complete, if rather limited, flora and fauna. The east, north, and western shores were mountainous, although none rose to great heights. In the west, the chains formed an outline of a discus thrower, or javelin hurler, while the eastern ranges formed a concave curve open to the east and trailing off in the islands of the south. An interior range, a spur of the eastern range, enclosed a broad valley that connected with the interior in the north. The rest of the interior was a vast grassy plain. And far in the west, as if hanging off the bent leg of the javelin thrower, a small subcontinent was attached, joined to the mainland by a narrow mountainous isthmus. It seemed pleasant and habitable, and was so reported when the Logline freighter Y-42 reached settled regions again.

As always the case with a new planet, at first the explorers and settlers came, although Oerlikon attracted no great numbers owing to its isolation and the reluctance of star-captains to make planetfall at such an out-of-the-way place. Once there, these early immigrants were able to see for themselves that there were normal quantities of metals, a biosphere of no great novelty, although some of the forms were odd, and the oceans well-stocked. The large continent, Tartary, was severe in climate and sparse in vegetation, and only the hardiest souls went there, prospectors and herdsmen, hermits and misanthropes, where they built sod huts on the treeless steppes, or erected frowning castles of the native shield granite, and remained to brood under the iron-gray skies.

Others, more sociable, moved on to the smaller continent, and settled places soon appeared, including a fishing and trading center which grew in the delta of the great river of the interior, and soon became a sprawling, disorderly city, which the locals called Marula, from one of the notable early explorers, Esteban Marula. Oerlikon had a city, and to the northwest of Marula, between the marshy land of the delta and the bones of the hills, even a spaceport of sorts.

But Oerlikon was not popular, and the immigrants were few, a mere trickle. The land available was not great, the climate bland, in short it was a world too much like the ones they left behind. For a fact, Oerlikon would have remained a bare, underpopulated world, had it not been for a certain sect hearing of it, and deciding that this empty little world and its isolation suited their desires exactly. These were the peoples who later became known as "The Changeless."

Who were The Changeless? They gave allegiance to no flag, for they came from every sort of state, principality, crank empire, and gimcrack commonwealth and idealistic union. Nor were they of a single race: every color, hue, and possible physiognomy was represented. Their tongues were Babel, and their home cultures as diverse as fish in the sea. But for all their disunity, they all held one thing in common with a belief that would not die, that the rate of change that was the pace of Time had run out of control, and they knew the present was inferior to the past, and growing more so daily, and they wanted no part of a future they neither understood, liked, nor profited by. And when they heard of Oerlikon, they knew they had found El Dorado, an obscure planet in an obscure region of space, where they could go and let Time pass them by forever.

And so they came, settled, and many survived; Oerlikon was neither rigorous nor poisonous within the smaller continent, nor on the tropical islands off the southeast cape, which they called the Pilontary Islands. And little by little, they gathered strength, were soon a majority, and the ships began to call less often, and then rarely, and soon not at all, save an occasional tramp trader from the remotest regions. No one went to Oerlikon. And no one left.

In a sense heavy with irony, which The Changeless neither understood nor appreciated, it was only with the arrival of the Changeless that history can be said to begin on Oerlikon. For, before the arrival of The Changeless, the smaller continent had only known isolated settlements, hunters and prospectors, and leagues of wild lands. But the newcomers, full of boundless zeal, quickly established growing and highly organized enclaves, and slowly excluded the old settlers, who either went further into the wild, or began drifting toward the subcontinent far to the west, or to Marula.

They ignored the wilds of Tartary as too stern a land, but moved in force onto the smaller continent and the Pilontary Islands. Their growing enclaves became autonomous regions, and developed names.

Now for some time, the smaller continent had been known as Karshiyaka, which meant, more or less, in Old Turkish, The Opposite Shore. But early on, The Changeless invented their own language to make sense among themselves, and they preferred their own names, some in echoing evocations of places they had once been to, and some in the harsh sounds of the new way of speaking.

North of the mountains (that formed the arms of the javelin thrower), the lands enclosed by spur ranges became Grayslope, rugged slopes and defiles covered with silvergrass falling to the gray turbulence of the polar seas. East of the thrower's left arm, there was a still sterner land that they called Severovost. In the west, facing the blue waters of evening, along the right arm and down the trunk was the land Zefaa, from its winds; and from the place where the ranges divided, and formed the legs of the thrower, the right leg became The Serpentine, a narrow isthmus connecting the continent with a smaller land somewhat farther west, called Clisp.

Between the legs was Zolotane, the land of gold, an arid country. The Delta became Sertsa Solntsa, the "Heart of the Sun," and the inside of the long point to the southeast became Priboy—"The Surf." The rest of the peninsula was Zamor, and all the east coast was Tilanque, save a tiny enclave in the northeast, which retained the old name of Karshiyaka for itself.

And in the interior there were three lands. The strip between the parallel ranges, the hidden land, was Puropaigne. Across the north along the south slopes of the mountains was Akchil, the Dales. And all the rest, so goes the saying, was Crule The Swale.

Of large cities there were only three: Marula, renamed Marulupol; Symbar, renamed Symbarupol, between Puropaigne and The Swale; and in Clisp, Marisol.

For a time, each area retained some identity, but a powerful process was at work among the stern and relentless Changeless; for one of their main drives was naturally toward orthodoxy and uniformity, and so a gradual pressure upon

11

the old settlers began, and increased, and the more sensitive to it began moving away, drifting out of the old lands and into fringe areas: Clisp, in the far west, arid and mountainous. The tropical Pilontary Islands, where life was too easy to worry about doctrine. And Marula, which had always been a gathering-place for the riffraff of all Karshiyaka. A few hardy souls set up exile regimes in Tartary.

The impetus for unification emerged from the center—The Swale and Puropaigne, joined shortly by the men of Akchil. Once these areas were cleared, things moved swiftly, and with a small action that wasn't a war, and wasn't a coup, but was something of both and of neither, and which the Changeless called "The Rectification," all Karshiyaka, save only Clisp, became one land, a nation its inhabitants named Lisagor— The Alloyed Land. Then, too, was when they renamed Tartary Makhagor—The Lawless Land. Clisp, free and full of ferment, remained independent for almost two cycles* longer, until it, too, fell, and was renamed, with malice aforethought, Vredamgor—The Conquered Land.

With vast relief, Anibal Glist departed the communal mess and made his way down the winding exterior stairs to the Level, which functioned more or less as the Lisagorian equivalent of a street. Glist stepped off the last of the narrow, whitewashed masonry stairs into the cool darkness of the street, and caught himself reflecting that now he only rarely thought in terms of "equivalents." He had been on Oerlikon for a long time, and was well on the way to becoming native in his patterns of habit and thought. His retirement would be not far off, and more than once he had considered taking his retirement here. Staying. Not entirely impossible. Novel, perhaps, but not impossible. He had grown to like it, this impossible planet and this even more improbable country which dominated it, Lisagor.

The one custom he found hardest to get used to were the communal meals, served to the tune of popular songs, sung

---

* Cycles: Time on Oerlikon was computed on an arbitrary calendar which used the ancient Mayan computation as a model. The "Years" thus computed had no relationship with the orbital period of Oerlikon or any other known planet, but instead were an elegant construction of four Prime Factors, twenty-three, eleven, thirteen, and thirty-one, which provided, variously, a Ritual year of 253 days, and a Great Year of 403 days, which cycled together to produce a Cycle of 101,959 days —253 Great Years. Time was counted from the day when Lisagor was proclaimed. The present, within this story-frame, is within the seventh Cycle.

badly out of key and time, but sung together nonetheless. The food, at least, was good. Next, of course, he would return to his cell, essentially an apartment built on an artificial hill, reached by means of the winding stairs. Lisak towns were clusters of these hills, connected by narrow streets made as level as possible without regard to the curves this might produce. How did one get from one part of town to another? Afoot, or on ludicrous variations of bicycles called velocipedes, in which the rider sat on a triangular truss framework between the wheels, low to the ground, and pedalled with the legs held horizontally out in front. Odd, and with little outrigger wheels to help get started, which were retracted once balance was attained, but fast and little work. They were expensive, though, and distinctly a luxury item.

At the velocipede rack, while unentangling his own vehicle, Glist happened to find himself next to a young woman engaged in a similar task. Glist knew her, of course—she was one of his student observers, by name Aril Procand. But as far as the Lisaks about him might know, she was only someone who had been at this particular mess hall, and by chance was near him at the velocipede rack.

Glist spoke casually: "A fine speech tonight by Primitivo Mercador, the First Synodic for Trade and Equity; almost as good as if the Prime Synodic, Simonpetrino Monclova himself, had been with us."

The young woman disengaged her velocipede and nodded politely, adding, "Monclova is more restrained, but of course sees further. Still, it is an honor to have Mercador." Her motions with the velocipede brought her fractionally closer to Glist, and she said quickly, in a much quieter tone, "Enthone Sheptun tells me he has an item for you which is most urgent. He will follow you, and meet you along your way to your cell, on the Level."

Glist nodded, and said no more. He did not have direct relations with Aril Procand, a fact which disappointed him as he risked an appreciative glance at the young woman's slender figure, and curly brown-gold hair. A shame. Glist evaluated her reports, of course, and knew her to be a fine young operative, a keen observer of events on this peculiar planet. Oh well, he thought ruefully, someone younger will doubtless be having a covert affair with her—most likely Sheptun, a romantic fool. Glist continued readying his velocipede for riding, as Aril mounted hers with youthful nonchalance and sped away into the night, the soft night of Symbarupol.

The news set something uneasy stirring in Glist; Sheptun was one of his more deeply buried operatives, not a mere observer, like Procand, and also unlike her, not on student-probationary status. Sheptun also reported much, as part of his duties here, and the reports were always quite good. If he continued, there was no doubt he'd have Discretionary Authority before long. Not his successor, of course: that was already arranged, and it would be Cesar Kham, who was now working on something in Marisol, in Clisp. Vredamgor, he corrected himself.

Glist settled into the machine, prepared himself, and set off onto the Level, retracting his outriggers and turning on the lamps, working up through the gears into a comfortable pace. Still, he wondered what Sheptun could have on his mind. Although contact of any sort was discouraged among the members, other than through the channels already established, it was not prohibited, provided certain assumptions were always borne in mind, the most important being that the Lisaks must not, under any circumstances, learn that there was in their midst a sizable body of off-planet visitors engaged in studying and manipulating their odd, retrogressive society.

He had not proceeded far along the Level, when, in the light evening traffic, another velocipede joined up with him and proceeded alongside in formation. Glist recognized Enthone Sheptun immediately, and followed him without comment, when Sheptun pedalled ahead, and turned into a narrower side-level which ended in a teahouse and a reside-hill across from a Dragon Field.* Sheptun stopped, extended the outriggers on his machine, and went into the teahouse, and Glist, slightly behind, did the same, as if he had happened to be going that way.

Inside the teahouse, a bluish haze in the air from the charcoal heaters and the water pipes which the patrons enjoyed blurred the atmosphere, and Glist had to squint to find Sheptun. Also, the place was crowded; a Dragon game must have recently broken up. By luck, Sheptun had found a table with two empty seats, in a far corner, and the constant hubbub and drone of conversation would bury their conversation. Glist made his way across the floor to the corner.

The Waiter brought tea, the commonplace Mixture #79, without comment, and left them, returning to the kitchen.

* Dragon: the sole public physical sport played in Lisagor and Lisak-dominated areas.

Glist looked about, a little nervously, and said, in a low voice which he hoped would not carry far, "Student Procand alerted me, and so I was awaiting contact. This doubtless will refer to something which could not be forwarded through the usual channels?"

Sheptun, an alert young man of some years, blinked rapidly and answered. "Much remains to be said through the normal reports, but I felt you needed to be alerted. I have just uncovered something you need to know, perhaps even advise the Policy Group about."

"Go on—expound at will, although you may not mention that group again in here. You are reckless."

"You will understand." Sheptun spoke without heat, calmly. Then, "For the last few days, I have been engaged in verifying a very strange tale: to the point, there is a weapon of some sort about to be released which will change everything here."

Glist carefully controlled his body movements, and his expressions. He looked musingly at the teacup and said, tonelessly, "What is the nature of this alleged weapon, and who is intended to use it?"

Sheptun adopted the same tonelessness, and the same blank expression, and said, "The nature of it remains unknown."

"You could not find out what?"

"The sources I tap do not know themselves. As to who will use it—presumably the Heraclitan Society."

"The so-called Underground, that favors normalization of the way of life here?"

"The same. Although there is inexactitude there, too."

"Inexactitude? In what way? Do they intend to use it, or do they support someone who will use it in their stead?"

"This may be hard to believe, but it's more as if it's something uncontrollable will be released, and they will be the prime beneficiaries of it. I cannot find its source."

"Or what it is. A Bomb? A Revolutionary Tract? That's difficult to imagine, for there is no widespread dissatisfaction for that to trigger."

"Just so are my conclusions; nevertheless, all my sources were certain, and very apprehensive. I tested them, all unaware on their part, and by Scandberg's Second Speech Reduction, they believe in it."

"But you have been unable to determine what it is . . ."

"As I said, they don't have any idea. But whatever it is, it

15

is coming to realization fast. That they know. And what they call it is significant, too."

"What's that?"

"The call it, 'The Angel of Death'."

Glist finished his tea and made ready to leave. "I fail to become alarmed. I do not doubt your conviction, but we need more hard data. More facts. You understand I can't act on night-fogs like this."

"Your pardon, Ser Glist, but my intention was not to request action, but to bring a matter to your attention, so that when the facts come, as I am certain they will, you can proceed in the best manner."

Glist nodded, agreeably. "Just so . . . I will be on the lookout for this, although I have seen nothing to date . . ."

"Perhaps you can obtain verification by contacting . . . you know . . . that deep-sensor."

Glist continued to look ahead, but he said, in a low tone, "That is something else that should not be spoken of."

"Can you?"

"It is not wise. That is perilous, that one. I would not now risk it upon no more than I have."

Sheptun said, "I feel you will hear from him soon. There is supposed to be something afoot that he will have high probability of having access to."

Glist stood up and prepared to leave. "Perhaps. I trust when he does, he will have occasion to be more specific."

Sheptun looked down, feeling a sly reprimand, and said, "You of all people should understand field conditions here, and know how difficult it is to obtain hard data."

"I understand very well how things are. But nonetheless, however they disguise it, at the core of every functioning society there is a social entity which knows and acts upon the facts. Even here. If a thing has a real existence, we can derive its nature by the traces and echoes it leaves, most especially if in use or prepatory to use. The motion of a thing is its reality, and the motion is what leaves the traces. Probe deeper."

"That in itself is becoming difficult."

"Remember the Credo of the Institute: *There is no such thing as a problem: there are many opportunities for outstanding solutions.* Your learning of these distinctions, these subtleties, will certainly result in advancement; otherwise . . ." Glist did not have to continue the threat. At best, he could have Sheptun removed from Oerlikon, and there were several other options he could use. He could, if circumstances required it, have Sheptun killed and disposed of, to protect the integrity of the net. Glist had done this before, and did not have pangs of conscience over it, then or now. It was a matter of protecting one's livelihood, and the way of life of uncounted numbers involved in the Watch of Oerlikon, by the Institute of Man, on Heliarcos.

Then he left the teahouse, and did not spend much more thought on the matter. Except much later, when he was climbing the stairs to his cell, negotiating the eccentric curves and twists and landings, that something floated back, of the conversation he had had with Sheptun. Odd: but Sheptun had said they had called it "The Angel of Death." Indeed, an odd name for a weapon. Still, he doubted if it would come to much. Because since the Lisaks were so much against change, they were no great threat in the technological sense, and so it was unlikely they could produce much of a secret weapon that would make any difference. These things always kept coming up, these superstitions, in many societies, but there was nothing like reality to dispel the shadows.

~ 2 ~

Midnight in the Mask Factory

Symbarupol: 23 Klekesh 5 Irgi Seventh Cycle:

In the conventions of the Mayan-like calendar which measured time on Oerlikon, the next day commenced at sundown, at precisely the moment of absolute darkness. And so, though Luto Pternam had waited only a short time for the return of his henchman, the counters in the Horologium had already changed over to the symbols for the next day.

The organization over which Pternam presided had an official title: The Permutorium. Its name, however, was less meaningful than what it actually did, which was dire enough. The Permutorium took in persons adjudged to be of either criminal or changist tendency, the distinction in Lisak custom being slight, and transformed them, by a number of techniques, into units of an army which would always be utterly trustworthy because all its soldiers had been totally conditioned to unquestioning obedience. Naturally, there was a tradeoff: their reactions were relatively slow, and the "units" retained little or no initiative, but neither did they flinch from pain, nor from unpleasant orders.

A considerable part of the energy expended within this department was devoted to a continuing program of research and development, which could in loose terms be considered quasi-medical, involving as it did the specifications of the human body and all its subsystems. Much had been done, which had borne fruit in other areas, but most in the area of what might be called the techniques of psychological control of a population.

Persons who were processed in this facility might reappear, but never in the lineaments of their old forms. Part of the program involved manipulation of the hormone systems, so that physiognomy aligned with function. This change was the reason why the office had a jargon name in the streets, which was never pronounced openly: "The Mask Factory."

Just so, it had been during the course of these researches

18

that Pternam and Avaria had happened, during review of the reports of routine experiments, to suspect a particular line of work, which no one had followed up. This they did, at first only curious, but later realizing what a weapon the line might lead them to. And so it was that a certain person had come into existence, under the long tutelage of Pternam, and a special cadre of assistants, carefully primed on half-truths and threats, a person who, in the terms usually referenced in Lisagor, literally did not exist. But in other terms, exist he did. And, as Pternam reflected on his creation, it was with a certain baleful purpose.

Pternam, feeling a chill in the night air, had returned to the inside of the residence, and was there now speaking with Orfeo Palastrine, his chief guard over the subject, over an antique communicator set into an alcove in the plain white-washed walls.

"Palastrine? Yes. Pternam here. How goes it with Rael?"

"Normal. He's up and about, working at his studies, but not at a real furious pace. Took a short nap after supper, he did. A fat job, may I say so."

"You wouldn't want it if you knew some of the things he'll have to do. This one pays his dues afterwards, instead of the usual case before." Then he inquired, "Is the sexual orientation still holding? No evidence of overlay?"

"None that we can see . . . He asked for a woman last night, and so we took a chit down to the local happy-house, and got him one, with whom he was reported to disport himself in the usual manner."

"Do they report anything?"

"This last one was debriefed without anything being noted. As a fact, if anything is out of the ordinary . . ."

"Yes?"

"Well, it's not so odd. They all say they would rather come here for this service than take their chances. They say . . . well, he's kind, and considerate, and, ah, how do they say it . . . 'shows them a good time.' Funny to hear that from whores."

"And no trace of overlay from another personality."

"Not that we can observe. Straight as a string is old Rael; he just addresses himself to one of those double-breasted mattress-thrashers and goes straight on."

"Naturally these are still being recorded."

"Of course. I view them personally."

19

"See anything?"

"Nothing outstanding. Standard male responses. No problems. I might say his frequency seems a little low, and he seems to want to keep them over the period allowed."

"You don't let him have them?"

"No. Straight by the book, Director. We signal when time's up, and he gives them up without a fuss."

"Good. You know what your instructions are in case he appears to have gained control over one of those women?"

"Yes, exactly. We flood the chamber with monoxide gas, and then incinerate what is left with oxy-acetylene. I know the drill: we check the reserve gas cylinders daily."

"I have some news . . . there may be some visitors tonight down there. No interference, no interruption. Avaria and I will be in there with them, and him."

"Begging your pardon, but . . ."

"I know the danger. The rules are still in force. Rael is supremely dangerous and must not be allowed to leave the chambers before his time. However, if all goes well, after this visit, he may be released in the future; possibly tonight, possibly much later. The use for which he has been trained may be at hand."

"Do you intend to pattern another one like this?"

"Decision has not yet been made. We lean toward not doing it again."

"Understandable. It is a fearsome creature, so the manual alleges."

"Rightly so. This is not something one would do casually . . . we can use the facilities for other purposes, and your people will of course be rewarded for this difficult service— just what they deserve."

"Ah, now, Director, that's fine to hear that. You know, some of the lads have chafed a bit at the secrecy and the isolation. Not the usual sort of duty."

"You still have security over your force?"

"Exactly. Positive control, all the way. No leaks. I know that."

"Good. We're depending on you. I'll call down later."

"We'll be here."

Pternam replaced the receiver in its receptacle and turned away with no particular destination in mind. He stopped and practiced an exercise he had often used, that of Confronting the Hidden Antagonist: he understood thereby that his anxiety was commonplace and related solely to waiting for his

20

visitors. Would Avaria find them? Would they come with him? More importantly, would they accept what was being offered here, something of high order indeed? Yes. That was the real issue, the one that would be resolved only as things developed out of the flux.

The doorward, a lobo especially trained for the post, by name Tyrono Ektal now, padded softly up the stairs from the lower level, taking, to a person with normal reactions, an excessively long time to assure himself that Pternam was in the room. Finally he said, in a measured, carefully paced monotone, "Ser Pternam, the respectable Avaria approaches through the outer barrier in company with three persons whose aspect is not known to me."

Pternam said, equally carefully, "All are expected. You may return to your cells and sleep. Your duty has been done this day. Go in peace."

Ektal nodded solemnly and turned and left. As he left the dim room, a rustle at the lower doorway indicated the approach of Avaria and three others. That would be them, doubtless. He faced away from the landing.

When he turned about again, there they were. Elegro, of course. And with him . . . Pternam knew the descriptions well enough. It was the three he wanted.

Avaria said, to the three, "We are secure here, throughout the Residence. You may speak as you will." As an afterthought he added, "Absolutely. We would not have anyone hear what we ourselves might say here."

One said, in a low, growling mutter, "Absolute control over a space? Unheard-of, it is. What would Monclova say? Or Femisticleo Chugun, our well-loved Synodic of Law and Order? This makes for islands of individuality, as they say."

Pternam recognized the speaker as Merigo Lozny: low of brow, head densely furred with bristly, unruly hair the color of cast iron. The nose and chin, however, were sharp, and the eyes glittered and flashed like cursed jewels. The torso was barrellike, and the legs short and bowed. He looked grotesque, and stupid as well, but Pternam knew very well that Lozny was exceptionally smart, and could be extremely difficult, even among his fellows.

There was a tall, rather athletic man with them. That would be Pericleo Yadom, the ostensible public figure, the front man, the one who spoke for those who manipulated the strings offstage. Were it not for the intense strain lines on his face, he could have been called handsome, and certainly once

21

was. The other, an older man would be Porfirio Charodei; if Lozny was the executive officer of the Underground, and Yadom the front man, then Charodei would fill the position of ideologue. That one had somewhat of the air and manner of a professor, off on an excursion outside his own proper field. But here, Pternam was not fooled, either: he knew from many reports that of all of them, Charodei was by far the most alert and the most dangerous. Yadom would be easy. Lozny would be won over by a logical argument that moved a little too fast for him. But Charodei would be the key to it. Pternam expected the real objection to come from that way.

Avaria said, conversationally, "We are late. Our contact point was to be a Dragon-Field, and of course, we had to mix it up a little."

Pternam said, "I am surprised no one accosted you. These visitors are not without enemies."

Yadom said, "It was arranged. Most of those present were our people, mixed with a few genuines."

Pternam thought, to himself, *So they used a Dragon-Field as cover, did they? That damned anarchic game. That would be another hiding place they'd shut off for good after they'd flushed all the insects out.*

They did not make polite introductions, for they were known to each other. But Lozny said, "You know what we are. My question is, 'What are you, that we should come here?' "

Pternam answered, as if feeling his way along the lines of an ancient ritual, "I am the alchemist who found the perfect solvent, and now lacks the proper container for this ferocious substance which attacks everything. I have brought the Angel of Death to Paradise Unending."

Lozny said, "It may be contained by Will and Idea. We have those."

Charodei added, "This thing we have heard distant rumors of: may it be seen?"

Pternam said, "There is no reason to wait. Come with me." And without looking to see if they were following, he turned and set off through the halls and corridors of the Residence, eventually leading them downwards, via stairwells of narrow aspect and precipitous turns, to a much lower level.

Yadom remarked, "You bury it deep; tell me, why would your organization offer the gift of a perfect assassin to those whom you know will use it without restraint?"

Pternam, leading the way, said back over his shoulder,

"Avaria and I have seen what must be, for the greatest good of the greatest numbers. Of the world—this world. We have lived in a dream far too long."

"But you would not use it yourself . . . ?"

"By giving it to you, I do use it. I place it where it will do the most good. So that you know it. But you will see; there is much we have to say here which will clarify things."

Pternam had conducted them deep under the Residence, and now they were at one of the lowest levels, in a dim landing. Before them was the confinement facility, a house within a house, so to speak. It was not crude, or hastily constructed. Here, everything was made and finished as well as the rest of the Residence. After they had all collected, he led them into a small antechamber, facing a large window of one-way glass. The view inside was of a large room, furnished for many activities—work, rest, relaxation. It was a cage, but it did not look like one. And inside the room, they could see a man, or what appeared to be a man, seemingly working at a desk, as if performing some study, occasionally writing short notes, or formulas in a commonplace notebook. This was the Morphodite.

Pternam stood back from the window and let them look, but he really didn't know what they had expected to see. Perhaps some scowling and grimacing savage, more brutish than the wildest Makhak? Or, a golden god-man, wearing a cape and striding back and forth like some frenzied orator? The Morphodite was certainly none of these; as a fact, he seemed to be so ordinary that the sight was disappointing. What they did see through the window appeared to be a mature man, no longer young, slightly worn around the edges, but above average height and with a slim frame that argued agility and self-discipline. His face was so ordinary it was difficult to remember it. He had lank dark hair, loose skin of a sallow-olive color. Except for the interest he showed in his work, he could easily have been one of the lobotomized trusties one often observed in the simple menial positions which were too easy for the labor pool.

After a moment, Lozny asked, "Can it hear us?"

Pternam answered, "No. Nor can he see who is here. But I may add that we have trained him to be extremely sensitive, and sometimes he is aware of observation . . . As in many cases of this sort, where one reaches into the unknown with both hands, the subject seems to be a bit more than planned."

As if to underline Pternam's comments, the figure at the desk gave a quick, flickering glance at the window, almost too fast to be seen, a mere motion of the eyes, and then returned to his studies, turning slightly more away from the window, as if desirous of a deeper concentration. The three visitors glanced uneasily at one another: the glance had held an instant of direst malevolence, of a glittering regard which reduced them all to something considerably less than human.

Lozny asked, "What is he doing in there now?"

Avaria volunteered, "Continuing to refine his main discipline, adding depth to the field we set him upon to study."

Lozny continued, "Which is? We have little enough time for dilettante intellectuals, as you may well know."

Pternam explained, not apologetically, but slightly sternly, "This is no idler, but an artisan, a craftsman, of a most subtle art. Here I must make my first exposition; you may have heard something of this, but only a little, for we could not let much of it out."

Charodei said, "Continue."

"Very well: throughout human history, or as much of it as we can reach here through the archives, the view has always been that key individuals are the shapers of history, that they hold a society together, make the special decisions that shape the pattern of events. Naturally, it has always been assumed that those key people are the leaders, and therefore the assassin's trade—that by removing the key leader, they could change the flow, divert the stream. But despite this belief, and the efforts of assassins, somehow things rarely changed according to those acts . . . in fact, a sober examination will reveal that assassins rarely have a better rate of success than ordinary murderers in changing societies—ordinary crime. This suggests an error in the view, and so we studied it, and arrived at this startling idea: that there are key people, but that they never show on the surface, that they are almost never the obvious leaders. Unseen, unknown men and women, who unknowingly acted out the ritual mythos of an era."

Lozny had been growing restive, and now he blurted out, "Nonsense! The masses make history! Currents move in the people, and those currents shape the destiny of the leaders, who are called into being by these currents—and dismissed by them as well."

"No. The absolute key parts, the balance-points, are hidden within the organism, within the machinery. There has been no way to get to them, or even find them. It is as if the social organism, the machine, is deliberately designed, to avoid tampering. But. Ah, yes, but. This individual has been shaped, inculcated, indoctrinated to this new theory. He has followed the initial idea out, and found the ways to make it work: you may view this as a precision tool to determine the identity of the key figures, and how to remove them, using the method calculated to be of maximum effectiveness. I will not enumerate all the forms of training he has had. I will say that he had to take what was a wild idea and carry it far beyond the bounds of what we thought we knew, what we suspected. This was self-training. He works at it yet. He is so far beyond us in this area that I find his explanations totally incomprehensible. So do the rest of us, who have been involved with training him. But hear me: we know for an undeniable fact that whatever he does, it works with a precision beyond our wildest dreams, and he does as he says he will do. He is absolutely dependable."

Charodei said, "You have tested him?"

"You may recall an incident a while back . . . in Vredam. There was a spectacular murder, I believe, which caused the surfacing and dissolution of a peculiar organization known as the Acmeists . . . That is a sample."

Yadom whispered, "The Acmeists were not of us, but they were valuable allies. That event evoked much distress."

Pternam stood his ground. Now was no time for apologies. "We could not risk using the weapon untested. And most certainly we would not have offered it to you."

Lozny snorted, "Hmf. Clispic scumbags, one and all. We are better purged of such trash. Pternam here, did us a favor. We would have made their eyes water ourselves, after we'd got the mileage out of them."

Charodei thought for a moment, and said, "I agree in part with Merigo, although I would not say it so definitively." And to Pternam he said, "How did you know to limit the test . . . or keep the results confined?"

"Those were the instructions we gave to the weapon."

Yadom said, "All right. So much is true. Still, it was a dangerous game that was played there. Pternam, if he's that good, why wouldn't you just use him yourself . . . you could even turn him loose on us!" Yadom already knew that Pternam wouldn't, because he hadn't. But the question was to uncover why.

Pternam answered, "True. We could do just that. But some

of us wish change, too, and if we turned him loose on you, then there would be no opposition at all worthy of the name. No. But more importantly, I have no vision of the world I would build, and I am not experienced in guiding others in such tasks. Tear down? Yes, we would help there, but no one has much of an idea for rebuilding. You have this, and have for a long time. There: I speak directly."

Lozny said, quietly, "So you offer him to us, because you know we'll use him. And we would, if he's half what you say he is. I understand. You came late to the truth. And you must know that there will be little use for an organization such as this, afterwards . . ."

Yadom said, "You must have used him to foresee things we cannot. If you are as high in the counsels of the State as we think you are, then you must know our fortunes have been poor the last few years, great and small."

Pternam said, "It is because of some of his insights that we conceived the idea to present him to you in the first place."

Charodei said, "In other words, you foresee through his program that whatever our present fortunes are, we have something like time on our side, and you want to make sure you are supporting the winning side."

"Not entirely. There is an element of chance here, and of choice."

Charodei was not satisfied, but he continued: "The words were whispered in the night, and the winds carried it. Night-things spoke of it, and in the darkness we also heard. And so also we heard rumors—that societies are founded on hidden, secret balance-points: unknown people, the crucial hinges. Pull them out and the structure falls."

Pternam corrected him, "Pull them out and the structure adjusts to a new pattern of stresses."

Charodei persisted, "Very well. Consider the theory as if it were true. Why not give us the theory, and let us use it— train our own people? Why do we need this dire creature of the night? Just give us the concept, and we'll take it from there; we have the material to do it with."

Pternam said, "It is not something I can give anyone, because I have not been able to comprehend it. It is alien to our most basic thought-patterns. I have tried, and failed. None of the other workers associated with this has been able to make any more of it. No: we told him, 'Here it is—develop it.' And he's done it, but he can't tell us how. He's so far into it that he would have to train us over from scratch so that we could understand it. This came early, and so we then trained him to the rest, so someone could implement it . . . all the arts of violence, mayhem, pain, death and disfigurement. And the best of all, that he can totally change his identity with the proper stimulus, and thus vanish after the deed."

Lozny said, "We heard somewhat of this. How so? Change? In what way—disguises are susceptible to penetration, as we have found out."

"Not disguise, but change. It came out of our studies of the hormone system. We have known for some time that certain aspects of exterior form of the body are controlled by hormone secretions—the shape of certain muscle groups, certain fatty areas, the distribution of patterns of facial and body hair. But there is more—the whole body is under these controls. It's just a matter of finding the key to the system. It's a little disturbing to understand it, but as real as you seem to yourself, you are not a fixed reality, but a wave in Time; every two thousand days, the cells in your body have changed, and so you are different. We found a way to uncouple this process from the memory and the controls built in, and reset the master control, as it were. You change, constantly, held in precarious balance . . . We found a way to speed the process up, to what you might call catastrophic change."

Charodei asked, "What kinds of time are we talking about?"

"Most can't do it, so we have to screen for those who can, and then train them to the degree of concentration required. At the extremes we have the subject attain, I have to refer to the state of consciousness as in intense trance state, something on the order of self-hypnosis, or yogic concentration . . . The process won't work at all if the time involved in the change is more than three or four days, and the release of metabolic by-products which poison the organism limits its shorter end to about a day—this is for the ones who can live through it. At the end of it, even the genetic code is changed, and the sex of the subject changes as a by-product, and the age as well, or rather the appearance of age. In fact, we have succeeded with only one. This one is the only one, and he's only gone through one change."

Yadom exclaimed, "Sex?"

"Everything." Pternam gestured at the Morphodite. "*That*

27

was originally a woman, an old derelict we selected out of the sloggers of the Labor Pool last-leggers. She was far gone, but somehow she responded."

Charodei breathed, "Woman! And now it's a man?"

Pternam said, "That was Jedily Tulilly, who is officially listed as being deceased. That is now an unregistered adult male whom we call Tiresio Rael."

Charodei said, "Tiresio! You dared name him that, or did you know?"

Pternam said, "The name was picked, so far as I know, at random."

Charodei explained, "In Hellas, on Earth, there was an oracle who was called Tiresias, who was said to have been both man and woman. And this Tiresio . . . Ah, I see, a most perilous weapon. I think I see. But go on. We are your guests."

Pternam reiterated, "This was a woman. Now it's a man."

Yadom asked, incredulously, "In every way?"

"As far as form goes, yes. He has all the requisite appurtenances, spigots, tubes and valves. Why not? All tissues are the same in either sex—they are controlled different by the hormone system."

Yadom continued, "To the sexual level?"

"To the DNA level! That's a man. There is no way to connect that with Jedily Tulilly—not by fingerprints, retinal scan, or DNA breakdown."

Lozny asked, "How . . . ?"

"Hypnosis, operant conditioning, severe stress, Will and Idea. We send it where we dare not go, and there it sets the Change off. And it also loses a substantial fraction of age, too. Tissue samples tell us that this man is about twenty of the old biological years younger than the old woman. The Change process apparently resets the timer running in the body. As I say, It has only undergone one Change, so we don't know how it goes after that."

Charodei exclaimed, "Then it's effectively immortal!"

Lozny added, "That's more important than revolution! Gehenna with changing things! Give us the secret of that and we'll outlive them!" He cast a burning, lustful glance at Yadom and Charodei, who nodded in agreement.

Pternam said, "Wait, before you ask for it. Consider that it is a gift you may not want: for one thing, it is painful beyond imagination. That one lost a third of its body weight

28

while growing a fourth taller. That was in the first day. And there is a lot of memory loss, or blockage. That one remembers nothing of its life as Jedily, whatever that was . . . Of course, we help it, because we did not want it to know. It knows that it can change, but it can't remember anything of its old life. And you . . . perhaps you would no longer be revolutionaries. And of course the Change makes it sick for a time. And consider that we who know of this—we do not elect to serve as subjects. Not a one. Think on that."

Charodei said, "Subjectively, then, to it . . ."

"Subjectively, the old woman died. And far below the level of anything we would understand as consciousness, *something* survived, and on that we built a personality . . . eventually, we were able to build a functioning persona, and of course we taught it much . . . but as far as the theory it operates under, it taught itself, and has done all the original work itself, and there is so much in that which is alien to us that it doesn't inhabit the same universe we do, conceptually."

Charodei said, "You mean it doesn't agree with us?"

"I mean we have a bargain with it, and its word is good—we've tested that, too. But it doesn't understand why what we've trained it to do is so important to us."

"But will it change?"

"Voluntarily? Yes. No doubts. Although that is another thing which separates us, because of course the process is a sort of death . . . its immortality is not escape from death, but the acceptance of many deaths, none of them pleasant."

Lozny mused, "Why is the ability of it to change so important?"

"Because it doesn't matter if they track it down and find it afterwards! There is no link between the two persons. Its origins can't be traced. It doesn't matter how public its act is. And rest assured we've given it an extreme education in avoidance."

Yadom asked, "And in what else?"

"All the tools of the trade for assassins. That one can brew poison from drinking water, make a pistol from trash, sabotage any machine made, live in the wild, maim with a gesture you can't even see, and use most conceivable weapons to a high level of accuracy, in addition."

"Why?"

"It told us that in the system it uses to identify its targets, it gets method as an inseparable part of the answer. It says

29

that the assassins of old were wrong in target *and* method, and that it must have the ability to implement the answer it gets out of its calculations."

"There is some sort of formula?"

Pternam said, "Yes. It makes no sense to anyone we've shown it to. Apparently it is using some underlying understood mathematical and logical concepts we haven't discovered yet, or can't imagine, blocked conceptually from them by what we already know."

Charodei interrupted, "You say, 'implement the answer.' You were speaking of method, but I sense there is more . . . the Target. Then we don't assign it a target, is this correct?"

"Exactly. All you have to do is agree—and we release it."

"It selects the subject, the method . . . ?"

Pternam said, "And the time to act. All of it. Remember, it sees our society as an extended schematic."

Yadom shook his head. "We heard tales, but this is even more fearsome. I feel as if I were comparing brushfires to surgery, our methods to its. Incredible! And what governs its loyalty to us?"

Pternam said, slowly, "You are to take advantage of the shift it creates. It is programed to remove the pin that holds this society in its present form. That is all. It doesn't understand what we would put in its place, or that we could. Only that it can do this. Neither you nor I have the option of controlling it once it is released. We can choose to release it, having given you advance warning, or we could destroy it . . . for we who created it fear it, too. My question is, do you think that you can take advantage of its release?"

Yadom didn't speak, but held his face immobile. Charodei looked away from the window, and also from the group. But Lozny, after a moment, solemnly nodded. "We can handle it."

Charodei said, thoughtfully, "You could have another choice, and set it loose on us . . ."

Pternam answered carefully, "No. That would require more retraining than we can do. Possibly we could pattern such a person, similarly to the way this one was done, but I frankly do not know. In the case of the Acmeists in Clisp, there were special circumstances involved. It told us of that situation; actually of three we could have tested, but we could use only one of them. It says that its actions disturb its own equations. In any event, I do not intend to use one against you. We went too far with this one, and we fear it also. There are serious restraints on this area. We simply do not take chances with it.

"Well," said Charodei. "Let's go visit with your fabulous beast, before we decide. I'd like to talk with it."

31

⌐ 3 ⌐

Meetings by Night

Anibal Glist was not the name he had been born with, nor
had his subsequent upbringing and education known that
name; however, it was the one he had been known by for so
many years that it sometimes slipped his mind what the old
one was. He actually had to stop and make an effort to recall
it.

Glist had made his way back to his cell, but he did not
rest, as he had intended to. At first he had dismissed the
alarming report by Sheptun as nothing more than fancy; for
this was a common enough trait among new operatives assigned to Project Oerlikon/Lisagor. They saw shadows everywhere. The trouble was that there was never any shortage of
shadows, so that the problem became to discriminate between
the real problems and the false starts, of which Lisak society
was overloaded. Who would believe a monolithic totalitarian
state still could erect itself and exist, and even prosper after
its own fashion, in these times? It was a tribute to some perverse human vice from the farthest reaches of the squalling
past.

But the more he thought on it, pacing back and forth in
his small cell, the more he felt uneasy. There was something
about this, some lunatic flavor that he had learned to associate, by dint of long experience on this planet, with some furtive glimmer of truth. And so it was that after a time, Glist,
donning a night cloak against the autumnal chill in the late
night air, set forth again, negotiating the narrow walkways,
stairs, and balustrades of his hill to the place of another of
his associates.

This was a woman, Arunda Palude, who served as the ar-
chivist for the Symbarupol Central Group. Having no contact
with the operatives, and insulated from all communications
save certain specified ones, she concentrated on retaining
data, for the reporting officials of their group to use. Most of
her files were in her head: she was a trained mnemonicist, so

that in case of emergency, there would be no damaging records found to link their group with anyone off-planet. She did not make reports herself.

As he laboriously climbed up a particularly steep masonry stairwell to her cell, Glist did not worry too much about being seen, or his presence commented upon, for another of the endless wonders of Lisagor was that despite constant antisexual propaganda by the government, and total absence of any public media stimulation, the major concern of Lisaks seemed to be devoted to the maintenance of numerous affairs, and exotic practices associated with them. He smiled to himself. Rather than resent, or even take note of his visit, any ordinary Lisak would probably admire his verve, and consider Glist's example as another goad to personal excesses.

At the cell door, Palude let him in without ceremony or comment, closing the door and bolting it. Once inside, she did not waste time or effort with pleasantries, but addressed Glist directly. She was a woman of mature but graceful aspect, tall and slender, with dark hair, streaked with gray, tied into a loose bun at the back of her neck.

She said, "Something would bring you out at night and over here directly; you're not known for lechery, and all the Dragon games have ended by now, so something's bothering you. What is it?"

"Direct as ever, I see. Well, I have heard some odd things tonight, and I thought I would stop by and check with you to see if you could make a tie to any of it."

"Go on."

Glist gave, in summarized form, a loose account of the incident in which Student Procand and Student Sheptun had collaborated in reporting odd circumstances to him. For a time, Arunda did nothing but listen, with a rather expressionless, passive face. Then she looked up and went to a small cupboard, from which she took a pad of paper and pen and wrote down short phrases.

Glancing at the list she had written, she began, "I have some items that may or may not connect with the information relayed by Sheptun. One. The Heraclitan Society central committee has been unusually active in recent weeks, doing a lot of moving around. Our contact has been sporadic and tenuous. There are indications that they have made contact with some other group, which has not been identified yet. Two. Vigilance was instituted, but the usual sources report negative. Other clandestine organizations associated with HS in

33

the past are disorganized and passive, and the Synodic of Law and Order, Ministry of Femisticleo Chugun, currently has no provocative actions in effect, except a very minor one operative in Marula, which appears to be unconnected."

She continued, "Three. Cesar Kham is working on this personally. There is an incident in Marisol, Clisp, which has very odd aspects. A very minor fringe underground group calling itself The Acmeists, was recently brought to light in the aftermath of a murder, and the group completely fell apart. They are hunting down the survivors now, but the group is considered completely purged."

Glist interrupted, "What is so odd about that? Chugun unearths one every other week. They don't amount to much."

Palude answered, "That's the odd part. Chugun didn't do it. It was brought into the open by an odd, motiveless murder, and at that of a very minor clerk of the group. The killing has all the marks of a very professional assassination, and naturally, the assassin has not been located. Chugun is not worrying much about the killer, since he's had so much fun rounding up the Acmeists. Another odd thing was that they were not really very secret, or very effective, or much of a threat. They had no known enemies among other factions, and were in fact rather useful as a sort of sounding-board. The usual sources in Marisol and throughout Clisp all report no contact, and in fact, all the local cabals are very busy denying it. They were all well-covered, so the fall of the Acmeists hurt no one except their own people, nevertheless, it caused a lot of nervousness, since no one seems to know where the incident that set it off came from. Kham went there personally to see if he could make sense of it. His last report is that it's as if something came out of the night and struck, and left the scene immediately. Kham also says that his investigation shows that this particular victim, although unknown and obscure, seemed to provide just the right impetus so that the internal weaknesses of the Acmeists caused them to fall apart in public. Chugun has written it off as a fortunate accident, and proceeded to clean up whatever was left of it. Kham suspects conscious motivation and direction behind the incident, but cannot identify the organization."

Glist thought for a moment, and then asked, "Is there coincidence in time between the activity of the Heraclitans and this incident in Clisp?"

Palude thought about it, and then said, "The Clisp incident was first. The activity commenced about ten days later. Also

34

Kham notes that the Acmeists were the only group in Clisp with no active connections with any other group. He plainly suspects a sort of demonstration, since they were relatively open and isolated, but by whom and for whom?"

"Kham suspects? If half of what he thinks is true, there's a finer control afoot than we've seen here."

Palude said, thoughtfully, "My material on the Acmeists is current, via Laerte Ormolu, and confirms their general harmlessness. This is why Kham is investigating. Somebody wiped them out, and they are manifestly not dangerous—there are much more alarming groups active in Clisp, and also in the Serpentine, which Femisticleo Chugun views as almost as bad as Clisp itself."

Glist reflected, "If a demonstration, it reveals extremely fine intelligence—that bothers me. We have Chugun pretty well covered, as well as the central organization under Monclova. If not from them, then who? Past reports indicate that there are few with that level of ability, or the networks to support the data base. Outside the police under Chugun, and the Heraclitan Society, everything else is local and pretty much ineffective."

Palude nodded. "I have one more item. Thersito Burya has been acting as a go-between with a person or persons unknown, this also after the Clisp incident. This activity is rated as unusual, and highly secretive. Well, and I should add that since the HS became active, they are no longer working out of Marula, but on the move."

"Not to Clisp?"

"Not noted there. Burya made a brief visit, but was gone in a day."

"Coincident?"

A pause. "Yes. Definitely possible."

Glist sat down on the edge of the bed and pondered for a moment. Then he said, "I suppose some watchfulness is warranted. If you can associate with this, advise me. I will try to scare up some data for you."

She said, "Glist, I know I am here to record these reports, but I have had an idea about all this."

"Speak freely."

"With that fine a control, do you suppose whoever it was could also *see* us—I mean, our mission, here? That's. . . ."

"I agree. We've never been compromised, or even seriously threatened. During the last testing period we ran our existence wasn't even suspected. We're clean with Chugun, and also with the HS. We had always assumed that they lacked the sophistication to penetrate our screen. Still, it's that fine control that bothers me. I will put the net on defensive alert until we can determine what this element is." He stood up and started for the door. "Tonight."

At the door, Pternam hesitated, for here indeed was the point they had worked for, but it also was a point of no return. There was also in this an air of chance. Rael *was* unpredictable, and he knew well how dangerous. Once they were in there with him . . . Still, this had to go on. There could be no stopping it now. He took a deep breath. "Are you quite certain that you wish to go on with this? I mean, once we penetrate the security system, we'll be in there with it, locked in, whatever happens."

Yadom said, "You have him under such tight security?"

"Indeed we do. This is the tightest security system in all Lisagor. There is none tighter."

"You fear it, then?"

"We had, past a certain point, to secure his active cooperation. To that end, we have a certain bargain with him, the details of which need not be told now, save this: if he's the man for the job, and if you are ready to live with the consequences, then we release him. If not, we'll keep him in there."

Yadom reflected, "You mean if we don't want him, then you keep him in there . . . why?"

"Because he can do what he says he can—what we say he can. Absolutely. And I will not release him knowing that the main underground group cannot rebuild from the ruins he will leave. And because once we turn it loose, there's no way to recall him. Or catch him. We trained him to be invincible and invisible." And here, closer than any other time during the evening's visit, Pternam was approaching the truth. They did not know for a fact that they could get Rael back, or stop him, if released. They had plans, but for this kind of contingency they had never been tested, not even in simulation.

"And he picks the victim! That's turning the whole program over to him!" Charodei was for once beside himself with agitation.

"You can waste your finest people and murder every member of the Council of Synodics, and not get the job done; he can do it with one stroke. In fact, an actual killing may not

36

be necessary, so he has explained it to me. But this is putting things where they belong: you claim to have a better way for Oerlikon. So, then. He's the thing that sets it off."

Charodei and Yadom lapsed into silence. Pternam continued, "I advise you to have a care with him, for I cannot predict his reactions to you; he does not perceive relationships as you and I do."

Lozny inquired, "It is rational? Does it talk?"

"Very well on both counts."

Charodei said, to his associates, "Perhaps it might be better if I phrased our discussions with it . . ."

Yadom agreed. "By all means. Do we need to wait further?"

Pternam said, quietly, "No." And he opened a small panel by the window and removed a handset, which he spoke into. "Tiresio Rael."

The bland figure at the desk did not look at the window, but spoke into the air, which they heard through the handset. "Yes?" The voice was husky and a little rough around the edges, but also it sounded curiously flat, unemphasized, distant, almost uninterested.

Pternam said, briskly, "I have some visitors who would speak with you, before committing themselves further. Is the time in phase for such discussions?"

The figure in the room leaned back from the desk, paused, and said, "The modes are aligned in an acceptable configuration . . . for many ventures. Not all, but more than is usually the case. I will admit four, no more, no less, and make no restriction of subject matter, even to Life and Death." Then he stood up and walked to a small panel in the wall beyond the desk.

Pternam replaced the handset, hurriedly, and said, "We are in luck! Things are not always so easy, where any but myself are involved. And of course, Avaria will remain outside . . . Elegro, you know what to do." The last was a statement, not a question.

Avaria looked grim and resolute, a vast departure from his normal choleric self. He said nothing, but nodded quickly, a slight, clipped gesture. And to the three visitors, there was something menacing in that brief exchange. Pternam added, admonishing them, "I will warn you only once: do not hector, or appear to threaten him. Say what you must, but do not expect a servant."

Pternam went around to the entrance side, and, motioning

the guards away, manipulated a series of intricate locking devices according to an order with which he seemed familiar; and after a moment, the door opened, and they entered the chamber, where Rael waited for them, standing in front of the desk, and holding one hand in the other in front of his spare frame. Pternam pushed the door shut after they had all come in, and they heard faint mechanical noises, as of precision machinery, as Avaria manipulated the locks. Rael nodded pleasantly to them, and made some adjustments to the panel at his left.

Pternam felt a sense of danger, now as he always did when he came in here, which was seldom. But it was low tonight. He glanced at the three leaders of the Underground; they looked uncomfortable. For a certainty, they would feel trapped here, totally at the mercy of a creature they couldn't begin to understand.

Rael said, in that same, distant, husky voice they had heard earlier, "There are chairs: please use them, that we may integrate as equitants. This is always pleasant, is it not?"

There was a faint irony to his greeting, but the meaning was clear enough: here, now, equals would negotiate. No one would give orders. Charodei understood this in the words, and the full implications of it. He said pleasantly, "Of course. Come, my associates; be seated, We are guests." And starting with himself, he introduced them all.

Rael started the conversation, "We have heard somewhat of your ideas."

Charodei answered, "We have also heard of you through our mutual friend, here, as a teacher might speak of a student who surpassed him. We would speak with you to learn how your expertise might help us achieve our goals, if possible. We might speak of your studies; perhaps it could be that we could ask for your assistance."

Rael began, "I have modesty and make few claims, however, there are few who can speak well of the things I have studied, so I must needs blow my own horn, as there is no one else to blow it for me. And you should speak plainly of the things you desire, as well."

Yadom said, suavely, "Men came to the world Oerlikon to turn their backs on the flux and pressure of the normal human universe, to stop things as they were, or as they thought they should be. We believe they were in error, and have harmed us all, and wish to remedy that defect."

Lozny said, "Generations of Lisaks have worked to this

38

aim, but therein is no accomplishment. They have built an impervious system to which we have not found a key."

Charodei said, "We wish to rejoin the human community, whatever it is now, which is rumored yet to exist out among the stars. To participate, to be. Our people are skilled and conscientious, and surely most of them would find a welcome."

To each one, Rael listened respectfully and attentively, nodding and moving his body slightly to the flow of the words. At the end, he said, "Is that all?"

Yadom began, "The People. . . ."

Rael interrupted, "The People? The People will suffer more from the change you have in mind that they have suffered in all the cycles since the Rectification. Can this be a gift: suffering and death and violent change? No. Let us not speak of the people, but of ourselves, for that is what we are here about. We will do this . . . for ourselves."

Charodei asked, "Of us, then. And what will you have of it?"

Rael answered, after a moment, "I will be free of a debt which I owe. One more transition, and then I will live out the life of the one who will come after me, innocent. Understand, I do not wish to destroy, but it is the only way I know in this mode. It is a weight."

"I understand. Then your cooperation is voluntary?"

"Yes."

"What can you do for us?"

"I can locate the keystone of the arch of civilization, break it and escape. I can dissolve this perfectly closed system. And they will never understand that what they find . . . could not have done the things they all saw me do. I will be changed."

Charodei said, perceptively, "There are to be witnesses, then?"

"There must be witnesses."

Charodei said, "There will be phocorders which will capture the image of Rael; can he be traced? Can they backtrack to us, or to Pternam?"

"Acceptable records are already in place for this contingency."

Lozny asked, "Why do you need the identity-change? Once you do it, it will all be over for the old way."

Rael said patiently, "There is a delay factor in time. The old will move for a time under inertia. There is a transition period which has duration. During that period, I am vulnerable. That is why the change."

Yadom asked, "Do you know who you will be, or is that blind to you?"

"The process I undergo involves manipulation of the genetic code. I become an ancestor, in effect. I have computed this ancestor. I know this identity, and have already had suitable papers drawn up for the contingency."

Porfirio Charodei could not restrain himself. "You will actually change, permanently? This grows more incredible each moment. This is a thing all our experience denies. Not even by miracle or thaumaturgy do men pervolve into women!"

The Morphodite acknowledged his amazement and said, "The obvious differences that you perceive are simple: by a readjustment of glandular balances, a reordering of hormone progressions, and a shifting of tissue structure, the process is accomplished. There is a penalty to the act, however—I lose the ability to form reproductive cells, and so cannot perpetuate my kind. A small loss, actually, which I do not bemoan excessively."

Charodei said, "And you know who you will be! That is also unbelievable!"

"I . . . ah, calculate the essential uniqueness of that identity in a similar manner to that by which I compute the identity of the target personality. It is a similar process," he said, emphasizing the word similar, "but in the case of my own identity, considerably more difficult. But I did so; it would seem logical to wish to know."

"Of course, of course. And so, having been apprised of what we need, you already know who it must be?"

"Of course." Here, the Morphodite allowed his features to settle into a complacent saturnine leer, an effect which Charodei felt disconcerting and threatening. He continued, "I know who it is to be, where, when, and by what method. Indeed, I can *see* it. After the act of calculation, it comes to me as if it were a memory, a remembrance. I call it premembering. There are some differences, which you need not know unless you would like to enroll in Dr. Pternam's program . . . I see you do not wish to, an excellent choice."

Charodei paused, thought, and asked delicately, "Is it permitted to ask . . . ?"

Rael shrugged. "One can ask anything. Anything at all. But one would not get answers. No hints, no oracles, no parables, no nothing. Absolute zero. I have been given the assay of the task, and I can do it: I *know* precisely what has to be done. Do you wish it done?" He paused. "It changes in time, of course, so that if too much time passes, it will have to be recalculated. . . ."

Yadom said, muttering, "This is a madman, and Pternam with him. How can we direct a sentence of execution when we do not know the identity of the condemned? Or when? Or how? We cannot mobilize our supporters . . ."

Pternam interjected, "When we made contact, your people said that the only thing you lacked was a suitable circumstance. A key to unlock the bound gate. We have a key. This much is simple and demonstrable. Does the key have to be used at your signal? Or are you, as your people have averred, ready to rush through the door once it's been opened? But if your resolve is in doubt, then let us await a better day, or perhaps less hesitant revolutionaries. . . ."

Charodei motioned Yadom to silence, and said, "You have a potent talisman here: one that could be turned to many purposes."

Both Rael and Pternam nodded solemnly.

Charodei continued, "Therefore a threat to us as well, infinitely more perilous than those ham-handed clowns commanded by Chugun. But yet you risked the peril of fervent idealists to show us this. Do you understand risks?"

Pternam was not alarmed, and yawned. "If I were sure three men could contain Rael, I would have them in here with us, and they would be armed. But no, we lock the door and surround this chamber with monoxide gas, and then oxygen and acetylene. I have no fears on that score whatsoever, and feel no anxiety."

Rael glanced at the three representatives and said languidly, "I am not aware of any threat you can offer to me. Here, or elsewhere. Now, or otherwhen. Perhaps you imagine to know something I do not. Perhaps. But they are not good odds upon which to gamble. I know you, but you do not know me. Thereby proceed with care."

Charodei breathed audibly and changed the subject. "Pternam, do you know who it will be?"

"No. Rael tells me that information contaminates the results. In fact, he tells me that the act of calculation makes the identity of the target somewhat unstable. And that to reveal anything about the execution of the mission to anyone causes a rapid shift in the identity. A tricky, slippery business! So I know nothing of who it is to be. There are, so

41

I am told, cases in which identity shift does not occur, but the other parameters change, such as time, or place. The more that is known, the more it, the knowledge, smears the result out."

Lozny said, "Then this is a form of knowing the future?"

Rael answered, "I would more properly describe it as a form of knowing the nature of things. Time as you look at it is not really a measure—in fact, you cannot do what I do because of the way you look at Time. And I cannot explain that further to you unless you become as I."

Lozny suddenly said, "But what if the target is one of us? We don't know! What if it's Pternam? Or someone else we value?"

Rael said, "This society you wish to bring down: if I can find the one person who is essential to the upholding of that society, would you not agree to go ahead, no matter who it is? Otherwise you do not wish a change. . . ."

Charodei turned to Pternam. "What if we don't take Rael?"

Pternam leaned back in his chair and said reflectively, "Nothing. We approached your group because you seem to have the clearest alternative course, and the organization to take up where the old left off. Somebody has to make the decisions. But if you don't want to act, then we'll use Rael in some other way. I have no plan for using him against your group, because the way things stand now, you are locked out and represent no threat to me." At this, Lozny glared, but Pternam added, equably, "As for normal assassins, I have quite adequate defenses."

"Then Rael is not for sale to the highest bidder, then?"

"Rael is not for sale to anyone for any price, including you. It is a possibility that I could have him redirect his calculations into the contingency that we would proceed without your group, entirely, and do it anyway."

Rael added, "In that circumstantial pattern, this group is not only locked out, but is precluded."

Yadom said, "Meaning?"

Rael explained, "When a society has a given orientation, the way it's assembled, it makes some alternative courses or structures either difficult to attain, or even impossible. The way things are now, and here, your group and its sympathizers are effectively prevented from assuming more than a nuisance value; if I go without you, the conditions that permit your organization to exist at all will fade, and there will be no Heraclitan Society. No violence. You'll just fade. The individuals involved won't even know why. It just won't work any more."

Charodei said, "But there's no decision on this alternative."

Pternam said, "No. Certainly not now. To be frank, we did not anticipate you'd have such cold feet, so no studies have been done, other than a preliminary scan by Rael. Certainly nothing strong enough upon which to base a decision about something of this magnitude."

Yadom stood up. "Very well. I'm satisfied. We'll take him. Lozny? Charodei?"

Lozny nodded, not without dour frowns, but he nodded assent. Then he growled, "I like it not, but let's get on with it. And once he does it, it will shift to us?"

Charodei thought that the remark was extremely perceptive for Lozny, and made an immediate reassessment of the man. He said, "Yes, I came to the same conclusion. Pternam?"

"That is correct. This was set up, as it were, not just in the 'What if' mode, but, 'To tilt in your favor.' Rael likens the process somewhat to the chopping of a tree—one can influence the way the bole will fall, sometimes with great precision."

Rael said, "With defensive-mode sociodromes such as this one, the analogy is particularly apt. This one can be caused to fall in a number of directions." Here, he paused, and smiled at Pternam. "Even to produce a successor even more defensive and highly-structured than this one."

Pternam said, before he had time to cut the thought off, "You never told us that!"

Rael shrugged and said, "You never asked."

Charodei asked Rael, "May we know who you will be, afterwards?"

Rael nodded. "The information affects nothing. This I will tell: In Marula, a younger woman called Damistofia Azart will come to your people for a position, after she recovers from a mysterious fever. You will see that she obtains a suitable position, not demanding, not in the public eye. She will be harmless. You have no fear of her." Here Rael rummaged through the papers on the desk, and shortly produced a pencil drawing of a woman's face and upper body, dressed. The picture was simply done, but skillful enough so that she could easily be recognized. "Here is something of her aspect."

Charodei took the proffered drawing and looked intently at it, then passing it to the other two. The woman depicted was substantially younger than Rael now appeared to be, and did not resemble him in the least. This one was of slight stature and subtle figure, pleasant enough, but not beautiful. The drawing suggested dark hair and pale skin. The face was crisp and well-defined. The eyes were large, dark, and slightly protuberant, suggesting an imbalance of the thyroid. She would be nervous, active. He said, finally, "This is to be you . . . ?"

"Exactly. That is about as close as I can get in a drawing. Of course, like anyone else, she will shift her appearance slightly with mood and circumstance. Diet as well. And she will come to you after recovering from an unknown disease. She will be slightly disoriented, understandable after her terrible struggle, and will need care and rehabilitation."

Charodei understood. He said, "Damistofia won't remember much, eh?"

Pternam said, "Ask him now what he remembers of Jedily Tulilly."

Rael said, unbidden, "Nothing. I know that such a condition was, but I do not remember it. I know more about her, Damistofia, now. Premembering. . . ."

Charodei said, with some satisfaction, "Then it's a one-time weapon . . ."

Rael answered, "Once is all you need, isn't it? And as for me, I don't fancy going through Change every three months or so as your resident repairman. Once I'll do, to earn my freedom. Not again."

Charodei said, "Very well. I agree. Let's do it. When does it commence?"

Rael considered, and said, after a time, "There will be an event you can't mistake. On that event, you move. When you see me again, you'll know."

"There's no signal . . . ?"

"The act itself is informative."

"And when?"

"Not disclosable. I pick the time, and I don't tell you in advance. Attempt nothing before that. Remain in your present configuration. If I sense that you are anticipating me, I'll recompute for it, because otherwise it won't work. And if you move too much, it can slip beyond my power to do it and influence it to your way. You understand how this is to work?"

The three conspirators nodded, almost as if they were operated by the same will, the same brain.

Rael said, getting to his feet, "Well, then, enjoy the remainder of the night." He turned away from them and began manipulating the locks of the room, to let them out.

Those inside the room shortly heard the slight sounds Avaria made, unlocking the outer locks, and afterward the door opened. Rael made no motions at all, but Pternam politely led the rest, after glancing at Rael, who made no attempt to follow them. After the door closed upon Rael, Pternam said, "Avaria can show you the way. We will not meet again, but remember how this was done."

They agreed, and Avaria led them away through the catacombs of Pternam's headquarters.

∽ 4 ∽

Night's Transition into Day

Excerpt from a routine report submitted by Anibal Glist to Onplanet Operations Director, Project Oerlikon, in Dorthy on Heliarcos, dated (Lisak Calendar) 3 Gul 11 Quillion Cycle Seven*:

Dragon: File under Games, Sports and Other Rituals.

1. Manislav's Conjecture states that the organization of games and sports takes an opposing structure to that of the society providing the players. Individualistic societies valuing excellence and competition favor highly structured team sports directed along military lines, while collectivist societies select sports of individual striving. With this in mind, we must consider the ramifications of the single sport known within Lisagor and Lisak-dominated areas as Dragon. (The name appears to be traditional and does not appear to have other symbolic connotations.—AG)

2. Dragon is a member of the tag family, which is rarely observed outside children's groups. Reflecting this relationship, it retains much of the lack of sophistication associated with children's games. In practice in Lisagor, however, there is nothing childish about it; indeed, it is played with a violent abandonment and lack of scruple not observed elsewhere. Dragon is the only sport played by adults.

3. Dragon is played generally in areas which have no use otherwise, or partial utility. No special areas are set aside, as arenas, coliseums, etc. The most common sites are vacant lots, dumps, junkyards, eroded and waste areas. The more irregular and broken the ground, the more it is used as a site. Places with suitable cover spots are preferred, i.e., those with small tangles of vegetation,

---

* In standard dating, this is approximately fifteen years prior to the events in this tale.

trash piles, brush dumps, or other refuse such as might be found in junkyards (which are especially popular). A group contemplating play will come to agreement on a site, go there, and demarcate the field with great exactitude. Anyone leaving the bounds is out of the game and may not return. Next, the group divides itself into "judges," "spectators" and "players," and money is collected and put up for the game, in the ratio (as listed above) 2:3:1.

4. The sole implement of the sport is a narrow, weighted leather sack with a grip handle at the narrow end, called "The Scorpion." The first Dragon (or lead player) is selected by scrimmage, the players linking arms and trying to reach the scorpion which has been placed in the center of the huddle. The winner of this free-for-all then displays the scorpion for all to see, delivering a monologue describing his or her qualifications and past triumphs, or virtues. During this speech, a harangue, judges take up positions, spectators gather in strategically placed huddles, and players attempt to conceal themselves or get as far as possible from the Dragon. At the conclusion of the monologue, the Dragon attacks whomever he pleases with the object of striking another player with the scorpion, either thrown or as a blow, whereupon that player then becomes the next Dragon.

5. Dragon is played in all cases in the evening or night, and play continues until all players have had an opportunity to be the Dragon. Each Dragon is authorized a monologue, and most take advantage of the opportunity, but only the first dragon is required to make it. The same rules apply as with the first: free movement is permitted during the speech.

6. There is no preferred mode of attack: the scorpion may be wielded or thrown. However, if thrown and missed, the intended target may capture the scorpion without becoming a dragon, and may do anything with it: he may throw it away, or hide it, or keep it as long as he can.

7. Individual style is all-important: some prefer stealth and subtlety, sneaking up on their targets and laying the scorpion on them gently, while others pursue their targets belligerently, screaming invective and curses, and then batter them to the earth. There are no rules

47

here and no fouls and no penalties. The dragon may act solely as he sees fit. Serious injury is not uncommon, and death not all that rare.

8. At the end of the game, agreed by mutual consent, the stake is distributed to players, judges and spectators, in the ratio (as listed) 3:2:1. Those players who were dragons often are awarded bonuses, which are taken from the spectators' shares.

9. No one is barred or refused. There are no membership rules, save a desire to participate in the risk of the game. Neither age nor sex is a factor. The only crime in the game is to enter and then leave the field, which event is regarded with scorn and ostracism, which may extend to real-life activities.

10. The alteration of personality upon entering a dragon game is marvelous to behold. Quite often, the local bully will become meek and skulking, while a civil servant of impeccable exactitude may rush about applying homicidal violence to anyone he may meet.

11. Certain individuals become well known as masters of the game or else as trustworthy judges. Others become equally famous for avoiding the scorpion, whereupon they are known as squids (traditional usage) and considered equally honorable. Another curious facet of the game is that despite the rigid organization of Lisak society, prominent public personages also play, and indeed, there appears to be a correlation such that the intangible esteem level of the player translates into major position within society.

12. Some of the operatives assigned to this project have entered the game and found it, especially in the context of Lisak society, pleasurable and exhilarating. However, in the light of its anarchic violence and irresponsibility, we cannot recommend its introduction in the Homeworlds.

With respect: A. Glist—Symbarupol.

Outside the Residence, Charodei, Yadom and Lozny all felt exposed and vulnerable. They had felt the risk was worthwhile before and so ignored their danger instincts; but now that the business was done, and the decision made, they felt, as one, disoriented and deflated, and so their previous feeling rose again; this was, after all, Symbarupol, the nerve center nexus of that which they would demolish and replace with a better world. They walked along the dark, curving walkway which led to the Residence, all wishing to have the last words said and be on their separate ways, to the ends of the world.

Yadom hissed, "Well, tell me: can we depend on this?"

Charodei said, "Improbable as it sounds, there's that insane ring of unspeakable truth to it. . . ."

Lozny said, a low muttering, "Hum. Likely so. But I'm going to ask us: with such a weapon, why does the owner of it give it away? Nobody gives anything away!"

Charodei answered, "Well said! But consider that he did not give Rael to us but wished to know if we would take advantage of a possible release."

Lozny snorted, "Dialectical hair-splitting. Rampant squidism"

"Ah, no—not acting the Squid, but the squum*, for in the distinction lies the germ of it. No doubt Pternam's got all sorts of oddities and freaks in there, some projects that never came to anything, others that failed too many times, transformations too difficult. But this one, against the odds, worked: a fearsome thing. Yet how would he employ it? It is a destroyer."

Yadom said, "He could take it to Clisp or the Serpentine."

Lozny huffed, "Wrong. Even Pternam is perceptive enough to know how tight a rein Chugun keeps on those places. No, it would not come from a *place*, but something spread throughout the system, as we are. And certainly, there is no other group who can claim to have the contact we do with all parts of Lisagor."

Charodei said, "No group we know of."

"Do you know of one?"

"No. But that does not delimit all possibilities. I say this because Pternam may have had alternate courses in mind. *He* may know of one."

Yadom said, "I think not. There was a do-or-die element to the proceedings."

Lozny said, "So we would believe."

Charodei said, "You don't trust it. Well, neither do I, but all the same, I am for preparedness."

Yadom agreed. "Just so. We wait, and then move. This may well be the chance we need. The improbable ally.

* Dragon jargon: one who demonstrably invites attack, to become Dragon.

Stranger things have happened. Who knows what his motivations are? And, for that matter, who cares? It will all be moot when we get control, because The Mask Factory will be the first thing to go."

Lozny nodded with grim satisfaction. "Right. And what do we do with the Azart woman? Leave her on the loose? I don't buy at all that line about not remembering. Perhaps the first time—all right. That one forgotten under trauma. But the second, when he's already predicted what he's going to turn into and can draw a picture of her? No. With that kind of control, he's built a fortress, so there will be something left over to achieve whatever it is he wants. And we definitely don't want something like that lying around self-controlled. What if she decides she doesn't like our way, and starts tinkering with our new order?"

Yadom said, "A dreary, dismal business, but those things can be arranged, as you know. After the change, she will be sick, and require care. . . ."

Charodei said, "But with the training it's had, and even partial retention by the subsequent persona, Azart, it could be dangerous to approach it, to attack it. It would have to be something other than a frontal attack."

Yadom purred, "I have just the thing in mind. We have a young fanatic in Marula, one Cliofino Orlioz, who, in addition to a most murderous disposition, is something of a celebrity among the ladies."

Lozny concurred at once. "Exactly! He has the face of a poet, the body of a young athlete, and the mind of a war criminal. We shall install young Cliofino as an orderly in the Marula Palliatory."

". . . A physical therapist. He will seduce her, of course. That way he can get close enough, I would suppose."

Lozny said, "Leave the details to me! We can handle it! I'll see he has backup, too."

"Not too many. We'll need them elsewhere, you know."

"As you say . . . And the signal can come from him, too: because whatever Rael does, if he appears as Azart, there's no doubt. Nobody can mistake that. So we'll have Cliofino give the alert too. Very good! So it shall be!"

Charodei suggested, "And now to our separate paths."

Yadom said, "Yes, separate. And Lozny . . . Make sure. If this is what is going to give it to us, we don't want it left for anyone else to use . . . and especially not itself. Let it do it, but afterwards, kill it! Under no circumstances must that creature run free!"

"As you order it, that's how it will be. Until next time."

Luto Pternam had returned to the chamber after the others had left. Orfeo Palastrine, his Commander of Guards in the section below the Residence, had tried, politely but insistently, to persuade him otherwise, but Pternam had insisted on returning. The danger, so he thought, was almost over. Most certainly, the time for release of the Morphodite was drawing near; perhaps was now. At any rate, he wanted to have a small talk with Rael before things became set in concrete.

In the chamber, there was a sense of tension departed: a relaxation and a fatigue, overlain with a wariness, a mistrust. Pternam heard the locks click into place behind him and observed that Rael this time did not lock the chamber from the inside.

Observing this, he said, plainly, "I see you do not lock the door."

Rael nodded, slowly. "This is correct; agreement has been reached, has it not? So I no longer restrain myself."

Pternam thought a moment, then said, "It is your wish that we open the way?"

"Yes."

"There is haste?"

"Were there haste, I would not be here now, asking."

Pternam thought of the massive building above their heads, the system of deadfalls, the guards, the cylinders of toxic gases and inflammables in readiness. Surely this . . . creature did not think he could simply walk out if he wanted. Yet he spoke plainly, like one stating a simple fact. Pternam ruefully considered that there was probably more in this Angel of Death than they had put into him, her, it. He moved his head once, as if to concur, and said, "Explain. You have trod strange paths since we first met."

Rael said, "And you have remained on the broad thoroughfare. No matter. I will explicTiate: Power consists of four components, which are in order of importance, Will, Timeliness, Skill, and Strength, weighted so that in that order, it is $4 + 3 + 2 + 1 = 10$, which is the Whole. The Strength a person has, his force, his resources: that is the least part of it —even Timeliness outweighs it. Here, you have arranged things so that my Strength is low compared with yours. But in all other things I have more. Some of that you gave by intent, some by accident, and some came of my own devising. Let it be so, for I have done what you asked, and made cause with the revolutionaries, as asked, and now comes the rest of it."

"Yes, my part of the bargain. Very well. . . ." Pternam made a hand signal to the observers outside, and when he heard no response, made it again, more emphatically. Then he heard the locks release. He said, "The way is now open."

"That is good."

"Indulge my curiosity: do you wish to leave tonight out of a sense of urgency, of Timeliness?"

"I appreciate your question, but cannot answer it. To answer is to contaminate the computation; to answer is to violate a basic fact of life, indeed all existence: things happen in their own time. If one has to hasten, it is already too late, is it not?"

"If you so aver."

Rael continued, "This computation I do is difficult, and complex and recursive: by that, I mean that there are stages in the process which cannot be compressed or jumped. A computer could do it faster, but not better. I would say that this would be wrong, inasmuch as the act of computation itself is included within the system of computation: how it is performed influences the result. In the end of it, it gives me a four-dimensional answer: place, time, method, circumstance, identity. I study the symbols, and by the knowledge of interpretation and isomorphism of this system, I come to *see* it, as a fact: premembering."

"It is not easy, then? I mean, practice with it has not made it easier to do?"

"The more you do it, the harder it gets. This contradicts common experience, yes, but that is how it is. You *see* more and more, and then the overriding problem becomes to stop the pattern . . . it just keeps on going, into deeper and deeper levels. No, I would not use a computer to do this; the speed of the computation . . . ah . . . makes it harder to disengage. I would fear for the safety of the machine, and for the fabric of local space-time—it induces strains. I suspect that at the maximum computational speeds, you would be *manipulating* the future—not just seeing it come to be, but changing it directly."

"That's magic, such as certain old legends speak of."

"I can comprehend that if you do it a certain way, what would occur would look like magic to an outside observer—

52

there would be change without apparent reason. Things would appear without cause. Disappear, too. I know of no way to do this and protect oneself from the field, if I may call it that."

"Some would call what you do magic of the direst sort."

"All call things they don't understand magic—usually evil magic. Especially the way of knowing."

"Interesting. I would like to explore this."

"I do not desire that you know it. One like me is quite enough for this corner of the universe."

Pternam felt a sudden surge of alarm as Rael spoke. Could this *thing* see that they had tried once before and failed, in this very part, and that the subject had evaded them. Harmless, true. It was a creature somewhat like Rael, but it had not been able to understand what they wanted of it. Could he see the past, too?"

He said, "Can you see the past as well?"

"I do not choose to look at it; no matter, for the past is embedded in the present. The present contains it entirely. I know this is a disturbing notion."

"Indeed."

Rael paused, and then said, "I must say one more thing, and then the time will have arrived."

"Say as you will."

"I normally would not, but there is something here I do not understand entirely, because I did not have the time to follow out the implications; I could *see* a certain condition, but not where its roots led. I think it is something about your world-line that you do not know about. Your actions indicate a blindness to it. Therefore I must inform you."

"Continue."

"A . . . condition of existence is a balancing of forces, a tension. I would expect a bipolar field for this place, this time. That is what the theory I have worked out calls for. But here, there is a third field, extremely subtle, but I sense power behind it, at a great distance. This makes the field here tripolar."

"Does that change what you do?"

"No. I act at the point where the three sets intersect. But hear me: something on this world maintains it, that is not of this world. I have not determined what it is. It is masked very well here, and extremely difficult to see. I understand that I will see it later, but for the now, I would have to run a special series to capture it."

53

"This maintaining set: it opposes us?"

"That is the odd part: it supports. Were such a thing to exist, I would think it weighted on the side of opposition, but this is not so—it maintains. Supports Lisagor as it is. You may wish to look into this."

Pternam said, "Why? By releasing you, I unleash Change upon the world."

"Just so—even the names of places will change." And then he said, "I have not determined your motives yet—that is another set of exercises I have not had the time or given the priority to do. Yet things are not as they seem to you, and you may wish to take some action or initiate a search."

Pternam shrugged and said, "You will change things. It matters not."

"Very well. Release me." Rael stood up, and began to arrange the papers and tablets on his work desk.

Pternam said, "What will you take with you?"

"My knowledge. I leave you my notes; you may study them at your leisure."

"Aren't you afraid that we'd learn how to do this ourselves?"

Rael gave a slight chuckle. "Not at all. If you understand what's in those notes, you won't dare. And besides, giving you this has no effect on things. Or not giving: it makes no difference. A rare find, I assure you, when it makes no difference."

"Very well. The door is unlocked, and the troops are advised. It is appropriate to wish you luck?"

Rael said, "I can appreciate the sentiment expressed." He looked at Pternam directly. "But in a sense, which I perceive, there really is no such thing as luck. Remember my equation of Power? Therein was no mention of luck . . . Enjoy your studies."

And with no more than that, Tiresio Rael went to the door, stepped through it as it was opened for him, and turned the corner. He was now loosed.

Pternam remained for a time in the chamber, gathering up in a slow, bemused fashion the notes, notebooks, and scratch pads which Rael had left behind; artifacts of some unknown process, whose validity Pternam seriously doubted. Still, he was certain that Rael would do something, however irrational it was. But he, Pternam, knew better. The basic idea they had fed Rael was false, and he had erected a science upon a totally worthless proposition; no matter—they had this world under control, and Rael was the last decoy. His key to the Inner Council, and with that the Central Committee. . . . He glanced down at the pile of papers he was gathering, and leafed idly through them, thinking to himself that they would make an interesting study for that section which specialized in delusions. Excellent material! But it caused him a peculiar emotion for which he had no name when his eye struck upon a short phrase close to the margins of one of the formulae-covered sheets.

It said, in Rael's meticulous printing, "It makes absolutely no difference whether one approaches the universe from an initial position of truth or falsity; it all comes out, if pursued far enough. And the Answer astounds either origin equally.—TR"

Anibal Glist was not accustomed to receiving visitors at late hours; he was one to retire early and leave alley-skulking to others of more ambitious bent. Therefore it was somewhat of a surprise to him to be awakened by a hurried knocking at his door, sometime, he imagined, in the hours between midnight and morning. He could not recall afterward what time it had been. But the subject soon made itself most memorable.

The visitor, meeting a very sleepy and out-of-sorts Glist, was Arunda Palude, the recorder. As soon as Glist opened the door and admitted her, she slipped in, motioning him to silence.

"Secure?"

Glist nodded assent, still half asleep.

"I'll be brief. I have had short-form communication with the inside man. A major assault in the works; agent, a human supposedly deep-trained in some kind of assassination science, target unknown, location to be Marula. Reference Acmeists in Clisp. Time unknown, to be associated with initiation of underground effort. I have recognition coordinates*, but although they are in stage-five form, there's a tag line attached that says they are changeable or tentative."

Glist now began to wake up. "That's a risk, sending all that."

* A technique of verbal description of a person utilizing that section of the brain devoted to recognition of facial patterns. Used when photographs or drawings would be impractical or dangerous, as for espionage operations. Use widespread off Oerlikon, unknown there by natives.

"He was quite concerned. Action Flash, Priority Grave—survival of mission at stake. So he said. I came immediately."

"You have the recognition coordinates?"

"Yes. Do you want them?"

"No. Take them to Sheptun, now, tell him to go to Marula and stop this person by any means available, and capture alive for shipment. He can take a few with him, if he wants. We don't want this thing to occur."

"No, we do not. But do you have an idea of what you are sending and what he will have to face?"

"I would send Kham, but I can't get to him, and even if I could, I don't know he could get there in time—we don't know when it is. Besides . . . we can't sent this kind of thing to our people in Marula until Sheptun gets there. That's one place outside Clisp they keep a close eye on. Marula, they say, a necessary evil, but evil none the less."

"It's the only real city they have. . . ."

"Yes and they distrust it mightily. No. We don't dare try to communicate direct. I prohibit it. Send Sheptun and tell him to recruit, and do it quietly. We don't want to set this off ourselves."

"As you say . . . right now?"

"Yes. Now. And tomorrow . . . I'll come to your place, and we'll translate those RCs into a picture and I'll see that it gets to Chugun's people."

"Won't that contradict our sending Sheptun? I mean, won't that create a confusion?"

"Possible. But I trust the Insider to set priorities accurately. He's no wolf-cryer, so much I know. I want everything working on this, so it can be stopped. Chugun will grind Marula to a powder, and he may flush something for Sheptun."

"I know the structure is in place, but you know we've never shipped a Lisak off-planet before. If Sheptun captures this thing, whoever it is, trying to get it off-planet may be more difficult than the plan has envisioned. There's a risk of exposure there. I feel an uneasiness about that."

"Risk, yes. But if the insider calls for action, then it must be something extraordinary. We need to have that person examined on Heliarcos, where we have proper facilities for testing."

"If he gets him, what will we do with him? The assassin?"

"Find out how he was trained and who trained him. Then dispose of him. Then dismantle the apparatus here. That's what I'll recommend, and at the moment I expect no diffi-

56

culty with Control. The prime directive is to protect the mission here *no matter what*." At the last words, Glist's voice shifted tone, to emphasize the words. *No matter what.* That was the key. Glist nodded, as if agreeing with himself, and he said, "Now go on; do it. And we'll meet tomorrow morning for the rest."

Arunda adjusted the hood of her night cloak and departed without further word. Glist closed the door behind her and returned to his bed. But he did not sleep for a long time, and he felt an odd emotion he could not recall ever feeling before, something to which he could not put a proper name. He considered several conditions before it dawned on him that the emotion was fear.

Elegro Avaria met Luto Pternam outside the chamber in which Rael had been housed. He said, excitedly, "I saw him leave!"

Pternam felt weary, bone-tired. He said, "Yes. It's done now. And now we wait. I'll arrange to have a small talk with Monclova about impending activity among the underground factions in Marula."

"You can't."

"Why not?"

"He's already there. Went down there to have that big public celebration marking the Liberation of Sertse Solntsa."

"What bad luck! Well, who's left behind?"

"He always leaves Odisio Chang to mind the store when he's out motivating the people, as he calls it."

"Chang's a shadow, that's all. He doesn't cast his own. Worthless for our purposes. We have to register it that we forewarned them. Chang is so busy covering himself that if he acted at all, he'd say it came from himself . . . look into this, will you? We have to find somebody now who will act for us."

"You are not worried that Rael will get Monclova?"

"Not at all. According to Rael, Monclova is the least one he'd be interested in. No—he says he's looking for someone ordinary, obscure, someone nobody knows, a slogger . . . No, I have no fears for Monclova."

"Very well. I will set to it in the morning. I'm sure we can find someone left behind."

"Good. And take these, will you . . . send them over to R&D Delusion Section and let them break a few computers on it." Pternam handed Avaria the sheaf of papers he had taken from Rael's quarters. "Also have housekeeping put some trusties in there and clean the place out. I want every scrap of paper; otherwise, strip it down to the bare walls and seal it off."

"Not going to try again?"

"No. It's just a feeling, but I think we came quite close enough this time. If this doesn't work . . . well, we'll try something else."

"I understand. And what about the guards?"

"They should be retrained, of course."

"All of them?"

"I can't think of any reason to make an exception. Them, the same way as the ones who set Rael up in that method of taking command of his own hormone system."

"As you say. That's a lot of people to put through the process, though."

"But there's nothing to connect him here, and that's the way we want it."

Avaria sighed deeply, shaking his head. "I'll see to it, and all the records and logs as well. Nice and clean."

"Good. See me tomorrow . . . about who we can place a hint to so they'll remember."

"I'll do it. Want a feedback from R&D, on those notes?"

"Only if they make any sense other than delusional." Pternam laughed at this. "Which I doubt greatly."

And with that last remark, they parted company, Avaria to his errands, and Pternam to bed. Before Avaria saw to the room and the guards, however, he made a short side trip to the Research section, in particular the computational facility, where he left the package of notes off, with a casual instruction to the night operator to "make some sense of it if you can." Avaria told the operator that the papers were some things done up by one of the subjects undergoing reorientation, and they wanted to know if any of the material was valid, by chance. Then he set about initiating another sequence of events.

Luto Pternam greeted the new day's daylight considerably sooner than he had hoped or expected, by being awakened by the earnest, excitable voice of Avaria at the bedside communicator. Its buzzing was soft, but insistent, and Pternam answered it with reluctance.

"Pternam."

"Avaria. I have a report to make."

58

"Make it, then."

"In person."

"Can it wait?"

"No. At least, so much I think. I urge haste."

"Come up, then—I'll be ready." And he closed the unit down with both disgust and foreboding. He hated being bothered after the events of the night before, but in the same manner, he knew that Avaria would probably not assay to bother him with senseless trivia. In a peculiar state of emotion, he found himself wishing that it was some trivial problem.

By the time Pternam had dressed, Avaria had appeared, with a disturbed look to him and an air of someone who was also awakened too early. And the report was by no means trivial.

Avaria came into Pternam's private chambers and did not wait nor did he pass conversational pleasantries before beginning; "The Computational Facility advised me early on this morning that the material in the Rael folder remains incomprehensible to them but that the machine considers it valid, coherent data which can be assembled into a system. They wish to know if you want it translated."

"Translated?"

"It is built of concepts which are alien to our present state of reference, and there is a program of re-education involved. So they are advised by the machine. It will take translation to make it comprehensible to us. Such a process is possible, but it will disrupt the operating schedule."

Pternam reflected and said, "No. So inform them. Return the material to me immediately, and purge the computer of all associations. We will destroy this."

Avaria, pausing for Pternam to permit him to use the room communicator, which he did with a slight inclination of the head, went to the unit and spoke rapidly into it. Then he turned back to Pternam and said slowly, "Done. Coming by messenger. Do you . . . ?" The question was unthinkable and unaskable. And as he had started to ask it, Avaria had realized that it was also unanswerable.

Pternam said, "Go on. No offense."

". . . They don't know what it is. It went directly to the delusion section, and was read out by the machine. So we can snuff that out easily enough. But about Rael. . . ."

"This means, Avaria, that Rael is in possession of valid

59

knowledge of how to do the thing we thought impossible—a delusion."

"That is my conclusion. And we have already released him, holding now an active weapon, not an imaginary one. I comprehend our error, but I don't understand how it could have been otherwise. Who would have thought such a thing: to attack the smallest and change the nature of a whole world."

Pternam said, "You are extraordinarily calm for such a disaster."

"I assume you know something I do not, that you have a program in reserve you did not advise me of. Such are the ways of one's superiors; otherwise they would not be superiors. Anything else is unthinkable."

Pternam's mind was racing at top speed, considering possibilities, but he did not miss the weight of the sarcasm Avaria had laid upon him, and of course the veiled threat behind it. He understood. This plan had entangled itself in its own nets of subtlety. And now they had a real problem on their hands. Onrushing, the future unthinkable was rushing to meet them, in the mind and hands of Rael the changeling, Rael the Morphodite who could vanish into another identity. Avaria was saying that Pternam was not fit for the position. But of course he had alternatives. They were not subtle, and they lacked imagination, but there was a chance they would work.

He said, "We aren't completely out of control yet; consider—we know Rael will do it in Marula, and we know he'll reappear as Azart afterwards. We may also deduce that it will be soon, hence he'll have to get there."

Avaria stroked his plump chin and said, "We can't very well count on the revolutionaries anymore—besides, what could we tell them? That our lie has become true? No. And as for Rael, you and I know him well enough, so I do not take him for a fool. Azart he may become, unless he lied, but I would not wait for him to present himself or herself to them."

Pternam said, "We'll notify Chugun that a prisoner from Reprocessing has escaped, believed headed for Marula to settle a grudge, highly dangerous, no remand."

"Shoot on sight."

"Something like that. But that's not all. We've some re-trainees here who would carry out a hazardous assignment. . . ."

Avaria looked at Pternam hard. He said, "You haven't got

anybody that good, to go one-on-one against Rael. I supervised that phase of his training; in that at least, he's highly dangerous."

"I don't expect them to win; just slow him down, enough for Chugun's goons to catch up with him. He's like a queen in chess, but even a queen may have to pause to destroy pawns placed in the way."

"Do you have any feel for how long we have to stop him?"

"No. But I do feel that we have some time, if we act now."

"Very well. I will see to it. I know the subjects you mean. We'll ready them, prime them and send them out."

"Use all of those in readiness state."

"All? Just so. And Chugun?"

"I'll do that."

"Fair enough. But there's something about this sequence of events I find makes me uneasy."

"Go on."

"Rael left the papers behind for you. And he said he wouldn't tell us anything that would make any difference. So by that, he's telling us he doesn't care if we know. That we can't stop him."

"You are filled with happy prospects today."

"Yes. Hindsight is wonderful; but there are things you can't know, it seems, until you reach for them in reality."

"And everything else he told us in the end?"

"That, too. Well, to work." And Avaria turned and left Pternam's private quarters.

Pternam, now alone, waited a bit before calling Chugun. For a time, he thought bleak and private thoughts, his mind still racing. And in rehearsing exactly what he was going to tell Chugun, he quite forgot one thing Rael had told him. It hadn't seemed important at the time, and was even less so now. Something about an unseen party maintaining the Lisak world. It hovered, this thought, just out of sight. Something important, but not right now.

And when he had finished his call to the offices of Femisticleo Chugun, a nagging thought kept ticking away at the corner of his mind that there was something else he should have said, but he couldn't quite place exactly what it was. No matter. The forces were now in motion, for better or worse.

～ 5 ～

Tiresio

Seconing. Rael read the signboard and paused a moment to allow some sense of spatial orientation to assert itself. He had come in the night, using these first few hours of freedom to put distance between himself and Pternam. But on foot there was not much he could do except disappear, which he could do well enough. Seconing. This was a distant suburb to the south of Symbarupol, a small and sleepy townlet concentrating on small manufactures, small crafts shops. Here, the buildings were more functional, and smaller, and the streets narrower. They favored plain wooden buildings here with large windows of many small panes, which now in the darkness showed only the dim glow of watchlamps. The streets were empty, shiny-damp with dew, colored with a bluish tint from the shops and streetlamps; Seconing tumbled down the last slope to the plains of Crule in pleasant disorder, with the hills close behind to the east. Far off out on the plains, he could hear in the quiet the passing of a beamliner running on its elevated I-beam, a rhythmic, steady, muffled sound.

The beamliner passed to the south. An express, it did not approach or stop at places like Seconing. Now he listened again, and heard, farther off, eastwards, deep in the hills, the night-cries of bosels, indigenous creatures of unpredictable habit. The calls had the odd quality of sounding profoundly artificial to the human ear, as if made electronically. There was a monotonous three-syllable call, starting on one note, then one higher, sliding to the original tone, repeated rhythmically several times. Another was a tinkling, tumbling sequence of no apparent order, and still another was a long wail, suggestive of profound loneliness. No one knew if that was what it really expressed; Bosels were alien, wild, and erratic enough to be regarded as demons by more conservative country folk. At night they prowled and called back and forth, sometimes making astonishing collations of sound, which the Lisaks wisely shut their windows to.

Rael quickened his pace through the dark streets, among the shops, avoiding the residential hillocks and their attendant racks of velocipedes, all set neatly in rows. Bosels were not unknown in towns like this in the night, so his recent education informed him, and against them his equations seemed to have no power. They were approximately man-sized, and could be dangerous; Rael felt no fear, but he did not wish to meet one. That was not within the desirable sequence of events, and would attract any onlooker. Not now.

There were short ramps connecting the levels of the curving streets, hardly more than alleyways, which Rael followed downwards, to the edge of the plains. At the bottom, he found his view to the west obscured by an untidy tangle of I-beams in sturdy metal posts: the local beamer switching yards, now mostly quiet, although here he could sense the suggestion of active life. He followed the lines farther south, not entering them, but staying in the street, until the local terminal building appeared; this a plain, workshoplike structure with a small windowed cupola at each end. Empty, dark as the rest, with a small lamp inside making only a weak glimmer. Closed for the night. Across the street there was a glimmer of light and movement, a small rest-place halfway under the overhang of one of the buildings fronting the yards and the station. A warehouse or storage depot. Rael detached himself from the shadows and walked slowly toward the rest, falling easily into the movement pattern of one who had nothing to do but wait. An easy walk, passing time, while inside he heard time running steadily, inexorably.

Around him, there was quiet, and, muffled and distorted by the buildings of the town, he heard a last call of a bosel, somewhere up in the hills on the other side: a long, rising, reedy tone, leveling out and collapsing at the end into a descending series of short titters. Eerie music. It bothered him that he heard it so clearly, for he knew that the humans on Oerlikon ignored or avoided the native life forms as much as possible. *Nerves,* he thought. After all, this, now was really where he emerged into the stream of the world. Now. Rael stepped out of the shadows into the glow of the overhanging streetlights and went directly to the rest-house, down a short flight of stone stairs, smelling of damp woollen clothing and stale beer.

Inside, it was a small, cramped room with benches around

63

the walls, and a counter along one wall backed by a fading mirror. It was early in the morning; predawn, and there was no tipsy night gaiety. The proprietor sat lumpishly on a stool and stared off into nothing. The room was crowded, but curiously empty in feeling. As if the people were there, but not in spirit. They filled the benches, their bundles piled beside them, waiting for the local beamer that was always late. Rael looked briefly at them, and then into the fading mirror, at the unrecognizable stranger who was the only one standing in the room, who looked back at him with an alien face whose set conveyed no meaning to him whatsoever. He caught the weak attention of the counterman and ordered a mug of hagdrupe, which was presently passed across the counter, reeking with the acrid flavor of the boiled potion. Rich in an alkaloid similar to caffeine, hagdrupe served the settlers of Oerlikon in place of coffee, which they had left behind. This was vastly overboiled and rancid, but he sipped at it anyway, passing one of the coins from his meager store across the counter.

Rael found the place subtly disturbing, familiar. Not that he had been in one before; not as Tiresio Rael. Perhaps as someone else who had been, once. He blinked. He could not remember Jedily; but the association set him to reflecting. He knew this world well, despite his loss of the other life which he had been, so they had told him. It felt familiar, all the sad nothingness of it, the sour flavor of the arguments the lifers* used to bolster their endless justifications to the poor sloggers*. He fit into it perfectly, and he did not know why in any direct sense. The logical explanation was that Jedily was familiar with this sort of life, and that there were ingrained habits even The Mask Factory could not erase, did not know of. Rael knew of one he had saved, hidden carefully from them, although it was covered openly in the notes he had left Pternam. Small chance, there.

What did Rael know? Rael's system of computation was paradoxical, like all good science, ambiguous, fleeting. He thought, *Science and Art are exactly alike in that. Ambiguity, a shimmering mirage.* It considered, on the one hand, that human faces were unique to a terrifying degree, even when broken down into component parts, and that a large section of the brain was devoted solely to the recognition of those unique patterns. It considered, equally, that music shared the

* The slang terms for the two main classes of Lisak society.

same sort of uniqueness; that what the uninitiated saw as a single persona was in reality a highly-organized group of disparate personalities gathered under the one roof of the body. And that whole societies acted as these complex entities, and that certain highly specialized statistical methods led one, by a crooked trail, into understanding, which integrated Time into the picture, a continuum that one could follow one's way through, with discipline and will.

He looked at the figure in the mirror: a thin, saturnine person, some slogger down on his luck, perhaps, insignificant, unworthy of notice. He looked . . . resigned, used to it by now. Oerlikon was the place where the Changeless gained power, and they had locked it into place for all time. To one tied within that perception, there was no hope, no possibility of change. But Rael had seen how it could be done within the holistic pattern his formulae had revealed, and he had seen much more there than he had told Pternam. Pternam! They had done something to him . . . not once, but many times. There had been pain and fear, later fading but never completely gone. They could always bring it back, if they wished. And as they had perceived a pattern emerging, so it had suited them to see that Rael could at least convince some that the incredible idea might be true. But they of course did not believe it. He saw that, understood it from the beginning; that made him all the more determined to make it real, make it work. And work it would.

It was exactly as Pternam had told the revolutionaries. That much. But there was more to it. Once he did it, the world would change, obeying its own laws about the speed of the reaction, but not as any of them imagined it. No. In the new alignment, there would be no Pternams, and the Heraclitan Society could not exist, would fade and be a curious note in the histories, if any were written. Those in the future, they would look back in astonishment, in gaping, slack-jawed wonder. And in this set of the world, Rael felt the pressure: he was not supposed to *be*. The orientation of a world that set a premium on Changelessness did not include one who could stand partly outside it, outside the *mythos, and* reset the balance point of the reflected pyramid so that it assumed a new set, a set in which Rael, or rather what he would become, would live openly, buried. Rael would make the act that would begin the Change, but not for Pternam or the revolutionaries, but to create a Set of World in which he could exist. It would be, of course, as Damistofia. It was fitting, he thought, for somehow he felt the Jedily had been pushed to the edge as well, in her own time, without knowing why, pushed to the edge and beyond, and would return to peace in a world he would make for one who would come.

Now he allowed the composition of the group in the nasty little godown to seep onto him, carefully, so that they were not aware of his attention. He heard fragments of small talk, small sounds of half-awake people trying to arrange themselves comfortably. He let his eyes wander, seeing what they would, careful not to allow the lingering of attention, anything which might alert some watcher who might be spotted in this group. The owner was harassed and overworked. To him the faces that pressed upon him daily were just papers in the wind, faded petals on a rain-wet branch; a handful of traveling reps of the trade guilds, or contact men for the small factories that were the mainstay of small suburbs like this. A couple of farmers from back in the country, scared of bosels by night and city sharpers by day, but on the way to Marula no less, where they expected to be cheated; one recognizable Proctor, one who was tasked with uncovering Change and arresting it. This one was old and tired and waiting for his pension after an uneventful lifetime of snooping and offering Pollyanna-pap advice, usually unsolicited, which never worked for those who needed it most. The Proctor was not even aware of him, and the rest were totally uninterested. He had picked a good group, bound for the distant City, one they hated and feared, Marula, vast, sprawling, trashy, fecund Marula, the City-as-Beast in the warmth of the southern province of Sertse Solntsa.

Rael relaxed into the disciplines of his craft, and began to read the group identity; this one was weak, but it was there for the initiate to understand: a minimum of awareness and coherence. As he *read* the group, he felt a sudden constriction, a knotting, a small awakening. He visualized it as an abstract plane surface with random undulating waves of low amplitude, which developed a bunching: he followed it, and understood that the Beamer was coming. They had heard it before they were consciously aware they had heard anything. He levered himself out of this state and perceived normally: he saw someone get up and stretch, while others began stirring, although it would be some time yet before time came to board.

They were rising, now, one by one, moving slowly, joints

stiffened from inactivity. One seemed to be having considerable difficulty with an unwieldy bundle which resisted all efforts to gather it for lifting. He looked closer, something catching his attention. Yes. Under the shapeless plain garments of a wandering agricultural worker, he thought he could recognize a girl or woman. She turned so her face showed: Rael saw that she was not particularly attractive, and no one seemed to pay her any attention at all—indeed, they seemed to avoid her. Could he contact her? He took a quick moment to *read*, and saw that he could, but that it would lower his position, such as it was. What was she? With her plain looks, she certainly was not one of the inhabitants of one of the happy-houses. He made as if to leave the room, and as if on an impulse, turned back and approached the girl, and asked, "You need help with that bundle?"

For a flicker of an instant, she registered fear, looking back to him, but this faded, and after a moment, she said, "Yes. Please; it was fine until I set it down."

Rael bent and grasped the bundle, and after a few tries, found it to be indeed uncooperative. He sat back on his haunches and said, "It doesn't work so well for me, either; what's in here?"

The girl continued to struggle with the bundle, and said, without looking up, "Cured fleischbaum pod."

He understood better why the rest ignored her. The fleischbaum, a scraggly, ragged tree, produced a pod whose fibers, properly cured, were of the flavor and protein content of meat. The problem was that the trees would not grow close to one another, which made orchards and plantations impossible, and the gathering was done from wild trees scattered through the wild. And for reasons which Rael did not completely understand, this was considered the lowest occupation one could take. He said, neutrally and as politely as he could, "You're a gatherer."

"Yes."

He said, "By the feel of it, it may take two to manage this bundle; it's shifted inside badly. Did you carry it here alone?"

She brushed a strand of curly, mouse-brown hair out of her face, now shiny with sweat. "Yes. For the markets. In Marulupol." Gatherers were the most solitary and taciturn of people, people of the open, the empty places, the stony wildernesses, people who heard their own thoughts in the silences, and who often had to run for their lives: from bosels, and from occasional bands of more integrated people who delighted in harassing solitaries, knowing there could be no retribution when none but the victim knew of the crime. Rael looked at her again. She was not a beauty, but there was no ugliness on her face. He could read it. Fear and despair and loneliness she had known, but not envy, impatience, rage, frustration, the marks of societal people.

He got a grip on the bundle at last, and lifted it. It was surprisingly heavy, and he felt more respect for the girl for managing to carry it alone; it was a load that would have taxed a strong man, yet somehow she had managed alone. He said, "I've got it, but it won't stay; it'll take both of us."

She picked up her end. "I had it packed just so—it wasn't hard. Now if we stop to retie it, I'll miss the beamer. . . . Are you certain you won't feel shame associating with a gatherer?"

"Will it disturb you to associate with a stranger?"

"What are you, that you would call yourself stranger?"

"I am Tiresio. Let us say that things have changed somewhat for me. Fortune, as it were. However it is, I now find myself looking for a new life of sorts, and in a land where things remain as they were, this can be difficult."

Now she smiled a little. As if she understood. Yes. Rael was someone who had been through Correction. Attitude Adjustment. He saw her in the light coming in from the street, seeing an open face free of guile or plot. Well-formed, though plain. She said, "And so you would take up with a gatherer, or a lonely woman? No matter—I need the help, so it would seem. Have a care, though: I'm an egg-stealer, too, and I've grappled bosels more than once and come away alive, and they don't volunteer for it."

Now that she was standing, he could see more of her shape and configuration; she was shorter than he, stocky and sturdy. He noticed that she moved well, confidently, with balance and no small amount of grace. He read truth in her words. She was extraordinarily self-possessed. She was exactly what she said she was. He said, "Very well, that is fair to say. And you know me as Tiresio. How are you called?"

She half turned away from him, shyly. "Meliosme."

Still grappling with the load, Rael made an artificially polite face. "Meliosme. May I accompany you to Marula?"

She gave him a wry smile, saying, "If you will help me get this thing to the fleischbaum bazaar, I will not complain, nor will I eat stinkhorns in front of you. But there remains a

68

thing—which is what must I do. You can see that I can pay little or nothing, and. . . ."

"I will be grateful for the company. I know no one now. Until Marula; I have affairs there."

"You could have one prettier, no doubt, if for hire, from the happy-house."

"Perhaps." Here he raised one index finger dramatically. "True. But *they* will not ride the beamer to Marula. Moreover I have little enough in the way of money. . . . And last, you are by no means homely or fearsome, or one to be called a bagger."*

"Gallant as well! And with the words as well. Are you a fugitive?"

"Not yet."

"So. Very well, then. But few seek such as I, and I'll sully your reputation, such as it is. Others may sneer. It's said that when a slogger associates with a gatherer, it's the gatherer who's in bad company, for who would stoop so low. . . ."

"I accept. Let's go."

They were the last of the group to leave the dim little godown. The proprietor remained behind the bar, glum and absorbed in his own concerns, and ignored them and the irregular bundle they were struggling with. Outside, a weary daylight was seeping into the adyts of the world, like a winter sunrise through frosted glass, although winter was by no means near yet.

The beamer was still moving along its elevated track, very slowly, but the rest of the people were gathering at locations which they suspected from long practice would be where the doors were when the machine stopped. Unlike the express models which ran at high speeds out on the plains of Crule, the locals made no rhythmic, driving sounds evocative of motion and power but emitted noises of mechanical, electrical and pneumatic protest: the electric motors hummed and throbbed irregularly and joints squealed with friction; likewise, the air brakes emitted vulgar flatulent moans, ventings and hisses. With a last moan, the beamer stopped, and the passengers began crowding at the doors.

* Slang. Homely women were called "baggers" by the men, allegedly on the premise that they were so ugly they would have to put a bag over their head in order to have a liaison with someone. Even more extreme were the so-called two-baggers, in which cases the man would also put a bag over his head, in case hers came off.

Meliosme said, "No need to hurry; we won't get a seat with a sack full of fleischbaum with us, anyway."

"The baggage section, then?"

"Where else? But I accept it with resignation—at least I don't have to endure the lifers up in the fine compartments, or the sloggers on the benches with their envy. No—it's all just plain stuff back with the tramps and the thieves. All fools together. Never worry—they won't bother us. What I am can't be helped and you don't seem to have anything worth stealing . . . or else you're hiding well. Either way, you're not worth a risk. We'll have an easy bit of it."

Rael cast Meliosme a wintry glance from his end of the sack. "You inspire one to excellence with your compliments."

"I mean that you should trust me, for this seems new to you. There is something . . . out of place with you."

Rael said, "I would not say why, but I am as confident in my own resources as you are in yours. Let not the aspect deceive you."

She smiled, like a child. "Oh, I am not. Otherwise I would not have let you come with me. What I do, out there; it makes one sensitive to the quick judgment of people. I mean that you cannot de-egg a bosel's creche in the company of idle boasters; that kind of stuff shortens lives. You, now: I think you could do it, but you never have. You don't move like one who has done a sprightly step with a bosel buck, or better yet a great mother bosel in oestrus, but you are wary—a good thing to be. So come along now; never fear—I will not betray your direness, which hangs about you like a thundercloud. So long as it does not involve me."

Rael did not have to look. This was not his quarry. He said, "It does not." And then they were boarding, wrestling the sack through a door which had seemed big enough, but at the crucial moment wasn't. And after they had negotiated that problem, there were others to attend to, until at last they found an open spot no one else had claimed, and there set the sack down, and themselves leaning up against it from opposite sides. For the while, they said nothing, and presently they felt the jerky, erratic motions that signaled the movement of the beamer.

Rael sat in silence beside Meliosme and reflected on how fortunate he had been to meet one such as her. For however much he knew about the pattern of deed which he must do, it was in no way a revelation of the whole future to come. Meliosme had arrived by luck—pure aleatory hazard, a happen-

70

ing, a fortune; and by this hazard he had picked someone who was infinitely more real than those pallid phantoms moving about who thought they were people. And as an outcast type, herself, she would be acutely sensitive to the whims of the groups they passed through: a most excellent antenna tuned to the present, and an odd, intriguing mind as well. Now, for the first time since he had computed this course, since he'd *seen* this way, he felt like he could relax for a little. And he thought, as he relaxed, that he sincerely hoped that he could disengage from his cover, Meliosme, when things began in earnest.

The beamliner started up again, and moved out onto the elevated trackage leading south along the edge of the hills to the next small town, somewhere out of sight. It rode roughly; the beams were uneven and aligned poorly. Nevertheless, Rael saw, sneaking a quick glance out of the corner of his eye, that Meliosme was cat-napping, taking little short naps, broken by a slight movement, then relaxation again. It looked effortless, and Rael envied her the skill; he would like to have that ability himself. He needed rest, now. The moment of action was not all that far away.

Rael tried to compose himself by imagining how one could know parts of the future. He did not question the techniques he had been taught and had added to himself, so much as he failed, as everyone else did, to integrate such momentary flashes into a coherent theory of how the universe worked. He knew about prescient dreams, and visions people had under one circumstance or another. His method, while controlled, non-mystical, scientific, all that negated mystery, only opened up deeper layers, and was no less ambivalent, contradictory, incomprehensible. He asked a coherent system for answers, and it gave them. But only that. There was no linking; the answers were as unique as the stars, as a piece of music, as a face. *Do this at this moment and it changes.* He had free choice: he could refuse, or pass. *It did not matter: such chances to alter the lines of this world occurred over and over again. It was just a matter of finding the next one, finding the next act, or non-act.* But he could feel this moment coming, and this one was special, different from the others in the way that all such instants were: they had different reaches of influence. And this moment coming at him at the speed the beamliner was running was one in which he could reach all the phases that controlled Oerlikon. And as he thought about it, he saw something else he'd not realized before: that in reaching all phases, there would be a backlash here that would reach into the incomprehensible third phase, and institute change there, too, although he couldn't see that, or how it would be. Only that it would be.

The sun rose and morning began fading into forenoon. Small towns passed, and the line of the hills began curving off to the east. Now the stops were out on the plains, which were becoming flatter and more watery, although they were a good ways yet from Marula. Once Meliosme went forward and returned with some buns, which she shared with Rael. They were hard and crusty, but good. He was hungry. And sharing them made them better.

After one long halt at a place called Orgeon, the beamer started up again, and as soon as it was trundling along out in the open country, he stood up, stiff from long sitting.

Meliosme glanced at him. "Where are you going?"

"Want to move about. I'm getting stiff. Is there water somewhere forward?"

"All the way up."

She fumbled a moment, and handed Rael a small metal flask. "Bring me some, please."

Rael nodded, and leaned to take it. A motion of the car moved him off-balance, and he caught himself on the sack of fleischbaum, feeling for something he knew would be there. A pin in the fabric, holding a place together that did not matter much. A sharp pain met his palm, and he grasped the pin out and palmed it. Meliosme did not notice. As the car steadied, Rael took the flask.

Meliosme said, "Be careful between cars; they can pitch you out in the swamp. This is one place you don't want to walk it, especially nursing bruises or worse."

Rael said, "Bosels?"

She said, grimly, "No. Not here. They're hill-creatures, or at least they prefer firmer ground. Upper Crule. Here, you'll have Letomeres, Sentrosomes. Maybe Kidraks."

"I'll watch out." As if to emphasize his words, the car gave another lurch, which this time did not throw him off balance.

Meliosme said, "Well, you seem to be getting the hang of it . . ." And she shifted her attention. Rael turned about and started forward along the length of the car, toward the front

72

of the beamliner, somewhere unseen far ahead, negotiating the ill-set elevated beams which guided the train. Now. Between Orgeon and the next halt, Inenda. It was a long passage, the last long stretch between here and Marula. Now. He could feel apprehension pounding the blood in his ears. Now. He permitted himself a nervous little chuckle, thinking about Pternam and the revolutionaries, all curious, all certain that he would do it in Marula, because he had told them that Damistofia would be there. All wrong. Not in Marula. Before Marula. Now.

Rael made his way forward through the swaying cars slowly, deliberately, like one who had never been on one before, lurching, leaning, holding on as he went. In part, this was wholly natural, and also in part it was a careful motional disguise, which effectively made him invisible to those around him. In this way he passed through four of the cars before he found what he was looking for: one of the wooden bench seats, occupied by a single young man, who was now looking out the window at the dreary passing landscape, a passing panorama of sloughs, marshes, expanses of territory neither land nor water but an uncomfortable hybrid of both, dotted by random clumps of spikegrass in the water proper, and brackberry tangles covering the land portions with their stilt-legged arachnid stance.

He had not known which car it would be, but he premembered the scene perfectly, just as it was: the light from Gysa coppering the marshes with its afternoon slants, the clear aqua-blue of the sky, by which he knew that the seasons had changed. Now it was autumn. It would be cooler now. And the young man sitting on the bench.

Rael leaned forward and said, "Seat taken?"

The young man shook his head absently, thoughts clearly elsewhere. Rael sat down, softly, so as not to attract any attention. No one had noticed him. The young man placed an arm on the windowsill and propped his head up, leaning forward slightly.

Rael said, "Excuse me," and leaned over behind him, as if reaching to place something on the shelf over the windows, and with a motion that did not seem to deviate from those normal lurchings caused by the swaying of the car, drove the pin he had taken into the base of the young man's brain.

Rael felt the body stiffen, and then relax, as he resumed his

73

own seat. The body did not slump or fall, but remained in position, propped up; it would remain that way, the muscles locked, until someone moved him, which doubtless would not be until the last stop in the Marula transit yards. Rael sat back, blending into the background with the rest of the sloggers, reflecting, feeling conflicting emotions. He felt a pain deep in his heart, an emotion he could put no name to. It was without doubt that it was an evil thing to dispatch this young man into the darkness so coldly, not even in the heat of an argument, not in conflict, but coldly. Without warning, without anticipation. Yet at the same time he could see this figure as a nexus of powerful forces, himself obscure, a nobody, but paradoxically the carrier of the weight of the whole world. This was the one. This was, without doubt, the enemy. Rael did not understand, but he could see it clearly. This was the one. And he could see the rest of it as well, how he would place a slip of paper in the boy's hand, with one word printed on it: "Rael." They would have to know who had done this. Rael printed the word on the paper and placed it in the boy's free hand, now cool. Rael looked carefully at the face; the eyes were closed, as if the boy were napping along the way. Exactly the way it was supposed to go.

And the rest: Rael got out of the seat and caught the attention of one sitting nearby, who had also been woolgathering, studiously trying not to see others or be seen by them, and to this one he said, "Pardon, but my friend is sleeping. He's very tired, and will not need to get off until Marulupol."

The other nodded. "Right. Up all night with a lady before his trip to the big city, eh? Well, no harm there; it's not a flaw to nap on the way."

Rael agreed, the man continued, "He seemed to be looking for someone, a bit earlier . . . was he to meet someone on the way?"

Rael thought, and answered, "Perhaps he was. Maybe they'll see him when he gets to Marula."

The other nodded, and began sinking back into his own thoughts, already dismissing the incident. Rael began turning away, letting him sink back. That was fine. He would almost forget it, until incidents at the station caused him to remember. No matter. By then, Rael would be long gone, or so he planned to be. The deed was done now, in the only time-slot open for it. Now the clock was running. When the beamer reached Marula, there would be a confusion over the body, but sooner or later they would sort things out, and then the hunt would be on. Rael figured that to make a successful *change*, he had to get at least a full day ahead of his pursuers, better yet a day and a half. He started forward, to get the water for Meliosme.

～ 6 ～
Marula

The outskirts of Marula slid by, mostly beneath the level of the elevated beamer. In the baggage car, Meliosme glanced out the window from time to time, but did not keep a close eye on the city. Rael, on the other hand, watched intently, for to his knowledge it was a place totally strange to him. From his training, he knew in a rough sort of way how Marula was laid out, if that phrase could apply to an organism which constantly changed, as variable as the channels of the sluggish inland river whose delta formed its foundation.

To the Lisaks with the most correct attitude orientation, Marula was something of a necessary evil, but withal a place to be avoided if at all possible. It changed. And its people survived from day to day by managing, so the saying went, with changing channels, docks whose approaches silted up overnight, roads which sank into the soft muck without a trace, elevated beamlines which leaned crazily to either side of center, and were propped up with ropes and stumps. Unlike the other cities of Lisagor, there was no area within the complex which could be called a city center, a built-up area in which authority resided. Authority, such as it was, moved about according to where the action was. No one bothered to erect anything resembling a permanent structure; instead, they threw up temporary buildings which became semi-permanent by force of habit, some part of them in constant repair.

With so much change about, it was natural that the inhabitants would take on some of its aspects; to this end, large numbers of the infamous Pallet-Dropped Troopers were settled there in garrison, and were paraded through the streets often. Those who missed their attentions did not complain, but expressed a sigh of relief that they had not been given over to the mercies of the troopers. There were also numerous officials, proctors, attitude patrols, informers, spies, and investigators, the result of which was that Marula, for all its diversity and sprawl, was effectively and tightly controlled.

Perhaps it was controlled, but it was not run very well. Marula was chaotic and disorganized, a fact Rael hoped to use to his advantage. Here, even with modern communications, things proceeded slowly; slowly enough so that if Rael could get away cleanly from the beamer, he could count on being able to gain the lead on them he needed.

Here, they did not bother to build the little hills on which the living-quarters grew which were traditional with other Lisak cities; the land wouldn't support them. Instead, they fashioned small enclaves resembling labyrinths in which one-, two- and three-story buildings proliferated. Inside the enclaves the streets were hardly more than alleys. Low walls separated the enclaves from the rest of the land, which was given over to other uses, mostly industrial.

Rael said, "Where are we now?"

It was evening, and the sky was becoming overcast from the southwest, washing the outlines of the city with a soft, weak light that obscured much of its harshness. It seemed, in this light, slightly magical, strange, exotic, a place where odd events might succeed.

Meliosme said, "This district is called Sango; the beamer won't stop here. The next named place is Semora, which is where I leave."

"It's close to the markets you have to go to?"

"Closest for this beamline. Got to walk a bit more."

"You'll still need help. . . ."

Meliosme looked sidelong at him, an odd coy look. "Still?"

"I'll trade you that for you telling me a place I can go and be unknown for, say, two days. After that . . . it won't matter."

Some light in her face faded. She said, "Plenty of places like that in Marula, in fact, if you're willing to move, you can keep ahead of them very well indefinitely . . . I know of something that might do, near the markets, if they haven't torn it down, which they often do here, but it will probably do. I'll trade."

"What will you do after you sell your fleischbaum?"

"What else? Go out again for more."

"Back to the Symbar area?"

"No, I'm a wanderer. I'll probably go on over into Tilanque, more southerly than Symbarupol. Winter's coming on, cold nights and the like, and I flow with it. You wouldn't

77

catch me working Grayslope or Severovost in the cold season, no. . . . And what are your plans?"

"After a day or so, I'll seek out a position here for the time. That will be enough."

"You wouldn't care to wander?"

"Not now."

"You look as if you could, and there's not many I'd say that to."

Rael chuckled, half to himself. "Not now, but if I came later, how would I fine you?"

"Not out in the field! But if you visited the markets, you'd likely catch word of me. . . ." She looked thoughtful, an attitude that made her plain face seem full of light and animation. "Mind, I offer little in the way of bennies*, but on the other hand, neither would you have to endure a preachy lifer, either. To be free. . . ."

"You don't have trouble with the authorities?"

She shrugged. "People want fleischbaum, and it's a lot of trouble to get it, so they leave it to people like me. Why not? We offer no Change to the sloggers. They wouldn't leave if they could."

Rael said, "They might have to, some day."

Meliosme frowned. "I know. I've heard, too, but it's just talk; it'll come to nothing, all that. They'll throw out Monclova and Chugun, but who'll come along but someone just as vile, with the same kind of boseldung, promising, promising, but the end of it is that there'll still be lifers running things and spouting slogans, and millions of sloggers keeping them afloat, all idiots. At any rate, they won't do a night-trot with a bosel, and so much for them,." She looked at Rael again. "Surely you aren't after all that."

Rael answered her straightly, more honestly than he knew. "I need now some time to think, to wait. But after that, well I might come, at least for a while."

She looked at him critically. "Need to put some weight on you, and some sun for that dungeon tan you wear on your hide," but she smiled shyly as she said it.

Rael agreed. "That wasn't a seaside resort I was in, that's a fact."

The beamer went through an alarming series of junctions

---

* Bennies: "Benefits," *i.e.*, of accepting an income from State Service as opposed to making your own living. These included food, clothing, housing and job security, all of which demanded a careful attention to one's allegiances and remarks.

which felt rubbery and insecure, and began slowing down. Meliosme glanced through the window quickly and said, "Semora coming up."

"Does the beamer have stops after Semora?"

"Beyond? Yes. It goes to the yards, to the shops. The old terminal used to be there, and many people still go all the way in. Did you change your mind?"

"No. Just curious." Rael turned away from her and pretended to look out the window on the opposite side, to conceal the relief he felt.

The beamer slowed to a groaning crawl and proceeded through a district, so it seemed, down the middle of a broad street. To either side were drab, low buildings of many sizes and styles, but they all had that shanty atmosphere which seemed to characterize Marula. There were a lot of people about, most on foot, strolling about in the evening air, which was thick and flavored with many odd substances so close to the ocean and the marshes, and with so many different industrial operations. Yet they displayed a certain swagger, a furtive elan, which distinguished them from the rest of Lisaks, who generally favored uniformity and anonymity.

The beamer aligned itself in the platform area and stopped with a series of alarming noises, and finally a bump, which made Rael wince, as he thought of someone precariously propped on an elbow four cars forward. But he got to his feet calmly, and began working with Meliosme to grapple the awkward bundle, and eventually they got it up between them and struggled to the door.

Together they made their way through the streets where Meliosme went with an unerring sense of familiarity. Near the station, on the main thoroughfare, there had been crowds, who fastidiously gave them room, but as they left the station area the crowds thinned and grew less deferential, although no one bothered them. They negotiated a series of narrow alleys, poorly lit, and at last came to a cavernous shed which seemed to be abandoned but wasn't; there was a sleepy night watchman, who let them pass inside without comment, almost without notice.

Inside the shed there was a dim light from lanterns set at intervals along the walls, none of them bright. Meliosme picked a place by a dimmer spot along one wall and there they set the bag down. Rael now took time to look around. Scattered all over the floor of the shed were others with vari-

79

ous-sized bundles, some large and apparently unmanageable, others hardly worth the effort of dragging them here. Most of the others appeared to be gatherers like Meliosme, all rather ragged, most catnapping, or conversing in small groups, very quietly in low tones so as not to disturb the others. Now and then one might go out for some food, or a bottle of spirits. In contrast to the lively, wary activity outside on the streets, here was quiet and a sense of peace, in which he felt some irony, for these were the outcasts of Lisak society, the gatherers.

Meliosme arranged the bag, and settled down next to it, motioning to Rael to sit beside her. This he did, half-leaning against the wall behind them. In the semidarkness, with the soft mumble of distant slow conversations all around them, he was conscious of the solid warmth of her body next to his, and she did not move away. He said, after a time, "You stay here?"

Meliosme nodded. "This is the fleischbaum bazaar. The selling will commence at dawn. That is why you see little in the way of rowdying and roistering. You have to be awake then, or you'll wake up with little or nothing for a month's trip in the wild. No one, besides, wants a gatherer in their hostel or inn, so we stay here. You sell, and then you leave. I expect to make a good bundle this trip . . ."

"What do you do with it?"

"Replace worn clothes, boots, a new knife . . . If there's much left over, I'll get a place for a few days and enjoy some luxuries, like a hot bath; cold streams are fine, but everyone likes a little laziness now and then." She relaxed a little, softening. "You could stay here tonight without fear. In the morning, I'll show you how it's done and then I'll set you on the righteous path of being free."

"How do you know I could?"

She shrugged. "I don't *know*. You might work out badly—who knows? There are more women gatherers than men, why I don't know. But you have an air about you of one worth a chance. You are an outcast, that much I can see with my own eyes, no matter which Silver City* you were a guest in; and not so much one who'd make a good little slogger, not here in Marula. No! You've got to snuffle up to the

---

* Silver City: The exercise yard of a confinement camp, fenced in with a tinny-bright metal mesh, electrified, hence the slang term.

old bung smartly here to get along. And you'll not do it well. Admit it."

Rael found himself liking immensely this rough woman. He put his arm about her shoulders, and she did not move away. "It's true what you say, and I admit I'm tempted to go your way. . . ."

A noise from outside intruded on his train of thought, and interrupted his words. It was a sound of wheels, and a thudding, rhythmic compression, and a piercing little whistle, repeated at intervals. The noise grew, and then faded. Rael had never heard anything like it, but he noticed that Meliosme listened to it intently, and many others in the warehouse also listened closely to it. As the sound faded, he asked, "What was that?"

She said, quietly, "Police van. Something's happened. Sounded like somewhere near the station . . . not so good."

"Why so?" Rael whispered, so others wouldn't hear.

Meliosme sighed, "Anything happens, they sift the gatherers. We are always suspect, you know. And you and I were on the beamer. If it's something on the train, they'll be along presently . . . I guess we'll have to wait."

"You are not in danger . . . ?"

"No." But Rael suddenly thought of a pin, and that it might well be a common type used by gatherers. They had been seen together, and this was the place where gatherers congregated. He felt a sudden constriction of alarm.

"Meliosme?" He fumbled in his clothing and extracted a hidden wallet. "How much would you expect to get for your sackful, there?"

"What?"

He extracted some currency notes and showed them to her. "Take what you think the sack's worth. I can't explain it now, but we have to leave this place now and hide. Separately."

For a moment she hesitated. Rael hissed, "Take it. I trusted you: now you trust me. I know danger."

Reluctantly, she peered at the money in the dim light, at last selecting some notes, which she took and stuffed into her breast. Rael said, "I am sorry to have caused you this, but we must get out of here. And you must tell me how to get a place I can hide."

She stood up, and Rael stood with her. She said, "I don't know, but I'd guess you don't want to be caught, and if they see you, they'll know you. Did you escape?"

"In a manner of speaking. . . . Where do we go?"

Meliosme glanced at the large sack with some regrets, and hesitated. Then she turned to him, face straight and matter-of-fact. "Come along. I know the way, and with all the coming and going, no one will notice." She led him back to the entrance, where a group of gatherers was just coming in, and two were trying to get out, causing a confusion with which the watchman was unsuccessfully coping. In a moment, depending on the respect and good manners the gatherers showed one another, they were through the gate and into the heavy night.

Then they set off in another direction, traversing narrow ways and crossing broad streets, rapidly crossing several small districts, and the only thing Rael could tell about their route was that it seemed that they were headed away from both the station and the bazaar, to the unknown. They saw no one who looked at them twice; there were few out. But at last they came to a more habited place, a sort of neighborhood of small shops, taverns and inns, and a few walk-up dwellings. It looked rough, but far removed. Meliosme took them to a small, three-story hostel and engaged a room for them without comment, nor did the night man make any. Lisaks were as they were about their affairs, even in Marula. Night-clerks did not comment upon whom they rented rooms to.

When they had gotten the key and climbed the stairs to the room, they found it a little bare, but serviceable. And it had its own bath. Meliosme smiled at the single bed, and at the bath, and said, "Well, it's sooner than I planned, but looks like I get my hot tub."

Rael gently took her by the shoulders and looked in her eyes. "No. Believe me, I did not intend to have you in this; you must not stay here."

She smiled at him, exposing white, even teeth. "No matter. This is a good hideout. They'll never find us."

Rael shook his head. "There is something you don't understand, but which you must take and accept. For your life, you have to leave, and by a different way than we came in."

"No problem there. . . . If you didn't want me. . . ."

"That is the problem right now. I do want you: that is why I am telling you to leave. They will catch me. I only need to be ahead of them for about a day, and then it doesn't matter. But you can't stay."

"Why?" She set her feet, preparing to stay.

"Something is going to happen to me which I will not have

82

you see . . . and which will entangle you in something unimaginably bad. If you love your freedom, leave me while you can, now."

She relaxed, incomprehension on her face. She said slowly, "Are you going to be killed . . . or changed?"

"I may, both. I didn't want you in it . . . but I stayed because I felt good with you. But because of that I now ask you to leave and save yourself."

"I believe you . . . but I don't understand. Can you escape? Can you meet me somewhere else after this blows over?"

Rael knew he had won. He said, "I can escape, but it has to be alone. I will seek you out, no matter where you are, but I may look different. Would you still have me?"

"Would it be only the looks that changed?"

"I don't know. I think it's only that, if this works. . . . Go back to the wild, tonight. Marula's not safe for you this trip, but it will be later."

"Would you really come looking for me?"

"I think so now."

"You'd never find your way around Tilanque . . . I'll go from here northwest, into the hills between Zolotane and Crule. You know those?"

"No better than Tilanque."

"At any rate, it's closer, and you can find me better, I think. I'll go there for my next trip, work north toward the Serpentine. But how will I know you?"

"I'll come to you and tell you who I am, what we did . . . or almost did."

"Would you have?"

"I would have liked to very much . . . more than anything in the life I can remember."

"Very well . . . Good-bye, Tiresio."

"Good-bye, Meliosme. Good fortune to you."

"And to you. I think you need the wish more than I." She took his face in her hands swiftly and brushed her lips on his, ever so shortly. And then she turned quickly and left the little flat, closing the door behind her.

For a long time, Rael stood in silence and waited, counting his heartbeats, feeling the pressure of time. While he waited, he did a quick, shallow reading of circumstances, according to his art, and concluded that he probably had some time, but not as much as he had hoped to have. He breathed deeply, went to the door, opened it, and looked out. No sign of Meli-osme, and the hall was quiet. Rael retreated into the flat, locked and barred the door. He looked about the room coldly. It wasn't much. A window. A single narrow bed. A table with a washstand. A bathroom, an unheard-of lux-ury. . . . Still, a shabby little room. He nodded, as if confirm-ing something to himself. It would have to be here, then.

Rael felt hungry, but he knew that didn't matter now. He went to the window, looked out on the street below for a few moments, and then went to the bed and wearily lay down on it, placing his hands behind his head, and staring at the dim ceiling. He thought for a long moment, considering whether he had any regrets. After some thought, he determined that there were indeed some regrets, but that they could not make any difference. The thing would go forward, as he had both planned and dreaded.

Now he thought about what he had to do: that in itself was an odd, half-process—he knew with the certainty of long-practiced, perfected motions *what* he must do. The prob-lem was that he couldn't recall anything about what hap-pened as a result of it, even though he knew he had done it successfully once before. Nor could he imagine it. All the same, there was a somber sense of dread, of fear, of—yes, a special kind of horror—which he felt associated with the Change. Rael knew very well that the gaps in his memory were deliberate omissions purposely installed by Pternam and friends, when he did this before. They wanted him to forget as much as possible. But now he was aware of that problem, and had found ways around it. This time, he would retain something. One never knew, safety or not as promised for Damistofia, for since when on any planet had revolutionaries ever kept their word?

He began the exercise, by relaxing, as if preparing for sleep, consciously feeling each muscle group, becoming aware of its tension, and deliberately untensing it, one by one, start-ing with the feet and working upward along the body. But as he felt the rhythms of sleep, he carefully shunted them aside into another state, a concentrated focus of psychic energy that seemed to magnify his self and reduce everything beyond that to a meaningless fog. He felt the brightening and the dimming of the other, and now slowly began to increase the contrast between the two, brightening the self locked some-where behind the eyes, probably at the pineal junction, dimming the exterior, the outside, the body, everything. Sensations faded, became meaningless, and then vanished entirely. Rael was functionally blind and deaf, lacking sense of smell and taste, and finally touch. The outside faded, faded . . . and went out. The core brightening further, became painful, unreachable, unstable, a burning pinpoint flux, a tight coil of glowing threads, all moving, writhing. He could *see* it, but only gaps, short flashes. The motion was still too fast for him. He held on, brightening it more, racing now with the unimaginable time pace underlying the perception. The motions became more coherent, the matching moments longer now, recognizable now as short flickers of motion which he *saw* directly; and longer still. The concentration was intense. (A part of him still left rational reminded him that if he failed to synchronize with that painful bright motion, he would not be able to attempt it again for days, which was too late.) He made an effort he didn't think he really could, and matched with the flow, riding with it in time, and the bundle of bright worms at the center of his consciousness slowed, slowed, and stopped.

Now. There was a certain configuration there, which he had to change, while moving in this current, which he did, slowly, feeling a hot wash of dread and loathing as he did so. One of the threads had to go *this way*, instead of *that way*. Dangerous, subtle work. He turned it, feeling it resist, feeling resistance from the rest, but after an effort, it turned, and locked into position with a rubbery snapping sensation. Rael turned it loose and let it go, and fell away weakly. The center leapt into instant motion, writhing and squirming as before, and as it whirled away from him, he relaxed the hold he had on the center and let the brightness fade, feeling the outside lighten up again, come back. He let it come, feeling nothing but a vast fatigue, and a great sadness for something he couldn't quite understand.

One by one, his senses came back to him, and the intense self awareness faded. He looked down. He could see, he could move, although he felt weak, and he thought, *I don't feel any different; perhaps the whole thing is just another sham cooked up by Pternam. Nothing is going to happen at all. Nothing. I'll stay here for a while, and then they'll come for me.* He sat up on the small bed, and ran his hands through his hair, wearily. He took a deep breath, and stood up, placing his right hand on the windowframe for support. Other than a feeling of weakness, he felt nothing out of order, nothing different. Rael took a step, and then moved forward more confidently, first to the washstand where he picked up the metal pitcher, and then to the bathroom, where he drew some water from the tap. He came back into the room and sat the pitcher down, looking about uncertainly for a glass.

It was then that he did notice something not quite right. He found the glass, but only by looking away from it: there was a small hole in the center of his vision, in which there was *nothing*, not blackness, not patterns of light. Nothing. As if there was nothing there. Rael stopped, as if listening. Nothing else was happening. He breathed deeply. Probably some transient effect, an aftershock of the concentration, something similar to a migraine visual pattern. He poured himself a glass of water, and drank it, feeling a sudden thirst. He drank a second glass, wondering how he had become so thirsty. Then he stood by the window and looked out into the dark streets below. There was nobody there. It seemed an unreal, empty city. There were lights but no life. He started to move toward the bed, for he felt very tired, when suddenly he felt a sharp pang of intense nausea; he ran to the bathroom instinctively, opened the water-closet lid, and vomited instantly in powerful heaves that felt as if he were trying to tear his insides out.

When his stomach had stopped heaving, Rael sat back on the floor, shaking. He tried to stand up, and found that his legs wouldn't hold him: they felt rubbery, unstable, unhinged, as if he were being unboned before his own eyes. There was also a dizzy vertigo. He thought, *I'm sick. I have to get to the bed.* He tried again to stand and fell back, weakly. Undaunted, he placed his hands on the floor and began crawling, a little uncertain, but making progress. He managed to get about halfway there, to the middle of the bedroom, when the second attack came. A sudden sharp pain which felt just like someone had kicked him exactly halfway between the testicles and the prostate. Rael fell over, groaning, biting his hand to keep from crying out, tears starting from his eyes. He rolled over into a fetal position and grasped his organs which felt white hot, glowing. Then came a third; Suddenly his body jerked, and he felt as if every nerve in his body had shorted out at once. There was a buzzing in his ears, his eyes transmitted a view of a flickering random black and yellow checkerboard, his skin burned, and he smelled and tasted unimaginable things: burnt flesh, a sweet-pungent gas, like acetylene, and his limbs contorted into odd, rigid positions. His hands were like shrunken claws. Then there was another attack of nausea, and this time he didn't make it. In fact, he didn't even try. It was all he could do just to breathe.

After a time, the attack faded somewhat, and he was aware of things again, but in an altered way, as if he hallucinated. He could not move; his muscles were totally uncoordinated. He had chills. Then it eased a little, and he could move, although only enough to shift his position a bit. His skin was crawling, and he was sweating. He managed to have a short space of lucid thought: *This is Change—it actually worked. It will probably get a lot worse. I will lose consciousness. I might die here without help. Got to get clothes off. It'll be messy. Nasty. I'm going to lose about a third of my body weight in the next half-day. I premember Damistofia: she's small, gracful, almost petite. No other way—catabolism, destructive distillation, excretion by all available orifices and surfaces.*

Fumbling with his pants, Rael managed to get them partially off. He stopped and forced himself to look at his organs. Already they were swollen, painful, covered with a milky secretion. He fell back, gasping for air. And then the real attack set in, and the worst part of it was that he did not lose consciousness. Time expanded, engulfed him, and the seconds loomed like adamantine monuments stretching across the world. And it got a lot worse.

Thedecha was a word which described the unrolling intricate recursive calendar of Oerlikon, and also, not by chance, was the proper name of the immense long river which drained all parts of the continent Karshiyaka save those that sloped directly to the oceans. West of Symbarupol, out in the plains of Crule the Swale, it was lost in the limitless flat distances, or sometimes the hint of a shimmer on the horizon, a lightness in the air, a memory. Thedecha water described a large counterclockwise loop around the end of the mountains separating Innerland Puropaigne from Crule, and far to the southeast in the mountains of Far Zamor it began. And sometimes one could catch sight of it east of the city as it flowed into the north, before the turn.

This was such a morning; beyond the bulky stark structures of Symbarupol the sun Gysa was rising in a clear sky, and between the blank faces of the structures gold flashes could be seen out in the valley. Pternam always rose early,

87

but clear, cool mornings he would stroll about on the terrace and look across the city for sight of that fugitive glimmer. And he was not disappointed when he went out on the terrace, for in the shadows and illuminations he could see it. Soon, though, some ground mists rose and obscured the view. Still, he considered it worthwhile. And he added to himself, if they managed to get through this problem, he'd try to arrange that they built a capital closer to the water. Surely there was something about water in a great city that could soothe one.

Not long after, one of the house bondsmen brought breakfast, and he had hardly cleared the entrance to the terrace when Avaria hurried in, face florid, manner agitated, more or less as usual. Avaria was never calm about anything. Pternam nodded politely to him and continued with his breakfast. Avaria understood that he was to remain quiet, but his constant motions and nervousness finally chipped a path through Pternam's studied lack of attention.

"Heard anything yet?"

"Yes. I got up early and strolled over by Chugun's place to see. There's no secret about it—they were free enough with me."

"Therefore, what?"

"Rael made his move: killed a young fellow on the local beamer, near Marula, apparently, and then tried to fade into the city. They are. . . ."

"Did they get him?"

"No, but they aren't concerned; they have sealed the city and are doing area searches, eliminating areas one at a time. They know what part of the city he's probably in and they seem to think they'll ground him by evening. They aren't using the troopers, but very quiet methods, so as not to scare him until they have him penned in. It was odd, though—he left a calling card with the body. Signed it 'Rael,' as if he wanted someone to know. A subtle job, apparently done right under the noses of the passengers."

"Who was the victim?"

"Didn't get his name . . . but Chugun is looking into that, too. I mean, the job has all the marks of an assassination, but it doesn't seem to connect to anything. But the fellow Rael . . . ah, killed, has them hopping. They ran some routine checks to see if they could determine a reason, and this fellow's not supposed to exist."

"Enlighten me."

"He had identification and normal position-rights papers,

but they don't relate to any real records on file. Chugun's people think the victim may prove to be more a problem than Rael, because they feel certain they can eventually get Rael, but this youngster . . . what was he? Ostensibly somebody's agent, with a cover that would look perfect—so good no one would try to verify it."

"Certainly not Clisp or the Serpentine; that's not their way."

"That's the tone of what I heard over there. Doesn't feel Clispish, as it were. They already have determined that he's not with any known Lisak group."

"Could he be with the Heraclitan Society?"

"I don't know. Possible, but according to Chugun's people, not very likely. They have no links, at any rate. They think something further out—some obscure sect in the Pilontary Islands, or maybe Tartary."

Pternam commented, "There are some curious groups in the Far Pilontaries, but Tartary . . . ? Not likely, unless. . . . If this fellow was from Tartary, it would show up in his body parameters; the natives have taken on some adaptations to the severe climate. We haven't studied them much because we don't often get a specimen from there, so we don't know much. But enough to identify him as one, if in fact he is." Pternam reflected for a moment, and then added, "Rael said something, just before he left, about a 'third faction,' or something like that. What was it? He said, 'The field that maintains Lisagor is tripolar, subtle but powerful, probably the most powerful force. . . . Something not of this world.' Yes. It didn't make a great deal of sense then, and no more now. Surely he couldn't have been talking about agents from Tartary infiltrating Lisagor with that kind of sophistication; man, they can't even agree among themselves. Tartary is, for all practical purposes, anarchy, and being anarchistic keeps them from being either of interest or a threat."

"Did he tell you what this third force was?"

"No, and I'm afraid I didn't give it much thought at the time; I was convinced that the line we fed him was just that—a line, nothing more, and so I didn't follow it. He might not have answered had I asked."

Avaria rubbed his chin and said, "No, I think that if you had asked him, he would have told you, at least as much as he could calculate of it within his system. He always gave straight answers if he answered at all; that was his way."

"Hm. Well, my guess is that Chugun's people won't get him; he's probably found a hidey-hole and initiated Change. They won't find anyone like Rael. They will probably find Damistofia, treat her, rough her up a little, and release her; she won't connect."

"Exactly . . . should we try to get her ourselves? I mean, sir, that she may remember . . . and if we can get her we can scrub her clean. As long as that relic lives, someone will know what part we played."

Pternam sat back and gazed into the distances of the east. "I would normally be tempted," he began. "But we don't want to show any interest at all to Chugun's people. I don't like this unearthing they are doing, and I definitely don't want them looking this way. You see, we can't get her, ourselves. We're blocked. They would want to know why we want her right off, instead of having her remanded to us after all the interrogations."

"We still have our own people looking for Rael. They are still under controls, and could be reaimed."

"Blocked there, too. They are not well-covered, and shortly after they got her someone would ask, why does The Mask Factory intervene in a case it's supposed to know nothing about? And once they ask one, they'll ask some more. And ask and ask, and there won't be enough we could say that would end it there. Oh, no. But I will have them ordered to make contact, observe and report. No action, though—make that certain. And they are not to be seen themselves. Valuation: if the mission would be compromised, break off contact with the girl. We can follow her through Chugun somewhat, if we have to."

"Aye. So it will be done, as you ordered. And what about the revolutionaries?"

"I've heard nothing. If they know it, they are sitting tight."

"They wouldn't tell us anyway."

"No."

Pternam reflected again for a moment, and Avaria sensed that it was not time to leave, just yet.

Pternam said, "Take the best one of those we have on Rael's scent, and have him stand by, well back out of sight. If they let her go, we might have a chance."

Avaria said, "I see. . . . Bring her in?"

Pternam smiled, an unpleasant facial gesture he rarely used. "Oh, no. Not to bring her here, or anywhere. If we can, kill her. We still don't want something like that lying around uncontrolled. She may remember something from Rael. . . . We put it through Change before, but we had the control, and we made sure he remembered nothing of Jedily."

"You don't want to try to reestablish control?"

"I want that thing eliminated as soon as practically possible with the minimum commotion."

"As you say. I will set to it immediately."

"Avaria?"

"Yes."

"I feel a pressure here, of distant events unseen or at least unreported. . . . I wonder why Chugun's group is so swift to respond to this one boy . . . surely he was insignificant.'"

"As I understand it, they got an anonymous tip that something was about to happen in Marula. They couldn't very well prevent anything given the vagueness of the tip, but they were prepared to hop right onto whatever materialized out of the night, as it were."

"Of course they got a tip! From us!"

"Not from us is this one they're talking about. Somewhere else."

"But . . . that could hardly be, could it? There was only us. . . . Oh, yes, I see. The Heraclitan Society knew about it. That raises more issues still; why would they tip off Chugun?"

"Begging your pardon, sir, but it seemed obvious to me, that's why I didn't say anything. . . . They will have a couple of sleepers, you know, passives, buried in Chugun's department, and so they would alert Chugun so they could tell by the reaction when it happened. They might miss it, otherwise. Or at least so goes my suspicion."

"What's their reaction to this tip?"

"They are trying to find out where it came from, and they are looking into some odd corners indeed. Not to worry, we're not involved at all. Clear as the morning air. As a fact, they are rather more interested in the tip than in the assassination."

"Wouldn't that inconvenience the Revolutionaries? On the other hand, Rael did say it would go their way. . . .'"

"Begging your pardon again, sir, but that isn't what he said. He just said that it would change. The rest of the interpretation was added on by us. He didn't contradict it, but neither did he confirm; I asked him several times, and he said, 'no comment.' That was all."

Pternam stroked his chin and looked off a moment

thoughtfully. He mused. "Then that would indicate that, all things considered, the process Rael envisioned is already under way. . . ."

"So it would appear. But the world seems as solid as ever."

~ 7 ~

Morning in Symbarupol

Arunda Palude hurried through the same morning streets of the same city, Symbarupol, but her motions were not those of one at ease, as had been Avaria and Pternam, but those of one with a concern on her mind. She made her way to Glist's settlement and negotiated the stairs and walks almost at a run. There were few abroad to see her, yet.

When she reached the quarters of Anibal Glist, there was further delay while he woke up through her knocking at the door, and took his own time about getting there. She swore under her breath, thinking bitterly that Glist had, after all, been here too long, entirely too long: he was becoming just like the damned natives. He didn't care about Time.

Eventually, Glist opened the door a crack, saw that it was Arunda, and let her in. He closed the door, a heavy timber door affected more for aesthetic reasons than practical ones, and said, "You seem agitated. Surely it could have waited?"

"No. You had to be informed immediately: my evaluation."

"Continue, then. Deliver your report."

"I have reports from Laerte and Foleo, and. . . ."

"Laerte is in Marula, yes? And Foleo is currently in Symbarupol?"

"Yes, and yes. You sent Sheptun to Marula, yes? To capture that changeling? Something went wrong—Sheptun was killed on the way to Marula!"

"Killed?"

"Apparently by the creature he was supposed to find. He never knew who did it. There was a calling card with it. The creature's name was on it: Rael. That was all, of that."

"That's not good."

"The rest is worse: his documents didn't check. At all. They are now working on finding out who Sheptun was. And there was a tip planted with Chugun's people. . . ."

Glist interrupted her: "I did that."

93

"No matter who. They are now assuming Sheptun was connected with whoever sent the tip, and. . . . They took Aril Procand."

"How?"

"Checking, they found out she was Sheptun's girl friend, and went looking for her. Got her early this morning. Her papers don't check, either."

"Damn it, I told those idiots more than once to fix those temporary papers . . . they *knew* that stuff the organization makes up on Heliarcos wouldn't stand a real check—it's just supposed to look good, that's all."

"Nevertheless . . . Foleo had to disengage, but he had it on good report that Chugun was interrogating her himself. He thinks he's uncovered something bigger than a murderer. . . ."

"Chugun himself . . . Well, that's not so bad. He's a blusterer, and Aril was trained to resist that approach."

"Perhaps. But they have patience, and more than Chugun—he has assistants, helpers, flunkies, henchmen."

"Evaluation?"

"Lost. These people are raised on a diet of conspiracy from birth, and they rule all of Oerlikon that matters, and as they see it they don't share that with anybody. Our cover here is fragile; eventually, they'll get something out of her."

"Now?"

"Not as of last contact, which was about . . . an hour ago, I think. They are not in a hurry, because they don't know what they have, so I would estimate at least a full day."

Anibal Glist turned away from Arunda Palude and stared blankly at the wall. Still facing it, he said, "We'll have to contact Transport, and arrange for our people to be picked up."

Palude said softly, "We have too many down here to make pickup without revealing ourselves; besides, it will take days . . . even if we could. What about Kham, in Clisp? I can't contact him until he calls me, and he's not scheduled to for a tenday. Besides. . . ."

"Go on."

"We have no comm with Central. We're out of position for it: Oerlikon is on the wrong side of Gysa for the relay station. The only ship is the one that brought the last group in, the one Sheptun and Procand were on. They are well out of range now, without the Comus Relay."

"Then effectively, we are stranded. We should have comm back in twenty days . . ."

"In twenty days, if they are sharp, they could have all of us in The Mask Factory, and then we'd find out for sure what goes on in that place. So far all they have is one fellow whose papers don't check, and a girl who doesn't know much."

"She knows me; she knows you. She knows Foleo. Any one of the three of us. . . ."

"I know, I know. All right. I give the order: Initiate the Pyramid Course, commence sanitization of mission. Have all the operatives vanish into the background—whatever they have to do. We all get this in Indoctrination as a possible course. . . ."

"But nobody every thought it would come to this."

"True. But when you don't contact Central, on time, after Oerlikon comes back into contact position, they will know something's gone wrong, and so they will activate the alternate plan—contact through Tartary."

"When I first came here, I missed a contact; it was so hard to compute orbital years from this insane calendar they use here, that Mayan gibberish. And so I missed it, and when I finally did set up again, I was terrified because I knew the plan—that if there was no contact after a clearing, they would come get us."

"What happened?" Glist quite forgot to scold her for it.

"Nothing. They didn't seem to have noticed. As for now . . . it might occur to them after a time, because once we sanitize. we won't have comm with Central or anybody. But personally I don't think they will risk it; Oerlikon is a bit out of the way. So there's something final in this."

Glist continued looking at the wall. "Yes, I suppose so."

Palude went to the door, and paused, just before opening it. "I will initiate the pyramid, and sanitize, as you said. You had better leave here, as well. No point in making it easy for them. They'll come for you first, if Procand fails."

"Yes, of course. Where are you going?"

"Under sanitization, you are not to know."

"Yes, quite correct." Arunda opened the door, and Glist called to her as she was leaving, "What should I have done?"

She paused on the step, and said, "Everything was set with clear choices, of which you took the rational path. I may not criticize actions I would have done exactly the same way. You made the best choices—indeed, the only choices. It's as if it were fixed: you didn't have Kham, you had something you couldn't evaluate, and Sheptun never fixed his papers.

Then no comms. It has a flow. If we were vulnerable, it would be now. Something out there could see us, and he struck exactly where his blow would topple things—where and when. And with our mission gone, I can't say what will happen here. Save yourself."

And then she was gone. Glist started moving, slowly at first, but then faster, arranging things, picking up things, putting others down, things he wouldn't need anymore. He was ready to go in a remarkably short time, and about that, at least, he felt good. Clean, crisp. The tie severed. All these years of work: ended. And one last thought crossed his mind as he left his Spartan little apartment: that Palude had not said one single word that could have been thought of as anything personal. Nothing. The loss of the mission seemed something less by contrast.

He had thought he would go mad; stark, raving mad. It would have been, in its own way, a release, an escape. He hadn't. He also had thought he would die, that the vast dark night of death would be the end of it. That night never came. He forgot as much of it as he could, winning a victory over each microsecond as it came, and then meeting the next, which was usually worse, never better, or if the same, in a new place. Rael discovered new levels of pain, to an extent that he had left words far behind. His own body was undergoing self-initiated destructive distillation, catabolism, and yet through it all, there was something that watched, monitored, did not let go and did not take him to the breaking point. Up to it, within an angstrom of it—but not through it. His lungs erupted fluids, his bowels constricted spasmodically, violently, his stomach heaved; and also he wept, and his skin wept fluids, and then sloughed off in great, raw patches that felt like burns, and wept some more. His hair fell out early—first the body hair, then the pubic hair, and then the hair on his head. All went. But after that, through the changes, the head hair began to return, growing abnormally fast.

The night made transition into day, a sodden gray, overcast day, which he knew in some corner of his mind, but did not reflect on. In brief moments of lucidity he remained on the floor, waiting for the next attack, the next wave. That was all he knew. And the whole of the day passed that way: the gray light pressing at the windows.

But when the light had dimmed and the room was almost dark again, he noticed that it seemed that the stages of the attacks were not so strong, that they were shorter, and that they were coming further apart. During one of the quiet periods he actually caught himself thinking about moving, of trying to move his limbs again. And if he could move, he could perhaps begin to think about cleaning up the floor before they came for him. Rael had been lying on his side, in a compressed foetal position. He tried, experimentally, to straighten a bit. With great effort, he managed a little, and rolled over onto his stomach. It was painful, and it made him light-headed, but it worked. The only problem was that his body felt wrong, but he couldn't quite say exactly in what way it felt wrong. Just wrong. The muscles worked, he rolled on one hip, but it didn't feel right. He didn't think about it deeply, just then, because another attack started, and he concentrated on fighting pains that flickered over his body like summer lightning.

Later, there was a more lucid period, in which he felt much more confident, although very weak and very sick. He struggled for some moments, fighting a profound sense of strangeness which affected every move he made, however small, and at last attained a sitting position, legs sprawled. He managed enough coordination to look down at his body: he expected to see a riddled, tumorous, burned wreck.

It was not exactly that way. His feet were smaller, and not so angular as he remembered them. The legs were shorter, more rounded, and the skin was smooth and, under the filth, the color of pale cream. The knees were delicate, the thighs following the outlines of the rest, a smoother shape. He looked directly at his crotch. There was nothing there.

Rael looked again. Nothing? No, not quite nothing. There was a little fleshy sprig where his penis should have been, and below that, a fold, still swollen, but obviously containing no testicles. His mind was dulled, insensitive; he saw, but it did not register. He looked more closely, down at his chest, his belly. There was no hair on his chest or belly, and in place of hard pectorals and small, non-functional nipples, there were soft swellings, and the nipples were much larger, darker. A wave of dizziness passed over him, and painfully he tried to stand, to walk. His legs felt rubbery, and the hips felt *wrong*, looser, more articulated, the muscles hard to control. But one step at a time, he managed it; he crawled into the bathroom, and climbed up, pulling on every available handhold, until he could look in the mirror.

Rael looked into the reflection, and he saw there a softer,

younger face, with a small, delicate chin, a wide, blurred mouth, a sharper and larger nose, deep chocolate eyes whose whites were still swollen and red. It was the face of a stranger, and yet it was also a face he knew well enough to draw, although he was not especially skilled at drawing. The face belonged to Damistofia Azart. The next attack came then, but he could sink down to the cold floor slowly, and this time he slept a little, or fainted; he was not sure. She could not say.

Achilio Yaderny, Team Leader of Marula Squad Forty-Two, Bureau of Remandation, looked about the small and shabby room with a nagging sense of irritation and incompletion. Certainly this was the place where the murderer had to be; Rael. They had traced him to this building, and through the terrified night-man to this very room. There could be no mistake. And yet there was no Rael. Instead, there was a girl with no papers who was extremely ill, with God only knew what sort of disease. Give her credit: she had half cleaned the place up, but you could tell it had been rough.

And her story, what they could make of it, during the occasional lucid moments she had, would be impossible to check. She met him, and agreed to meet him here: he let her in and then left. She had been sick then, coming down with it, whatever it was. He hadn't come back. He'd taken her clothes, too. Small chance he'd use them as a disguise, because according to the description they had, this Rael was tall and gaunt, whereas this girl was small; and as wasted as she was, she looked even smaller. All probable, no doubt, and so there would be a report back to the prefecture, and there would be no end to it—a royal pain in the arse, up all day and all night, too, trying to figure out where the bastard got to.

Yaderny glanced at his men with a weary gesture, raising his eyebrows and glancing at the ceiling, and removed his communicator, inserting the earplug, and pressing the Headquarters Call button.

"Yaderny here."

"Yes, we are there. No suspect. We have a girl whom he picked up on the way, but she was sick when she met him here, and he left and took her clothes and papers."

"Yes, she still has something, although she says the worst

98

of it has already been. No, she doesn't appear to know anything about him, or where he might have gone."

Yaderny rolled his eyes and made sputtering motions without sound before replying. "Yes, of course. Definitely. We will bring her in, but she should be put in the palliatory for observation until it can be determined if she's contagious or not—we don't want the whole city down with diarrhea—Marula's not that high above sea level."

"No. No trace whatsoever. He didn't leave anything here. No one saw him leave . . . but that doesn't mean much in itself. We will check the rest of the building, it's not large, but I'm sure we won't find him. This taking the room was a decoy operation, as obviously was the girl as well."

"Yes. Send a medical team to move her, she's not in walking condition."

There was a moment during which Yaderny listened intently to the communicator, and then, shaking his head, he replied, "Yes, we could, but as I said, I don't know what she has, and I don't know if we can move her without losing her. She's not much good to us, but she's no good at all dead."

"Fine, then. I'll wait. I'll personally watch her, and send the rest out in the building. We'll be in shortly. Out."

Yaderny kept his distance from the girl and looked at her. She was asleep now, or unconscious, at any rate. Sick as she was, he didn't think she looked like much. Pale, and very thin, with a metallic sheen to her skin that spoke of recurring high fever. Poor kid, someone who was looking for a little fun, and met up with a cold-blooded maniac who killed with a pin, and then vanished, leaving her. She was in a tight spot, no doubt about it. No papers, no clothes, sick, probably a stranger—yes, she said she wasn't from Marula. Came here to die. Well, probably not die. She was breathing evenly enough. He turned to his men and told them what more they would have to do while he waited for the medical team to come for the girl, and they nodded, not complaining, because their patience was endless, and they were thorough, and they obeyed. And they filed out of the room quietly.

Yaderny went to the window and looked out onto the street, where one of his outside men was waiting. That one looked up and saw Yaderny, and made a small sign, signaling that everything was quiet on the street, that no one had come or gone. Good. At least they could depend on that for a fact.

After a time, Yaderny's men came back, silent and glum,

shaking their heads. Yaderny did not rage and rant at them; it would do no good. No—they had looked, and they had found nothing. No trace. That meant that somehow Rael had slipped out of the building sometime between the time he had come here and the time when they had traced him to this place. That wasn't much, and it meant that he'd still be in the city, unless he could make contact with someone who could smuggle him out. Not likely, but still possible. But Yaderny was a long-time squad leader, he had instincts, and this one told him strongly that Rael had not left Marula. Indeed, he was sure that Rael was somewhere nearby, hiding, after leaving them the dummy trail to run to and cover up the real scent with their own tracks. Yes, he was certain: Rael was close by, probably within hearing of a speech-projector.

Yaderny shivered with anticipation at what the captain would say—that it was all a lot of superstitious nonsense, that they had missed the assassin and that was that. But Yaderny would argue, and eventually he'd agree to send a team back to this neighborhood. But by then, dammit, it would be too late. That was what the bastard was waiting for. Now! They had him pinned down somewhere, somewhere close, damn close! So close he couldn't move until they left. And they'd told him to come back to headquarters! Yaderny took the communicator out again and put the earplug in once again, noticing as he did that the medical team was arriving to pick up the girl. Good. He keyed the Headquarters relay.

"Yes. Yaderny here. We didn't turn him up in the building, but I'm certain he's not left the neighborhood. We covered it too well."

"Yes, it's my instinct again, but I could tell you how many times that's been right, or nearly. . . ."

"You say stay and do house-to-house? Thank you, sir. I will do it. Please seal this area off. . . . You already have? Good. I'll need some more troops, have them report to me directly, I'll turn the locator on so you can trace me. Good, and thank you again. Yaderny out."

By this time the medical team was at the door carrying a stretcher. Yaderny turned to them, pocketing his communicator. "This girl we believe to be associated with an assassin, and so she is under remandation." Yaderny produced an ID card which the medics acknowledged by nodding agreement. He continued, "She has no papers, also. She claims to bear the name Damistofia Azart. She has had some sort of attack,

100

of what we don't know. She'll need quarantine, and isolation, and guard."

One of the medics said, "Your people, or the Palliatory staff?"

Yaderny thought a moment, and replied, "Yours, until we have something else on her. Right now, she is a low-grade suspect. Keep her confined. I think that whatever she had, the worst of it seems to have passed, but I'm no medical, I don't know what she has. Fever, vomiting, diarrhea. . . ." He made a gesture as of picking something loose out of his pocket and handing it to them, as if for their choice. "With those symptoms, it could be anything: Mercani's Ague, Bosel Fever, Chorylopsis, Battarang, Vyrygnenia, Nasmork, Tifa. . . . I assume you can find out there."

They nodded, and the one who had spoken before said, "Hope it's not Tifa; but doesn't look like it. We'll keep her locked up good, never worry." And they went to the bed and took Damistofia from it, wrapping her up in the sheet she was already covered with, laying her on the stretcher carefully, almost tenderly. And they took her out without further ceremony. As they were taking her out, it seemed that she awakened for a moment and looked at Yaderny briefly, but it was an unfathomable expression, one Yaderny himself could assign no meaning to.

After that, he told his men what they were going to do, and they left the shabby little room in the rooming house and rejoined the men they had left outside, on the street. Soon they were met by the first of the new troops, and Yaderny threw them into the search immediately, with the elan and verve of one who knew that they would pick up the trail again, very soon. There was great excitement as they began, spreading out. Yaderny threw himself into the chase wholeheartedly, not content to let the underlings do all the work while he stood back and supervised.

In fact, he didn't slow down until they had gotten a couple of blocks away. They had just cleared a small commercial building, with unused warehousing facilities on the upper floors, and they had come out in the street to take a short break. Yaderny sat down on a curbstone, just pausing for a moment to think where to hit next, and then his instinct suddenly rose within him again, quite out of nowhere, for no special reason, but he knew. He *knew* that somehow Rael, the assassin, had escaped them, that their search would turn up nothing. It came to him with the utter certainty he had always known and employed when he could, with a general pattern of success. That was why he was a Squad Leader, not just one of the foot soldiers. *But he knew it.* Rael was gone. He sat still for a moment, thinking. They would continue, of course; foolish to recall the teams now that they were already working. But he already knew the outcome: their quarry had moved, and was now outside the area they had under control.

One of the team members, long accustomed to the moods and intuitions of the boss, noticed a change in Yaderny's general demeanor, and stepped close, to speak to him. "Something wrong?"

Yaderny said, "Yes. I think we've missed him. The trail's cold now."

"We haven't covered much, and that area back there is still sealed. He can't have gotten out of it."

"Yes. You're right . . . but I don't think it was like that, that he was there and we missed him, and when we left, he moved. No, nothing so simple. No. We moved a certain way, and our move made it clear for him. And you know what?"

"What's that, boss?"

"I think it's for good."

"But you felt sure back there; you thought. . . ."

"I *was* sure. He *was* close. Damn close. Or somewhere we could have seen if we had only looked. But not now. No. Rael, whoever he was, is gone, and we'll not find any more trail."

The squad member reflected, "All's not lost: we have the girl, Azart."

Yaderny replied, without heat, "What do we have in her? Not much, I'll bet; oh, I'll have her checked, but not hard. You see, we already know she wasn't on the Beamer with Rael, or at least as far as we can determine. No, we'll hear her story, and they'll probably give her some correction for losing her papers, but she doesn't know anything: she was part of the decoy setup he arranged. We would spend enough time with her, just enough a delay, for him to get in position, and then when we moved, then he'd move. I'm sure that's the way of it. Too bad. I'd like to get a handle on this one—there are a lot of problems with this case."

"Yes, so goes the rumor. And as far as the girl having no papers; that's not all that uncommon, either. There's quite a few of them wandering around, you know. . . . I'll bet she didn't figure on running into this, or us."

Yaderny added, "Or getting sick, either. Now under guard,

in isolation, and under quarantine. Poor kid! But that's the way it works out: you never know what's going to crawl out from under a rock and bite your arse, do you?"

The squadman chuckled. "No, no."

Yaderny said, "Let's get on with it, for the sake of form; take your men and work that shop across the street. Take your time. We aren't going to catch him, or see any trace of him."

"You don't think we'll pick him up from another job, later on?"

"No. He's gone, that's all. Just vanished. I don't know how, but he did."

"What about the other guy, the one who Rael cooled on the Beamer? The higher-ups going to work on that?"

Yaderny said, "I hear they are working on that with a will. In fact, it wouldn't surprise me to see them turn on that more than this; that's the sort of talk I've heard."

"Yes, me as well. But now . . . we'll go do it." And picking up his partner, the squadman walked across the street to search the place there. But Yaderny knew it was all over. Too late. And what bothered him was that he had been so certain they were close to him, once. *Close.*

For Damistofia, Time, once a string of crystalline beads, now mutated into an undifferentiated grayness, which displayed random and subtle variations that communicated no meaning to her whatsoever. She was taken somewhere, across Marula, so she thought, but it all looked the same to her. There was a place that was quieter, removed from the street noise, and there, things were done to her, which she did not resist; they were not especially gentle things, but she sensed there was no deliberate intent to cause pain, and the rough treatment seemed to help, after its own fashion. She slept. She was fed and washed and examined under the guidance of what passed for medical arts in Marula, in Lisagor.

There was a doctor who came and examined her, and talked with her some, and who eventually told her that her case had them baffled, that she had apparently contracted some factor which had caused her to, as he put it, "purge herself completely." And that, save from some drowsiness and temporary confusions, she was completely healthy, and would need only time to recover. That she was vague about her past they wrote off to amnesia, and after a few desultory attempts to penetrate it, they gave up, and recommended that upon discharge from the Marula Main Palliatory she be assigned to retraining and given some simple task to do, along with a suitable probationary period.

The police came and talked with her a few times, but as Yaderny's assistant had remarked, when everything was considered, the loss of papers wasn't the most serious event in the world of law enforcement, in fact. they did have much more pressing problems than an unidentifiable girl who had had a momentary association with a mysterious assassin. What these problems were, they did not say, and Damistofia did not ask, although a part of herself she kept under rigid control thought she knew. For a time, Yaderny seemed to show an interest in her, but more and more he delegated his work to assistants, progressively lower in the police chain of command, and at last, she was talking with either disinterested flunkies or confused students, neither of which profited by the experience. They pursued things as far as their priorities permitted them to, and then they quietly gave up on her and instructed the Identification Bureau to issue her new papers in the name she claimed to be her own, in the full form favored by the Bureau, Damistofia Leonelle Azart i Zharko, Resident, Marulupol, Sertse Solntsa, Lisagor.

They moved her from the largely empty violent ward to a more relaxed part of the Palliatory, still somewhat isolated, where she had a small cubicle of her own, and where she spent the days attending retraining, eating and sleeping, and exercising; they had insisted on the last, because of the condition she had been in.

Her appearance, at first curiously mutable, soon stabilized; after that she began to gain weight and take on an appearance of more health and normalcy: a slender young woman somewhere in her late twenties or perhaps early thirties, slight and graceful, with pale skin and dark hair and eyes. The face was oval, with large, slightly protuberant eyes, which lent her an intensity she did not, on acquaintance, seem to have.

Internally, she practiced on herself a self-willed amnesia almost as thorough as the one they thought she had; this was necessary to make a clean transition from Rael to Damistofia, because she soon discovered that thinking as Rael, which she tended to do without being aware of it, brought her into conflict with the realities of the body she inhabited: there were too many discrepancies. The weight and mass of Damistofia's slight body was distributed differently from that of the lanky but powerful Rael. Thinking as Rael, she wanted to swing her shoulders more, and walking was a problem because of the feel of the placement of the thighs and hips. Men walked spraddle-legged, compared to women, because their hip joints were closer together and they needed to leave space for the genitals. Women walked with their feet together, and did not need to counterbalance the heavy legs with motions of the upper body. This was something normal people learned unconsciously, or instinctively, but Damistofia had to practice it constantly until it became routine.

Another problem, which showed less but bothered her more, was sex, or more precisely, sense-of-sex. Rael had learned, whatever he had been before, to enjoy women, and sex. This sense of desire, part of the psyche, made the transition with Damistofia, but the realization of it was a constant difficulty. It was difficult for her to grasp, especially in the location of the impulse. She experimented a bit, to get the feel of it, touching herself, trying to imagine . . . It was like, and unlike. Desire was as strong, when she encouraged it, but curiously diffused, unspecific, unlocalized; more, it didn't drive her to assertive motion, even though she could recall that clearly enough; rather, it made her lethargic, with an odd undertone of tension that would often culminate in a headache. And she tried to reach back further, to Jedily, whoever she had been, but there was simply nothing there. Whatever they had done to the original subject at the Mask Factory, their work had been complete: Rael could not remember Jedily, and now Jedily was even farther away. Damistofia knew, fatalistically, that whatever sexual orientation she settled on, she would have to do it on her own.

In the wing where she was assigned, there were others about, men and women, girls and boys, patients and employees, and those she watched closely, trying to build an identity by using the hints of their reactions to her; equally importantly, she worked at erasing old patterns which were Rael's habits, and learning new ones, but that was also hard.

But, little by little, it began to form. She thought that she would carry it as far as she could in this place, and then, outside, on her own, develop it fully. Because she knew that to vanish completely into the anonymity of the population, she would have to become what she seemed to be; she did not wish to be singled out for any deviation, however insignificant. For she knew very well that the machinery that was Lisagor might be inattentive from time to time, but it could be roused into full alertness very quickly. Rael's odd science: she still had that, and his martial and survival skills, but she hoped that she would not have to use them. She wanted most of all to be left alone, and vanish.

And she wanted to forget what Rael's price had been, what he had had to do, that he could see from the beginning. She felt shame and regret, even though she still knew completely that Rael's target had been the right one, the pivot point, at that moment. It helped for her to feel a guilt about a cold, calculated murder of an attractive young man, and not as the breaking of a connection holding Lisagor together through the imposition of a third force she had not bothered to trace out, although this lay within the limits of the science Rael had devised.

News from the outside world was particularly difficult to get, which suggested that her wing was a sort of mental ward; they kept it that way on purpose. Reasonable enough, considering that most of the patients there would have been retreating from the outside reality anyway, and being led back to it was a subtle, gentle task, at which they took their own time.

Nevertheless, there were hints that something wasn't quite right outside. Often, and then more often, she would surprise the normally reserved orderlies, engaged in heated discussion, not the less energetic for being conducted in whispers, which would stop as soon as they caught sight of her. She tried to read it, but the data was too thin for her to build an image: Rael's science built answers like holograms, reconstructing virtual images from the interference of wave fronts. But unlike a hologram, there was a lower threshold limit for assembly, and what she was receiving in the Palliatory was below that limit. Still, it teased her because it seemed to have a particularly dire import for those who talked about it so earnestly. Whatever it was, it seemed to mean some kind of trouble, outside, and it wasn't getting any better.

It was about this time that they changed her routine, and put her on outside work, in the landscaped gardens surrounding the Marula Main Palliatory. That was a pleasant change, although it was growing somewhat chill and damp early in the mornings, and in the late afternoons.

One day, under a high, silvery overcast, she had been working with a small group, finishing a planting set in an odd and random grouping of cast concrete pipes and pipe-junctions. The larger plants had already been set in, and the tubs filled with soil by a detachment from the local labor pool, so that now all that remained was the planting of ornamental creepers and small accent plants, mostly evergreens. Damistofia enjoyed the activity, and being outside; she felt almost normal, although most of her associates seemed to be a dispirited group, with minimal motivation.

Some she knew by sight; others, not at all. But as she worked, she also watched the others, trying to imagine what circumstances might have brought them here, and what their ultimate fate might be. It saddened her to comprehend that most of those working on the planting didn't have much of a future: they were withdrawn, passive and resigned to their lot, which was to remain here, doing odd jobs, until some use was found for them, either in the labor pools for the most stultifying jobs, or else material for the Mask Factory, where they would be purged and made faceless servants of the Alloyed Land. That reflection motivated her a bit more, and so she worked more diligently.

By afternoon, the others on the crew had become familiar to her, so that she knew them as separate personalities, even though she was not interested in them. But one, an older man, she worried about. This one retained some traces of a former high position, but he was the most severely withdrawn of all of them, often talking to himself inaudibly. None of the others seemed to pay any attention to him, and his contribution to the planting seemed to be minimal. When she asked about him, she was told by the more communicative that they knew nothing about him, save that he'd been picked up after a disturbance near the docks, dazed, wandering in the streets, mumbling all things about getting to Tartary, and raving about his agents. They said that he claimed to be the leader of a group of spies, representing vast powers from the Void, but he couldn't explain how his position had led him to be picked up and unceremoniously assigned to the Marula Palliatory, Deranged Section. They ignored him.

It was customary to have a midday rest in Marula, and the custom was allowed for the inmates as well, and so, after lunch, they all spread out a little to find sunny spots beside walls or large ornamental rocks, to stretch out, and perhaps to nap a bit under the eyes of the distant supervisors. Damistofia saw something different about this one man, something she needed to do; he was clearly not on a course that would encourage survival. And so after she had eaten the buns they

107

had brought out for lunch, she found the older man, and sat down beside him. She didn't know exactly what she wanted to do, but she thought if perhaps someone paid a little attention to him, he would come back to himself.

He paid little attention to her when she sat down, still mumbling disjointedly, and gazing longingly at the low wall that separated the park from the streets of Marula, a wall that might as well have been as high as the sky, as far as getting over it successfully went. She tried to talk to him, but he didn't respond, so she let him go along as he would, and gradually he seemed to notice her and turn his remarks more toward her.

". . . the only hope was to get to Tartary, but that's gone, now, too . . . all gone . . . everything . . ." he said. And, ". . . The fools, they are overreacting, just as we knew they would, and it's going critical now, feeding on itself, injustice and revenge upon injustice and revenge . . . I tell you, I know these things, once the people get revenge in their heads, nothing but the deaths of millions will get it out. . . . We could stop it, the fools, they won't listen. . . ."

Damistofia said, softly intruding, "Stop what?"

The man glanced at her with the hunted expression of an animal at bay, and then said, "Listen; this is a world whose people undertook an impossible task—they set their task to totally stop change, evolution of society. They failed, of course—for nothing will stay the same, but they slowed it! They slowed it to a negligible amount! Now all that pressure has been building up for generations. . . ."

Damistofia thought she had his attention now, and so she prodded him a little: "I know, I'm from these parts myself. We don't change; that's the way we made this world when we came here. Every child in the schools knows that. Why does it fail now?"

"They had help! That's what. Help. For a long time. Some people from far away came here to see if it worked, and it was close, but not enough, and so they helped a little, influencing here, pressing there, dampening this influence out here. And then the worst possible combination of chance happened, and we were cut out as neatly as by a scalpel, and now human nature takes its course."

"Why don't you tell the higher-ups? Surely they don't want change."

The man shook his head. "Only worked as long as we were

108

unseen. When we intervene openly, it changes the balance, and we ourselves become part of the process of change."

She looked curiously at the man now. And she remembered, as Rael, sitting in a cell poring over odd equations that identified a third source of power on Oerlikon, in Lisagor, a hidden, concealed power. And here it was, right in front of her, somehow scooped up off the street and lodged in the Demented section. She asked, "Why would these people want to help us achieve our goal of changelessness? What could it be to them? If they wanted to live like we do, why couldn't they just come and *be* us. I know no one's done it for a long time, but the immigration laws are still open . . ."

He said, after some thought, "I'm not sure I could explain that; these people, you see, they didn't really want to live here. This is in many ways a primitive little world. It was . . . we developed an interest here, for ourselves. As long as Lisagor stayed changeless, then we who were in the project had something. And if it changed, then we no longer had a place. . . ." He stopped, and lowered his face to his hands, and after a bit, mumbled, "I've told you too much, and besides, you don't believe me any more than they did in there."

Damistofia said softly, "If I did believe, what could I do about it."

"Nothing, nothing. It's too late for us, that's all. Too late! Nothing can salvage the mission here: that's gone forever." He looked at her craftily. "You could help me escape."

She shook her head. "I've been unable to escape myself."

The man looked away, now, and seemed to withdraw internally from her, although he still continued to talk, "Well, so much for that; but it just drives me almost crazy to think that some crazed assassin came out of the darkness and struck in just precisely such a way that it sliced us out of it, and now they're calling him a hero."

Damistofia became suddenly very alert. She said, cautiously, "I heard there was a murder, that they were hunting for an unknown assassin. But is this the same person?"

"That's right. You wouldn't have heard so much in here, if you've been here a bit. No, at first they hunted him, but now they call him a great hero, and they seek for him, to honor him. That's a laugh; when he struck, he pulled more than one world down! They grabbed a couple of our weakest links and they talked enough to get a purge started. We had started withdrawing, of course, knowing what would come, but some were still in place when Chugun's men came for them."

"Who were you?"

"Here, on this world, I was Anibal Glist, and I was the head of the Oerlikon Project."

"It is dangerous that you tell me this—I could identify you. Surely they are looking for you."

He shook his head again. "They don't seem to care about us, now. I have hidden, to be sure, but you? You are in as much trouble as I am; why I don't know, but you are here and that's enough for me. And they have much more dire things to worry about besides defunct spy organizations: Clisp is seething with secessionists, Marula is crawling like a maggot pile, daily the ideologues of the inland provinces call for more ruthless measures of expostulation. No, they don't really want me now. They have their hands full."

She said, "You can get out, eventually, if you do what they want you to; and they'll find a place for you. That is what they are doing for me—I think I'll be out soon."

"You don't believe me. . . ."

"No, that doesn't matter, that I believe or not. You've fallen, wherever you came from, into a different trap, and now you have to get out of it and live on."

Glist shook his head and looked away. Clearly, the choices before him were almost too much to bear.

Damistofia discreetly excused herself, seeing that Glist didn't notice her leaving, and went back to the group at the planter. Outwardly, she was quiet, just as she had been all along since she had found herself in this place, but inside, her mind was working furiously. Rael now called a hero of the people! What a blow: to have gone through so much to escape detection, and now this one says they are calling the unknown assassin a hero. Who would have thought it? But she remembered that in Rael's analysis of the timing and necessity of the act of *change,* there was nothing about waiting for honors. One could get killed waiting for honor, and neither Rael nor Damistofia wanted honors when they came posthumously.

But in the way that things would influence her, she passed that information up. It didn't matter to her; she was already on the safe course plotted long ago, and she had survived so far. What did interest her was the confirmation of the third force operating in Lisagor, unseen, unknown, generally on the side of those who wanted no change whatsoever. And that it was now inoperative, allowing nature to take its course, whatever that would be. Confirmation! And Rael had been guessing, or hardly more than that. That she could remember: one could feel the third unknown there, but couldn't identify it, without an exhaustive search. It had been vague, subtle, weak . . . but enough to tip the balance, and allow such monstrosities as the Mask Factory to exist. And, she added, for their cruel work to produce one such as herself.

And *something* was working out there: either Glist was a hopeless basket case, or else it was true—Lisagor was coming apart, unraveling from the weakest points: Clisp and the Serpentine, vast Marula, and the ravings of the intolerant Inlanders. What else, which he couldn't see, or catch rumor of? And that led straight to the next conclusion, flowing like smooth water—she had to get herself released from the Palliatory and out of Marula. Soon. A vast, massive organism was shifting its weight to another center, and she wanted very much to be as much out of the way as possible. If possible.

～ 8 ～
Marula Nights

The day's ration of work was over and Damistofia was walking back to her building alone. The silvery half-overcast had slowly evolved to a dense bluish overcast that promised rain; there was a scent of brackish water from the invisible estuary, a sea-wind, mixed with the odors of the city, the usual ones, too many people, dusty streets, odd chemical odors, and—something else, a faint sour reek she seemed to know but couldn't quite identify. A smoky odor that seemed to alarm her without her knowing why. Deep in her own thoughts, and pondering the odd odor, she failed to notice that someone was moving along the same walk, from behind her, and catching up, until he was quite close. When she turned to see who it was, he raised his right hand, as if in greeting, and so she stopped.

She had seen this one before, but never close. He was a young man of the Palliatory, judging by his clothing, which was the pale off-white of the staff. She didn't know his name, but she had noticed him; slender and muscular, he was quick and nervous, but also very precise, qualities that suggested an alert, predatory nature. His face was oddly delicate for a young man, almost girlish, very finely shaped, and he affected an odd sort of mustache that seemed to grow only at the corners of his mouth. He also wore spectacles, very large ones which seemed to magnify his eyes, which were a pale gray color.

He said, "I wanted to talk with you before you retired for the night."

"I've seen you, but I don't know you."

He gestured at himself. "Sorry. Cliofino Orlioz, Exercisist and Disciplinarian. I haven't worked with your group, either, but I have been observing you—part of the job, you see; we always keep an eye out for indications in our guests that indicate something exceptional."

She thought: He'll be one who watches for those who think they can fool the system.

He paused and went on, "Not what you may think. My job is to watch for those we can release . . . or perhaps use here. There is need of experienced people."

Damistofia laughed a little. "That's good! You will use recent loonies to help the real ones back to their feet after they've fallen."

Cliofino smiled, "And why not? Who better knows the condition? And who would wish to be more successful? All such a person needs is some proper training, and they find a rewarding position here. It is better, it need not be said, than going through the Placement Bureau and getting the luck of the draw. . . . But I diverge; I race ahead, I pass the real point: they watched you working with that old fellow this afternoon, and they noted how he responded to you, something we've not been able to do. He actually responded. They've not been able to get him to do that since he's been here. And so the suggestion is that you might be worth considering. . . . What would you say to that?"

"You're not serious."

"Oh, yes—indeed I am so."

"I know nothing of such matters . . . I acted by instinct, if you will; no one seemed to care for that man, who has the most remarkable delusion. . . ."

"We know his delusion; thinks he's an offworlder, in charge of some great windy plot. No matter. Forget about him. There are others who need Reality Orientation much more."

"How can you be sure I would do it well? After all, you might very well assign me to someone I would hate, or feel nothing for, or someone I might abuse."

"You'd be surprised how many in a place like this abuse them all with great random abandon; if you only abused every other one, you'd be an improvement over some we have on the staff!"

Again she laughed. "Come on! I've been treated well enough."

Cliofino grew more somber, which caused his odd mustache to droop comically. He said, after a moment, "Actually, that's for other reasons; your illness still hasn't been identified, nor have you, but in the absense of positive indications of anything, they are not looking closely at that. We don't know what happened to you . . ."

". . . Neither do I."

"Just so. At any event, you do not appear to be demented, but a victim of someone else's plot. The theory is now that you were drugged."

She said, "I have no recollection of what happened. I remember only some of it. . . . The earliest thing I can recall is that they took me from a room and brought me here."

Cliofino continued, "The police have lost interest in your case, although it is not closed. You understand that they have, shall we say, higher priorities now. So we can do this; actually easier than releasing you to general assignment or the labor pool."

Her mind raced, as she looked away, trying to hide the hope and the anticipation. Was this the way out? She said, she hoped with the proper shyness, "I don't know, now. This is sudden."

"Of course. That much I well comprehend. But you will consider it?"

"Yes."

"Good. Exemplary! I've taken the liberty of having myself assigned to work with you, so we'll have more contact, and we can discuss this more. And in the meantime, I can work with you on some exercises; they say you aren't completely well yet."

"Well, no . . . I tire easily yet, it seems. I don't know why."

"Lack of the proper exercises, lack of motivation. It's all easy enough. We could start tonight, if you're so minded. . . ."

Behind the easy words and the logical progression, Damistofia sensed a subtle pressure; nothing definite, but a pressure she couldn't recall feeling as Rael. Was he attempting to seduce her? She didn't have enough experience so that she could remember to tell if that was what he was after. She decided to be cautious, and said, "Tonight? Let me think on it. I am tired after today. Could we not work it in the regular exercise period?"

A momentary flash of annoyance flickered in his eyes, but he replied, pleasantly enough, "I'm still working those details out, shifting assignments, and that sort of thing. I do have others to work with I can't just let go."

She said, "I understand. Well, tomorrow I have no work assignment, and so I could do it after the regular day."

"Very good! We'll do it that way, then. I'll come after regular hours."

"You won't be getting into any trouble, will you?"

"Oh, no. And you won't, either. Just a little overtime."

"I want to ask you something . . ."

"Yes. Ask on."

"What is that peculiar burnt smell in the air?"

He looked off into the distant sky, and then said, "Burnt housing. And now is not the time to talk about that."

"You know about it?"

"Yes. Tomorrow. This is not the place."

"All right, then. Tomorrow. . . . And what do I call you?"

"Say nothing to your usual people; they would be offended. But Cliofino, if you're so minded."

She smiled at the informality, and reminded herself to watch him more closely, to see what he looked at. She said, "Good enough; and so I will be Damistofia, as opposed to Patient Azart. And so good evening."

Cliofino nodded politely and turned back to the way he had come. And Damistofia set out again for her own building in the dusk, now with a fine mistiness in the air that said, beyond a doubt, that the rain was here.

And later, after supper and a bath, she lay in her little cubicle in the dark and listened to the rainwater running and gurgling in the downspouts and guttering, lying awake for a long time, trying to understand the significance of what had happened to her today; she sensed hidden motivation behind Cliofino's words, which were reasonable enough, in themselves. And what if he wanted to seduce her? At first consideration the idea seemed odd and a little perverse, but she understood that as arising from her thinking as Rael. And she wasn't Rael anymore, was she? She ran her hands over her body under the covers. No, most certainly she wasn't Rael. And she caught herself thinking, *This wasn't quite the way I planned it, but after all, why not. I will have to learn to live completely in this disguise, which is permanent.* And, thinking about it some more, she concluded that Cliofino wasn't unattractive at all, and that if he could be used to get her out of here, it might be well worth the trouble of adjusting to the new experience. And on that note she slept.

The day opened gray and drizzly, with a damp chill in the air that seemed to soak in and make itself at home; an intimation of the winter of this southerly but not tropical city.

Nothing definitely cold; just chilly and unpleasant. Damistofia went through her routines of the day absentmindedly, trying to keep warm in the drafty halls and rooms. In her free time, it was no better—her own wing was no less chilly than the rest of the place.

Toward afternoon, she caught a whiff in the air of the same odor of burnt rags she had smelled the day before, but when she tried to see out the window to see where it might be coming from, she saw little or nothing she could identify. There was a plain, unadorned brick wall around the Marula Palliatory which shut out almost all the view of the world outside, except the tops of the taller buildings and some industrial chimneys. Certainly nothing nearby seemed to be burning.

And later, while that was still in her mind, late in the afternoon, actually in the early evening, she heard in the distance some very odd sounds; there was a mechanical droning, as of a large number of engines, which grew out of nothing, but didn't seem very close. The noise level stayed about the same for a time, and then faded, followed by another set of sounds that seemed to alarm her without her knowing why— a noise as of a large crowd of people in confusion, but it, too, was distant, and faded away. The droning came back for a short time, and faded away entirely. And with the dark, there came on the night air another odor of burning, this mixed with a sharp, sweetish chemical odor—something inflammable. The attendants put the more excitable to bed early.

No one seemed to bother with her, and so she wandered after supper to the dayroom, where there were a few late-stayers and persons as bored and apprehensive as she was, reading magazines and playing cards and dominoes to pass the time. Here, she settled in a corner under a dim lamp with a travel brochure about the Pilontary Islands, a place far to the southeast that she could reasonably hope never to see.

Damistofia felt the attention of someone watching her closely, staring; she looked up, and saw Cliofino across the room. When she looked up, she saw that he looked away, as if he did not want her to know he had been watching her. He was just a shade too slow. And just a shade too practiced on acting as if he had just seen her; but again, with him, she felt a confusion on trying to interpret his intentions. For a second, she felt like Rael, and felt like screaming, "Dammit, I can't make the assumptions women do because I don't know

116

how to be one yet! And so what's this Cliofino's game? Why is he so interested in me? It can't be ravishing beauty—I'm ordinary and plain at best—as a fact, I wouldn't give me a second look." The frustration passed, and she nodded to him, that she'd seen him, and he came across the room to her.

She saw that he was dressed differently from his workaday uniform; he wore dark clothing, dull and plain, except on one shoulder there was the emblematic figure of a dragon worked into the material in a low-contrast pattern of some different material. Again, she felt as if she were groping in the dark; the emblem was obviously intended to symbolize something, but it meant nothing to her at all. He was also damp, and there were rain sparkles on his clothing and hair—he had been outside, somewhere.

He said, "I signed out the gym for a while, if you'd like."

Damistofia put the brochure back in its rack and stood up. "Yes. I could stand some motion, some movement. I need activity, some kind of challenge."

He nodded agreeably and said, "That's right! Most of the duds are content with the routine, and they stay that way! But I thought it would be a good idea for us to go there, and have you work out a little; I want to see how dextrous you are, and check your reflexes, before we get too far into this. You might conceivably need to work on your general body tone before we can go on."

"I hardly need an examination to tell that; I already know it."

He looked closely at her. "But you don't remember what you were before . . . ?"

"No. But I'm not in the shape I could be in . . . and I'd like to have my figure back, at least, for what life I've got left to live."

He looked at her again, with an odd, guarded intensity that Damistofia found disconcerting. "There's nothing in general wrong with the figure you have now—nothing at all."

"You couldn't prove that by me, or my mirror, as I see it, but if you say so, that gives me some hope all was not lost. Well! Lead on."

Without further word, Cliofino turned and led the way out of the dayroom into the dim hallways and set out for the Gymnasium, which was located some distance away in another building. They traversed long corridors, now mostly untenanted, and then outside, for the most part passing under covered walkways from whose eaves the rainwater dripped into puddles. Only once they had to pass from one covered walk to another, and Damistofia felt the rain on her face, and in the air there were still traces of the smoke she had smelled.

She asked casually, "What's burning?"

Cliofino looked at her sharply, and waited a moment before replying. Then he said, "Settlement areas, squattertowns. There has been some trouble, and they've had a couple of pallet drops."

Damistofia shook her head, not understanding what he was referring to. "Please. Say again. I don't understand."

He reiterated patiently, as if recalling that he was talking to a woman who had lost a large part of her knowledge of how things were, "One thing led to another, and there was a riot among the people of some habitats. They restored order by landing several platoons of Pallet-Dropped Heavy Troopers on them."

Damistofia walked on for a minute, and then said, "And what do they do?"

"They hit the ground shooting; they are a force whose sole mission is to terrify and subdue. They carry sawed-off shotguns, flamethrowers, grenade launchers, and chainsaws, which they use as swords. Rumor has it they are recruited in a place called 'The Mask Factory' where they have parts of their minds removed to make them amenable to heinous orders, and then given glandular injections to bring their mass up. In this series of actions, of course they were successful and things have quieted down, but it is uneasy. They have gone too far, of course, and who can tell if the measures will work. It seems that people no longer restrain themselves."

He was clearly disturbed by the events, as he told them. Something of this showed in his voice. Damistofia said, "You say this as one who does not approve."

"Who could?" he asked passionately. "Many were killed, two habitats completely leveled, a third damaged so badly it will have to be pulled down and rebuilt. I mean, everyone knew that there was such a corps as the Pallet-Dropped Heavy Troopers, but they were never actually used against the people."

Damistofia said, "If one has a weapon. I would guess time comes to use it."

"Mind, we present-day people don't know if they ever did. They say they loosed them before, but all we saw was the parades in the streets. That was enough. Now they have used them in actuality; and they destroy everything. . . ."

118

"I do not remember what my feelings were before this, and I have not been allowed outside, so I cannot approve or condemn on the face of it; still, it would seem to be excessive. What brought that on?"

Cliofino said, "There are disturbances everywhere now, and they feel they cannot be slack with Changemongers, and so they strike at will—here, there. I know that long ago our ancestors came to Oerlikon to escape the relentless pressure of Change, but their desires built a system that cannot respond, and so resentment and pressure build up. There is no feeling of compromise, of finding the way that will work. The people say, 'we need,' and they say, 'no.' And when they gather to demonstrate, then come the troops. This is happening all over."

They had arrived at the gym door and now stopped before it. Damistofia said, "And what is your place in this? Or am I asking too much on so short an acquaintance?"

Cliofino opened the door for her, and said, "Something has gone wrong, and we must right it, to maintain the vision of old, that we came to this planet for."

Damistofia nodded, not speaking, and stepped into the darkness, which Cliofino banished by turning the lights on. He looked around, and then said, "And now we must work. How do you feel?"

"Good enough, I suppose; a little restless. . . . What do you want me to do?"

"I will show you—mostly some simple tumbling, and some light defensive methods I will show you. I will be judging your reflexes, your speed in learning."

She said, "I see. This is a test. I will see more if I pass. And if I do not?"

He said, in a low voice deliberately restrained, "That you ask that is your admission to continue."

They located some loose floor mats and put them together, and then Cliofino led Damistofia through a series of motions and short exercise routines that seemed ridiculously easy at first, something like dancing, but steadily grew more difficult. Still, she took on the activity and did as well as she could; she needed to capture the dynamic feel of her body, and this was an excellent opportunity. And moving, exerting a little, told her things more quiet routines had suggested—that she was now very different from Rael. Her center of gravity was lower, and she was more supple, once she ironed the kinks of inactivity out. And putting all of herself into the exercise helped her feel more at home in her body, and it began to feel more right, more herself, less an intrusion. And as this feeling of rightness increased, she found herself becoming more aware of Cliofino, who moved with her easily and with complete confidence. Their close proximity, moving together, brought forth responses from her body itself, and less and less she found them strange and frightening. And doing so, she found that it lessened some internal tension and made things easier.

Cliofino showed and demonstrated a couple of easy defensive techniques, and then stopped. He was breathing hard. He said, "Enough for now, I think. This will stretch muscles you haven't used. To the showers! Hot water, and then cold."

She sat on the floor and sprawled out awkwardly. "I am already stretched. Tomorrow I will be sore. And I must tell you that my clothes are all sweaty and I shouldn't want to wash and then put them back on to walk back."

"A good idea, that. Well—we can do it that way."

"I to my room, and you to yours. Where do you stay?"

"I have several places. I move around a lot. I would like to come with you, if I may ask."

She smiled at him archly. "You see me at my worst, which is not how I might have it."

He said, "There isn't anything wrong with your looks. You are fine. Act with confidence."

"Is this also part of the testing?"

Now he smiled. "No. For now, you pass." And he extended his hand and helped her to her feet. They put the floor mats back where they had found them, and turned out the lights. In the dark, illuminated only by the night-glow coming from the doors, Cliofino took her hand, and with an odd excitement she did not suppress, she did not turn it loose. And on the way back to the dormitory, she did not turn it loose, either, although they said nothing and he attempted nothing more.

The night air felt cooler now, almost chilly, as they walked along. Damistofia thought many things to herself; in one set of arguments, she sensed a powerful current of danger associated with Cliofino, an out-of-place-ness that bothered the old Rael instincts profoundly. Still she could not work these things out in her head. She would have to write things down, ensymbolize, compute, to determine the answers she needed. The likely computation was that he was a spy of some sort—but for what side? On the other hand, she felt this

whole encounter as another test of sorts, one she was conducting on herself.

She asked, "Now, what about the more that's assumed to be? Who are you?"

"A simple worker here, who has associates who believe that we can set things on the correct path . . . someone who has need of a trusty and agile friend. I would not say much more yet; but on that, would you want to leave, to get out before we go deeper?"

Damistofia breathed deeply, and then said, "No, I would like to see more. They have given me little enough here, that I would rely on it alone. That's just it; they don't seem to care very much what happens to me."

"Exactly. You cause them no problems, and the police are no longer interested. They have much more alarming cases to worry about, and so you languish. If it turns out that we will be able to work together, then I believe that I can get you out of here. And I think you should consider getting out of Marula; this is becoming a hazardous place to reside, what with the troubles, and the responses."

"Where could I go?"

"Lisagor is large, and it's not the whole world."

"But Clisp . . . say. That would be worse, I'd think. They will be bearing down hard in places like that."

"I will tell you a secret. The trouble came to Clisp first, and although there are still incidents there, they have written it off. They have trouble here they can't ignore. Don't worry about where, just yet. That can be arranged. What I want you to think of is wanting to leave here."

"And what of my old life? Perhaps someone waits for me to return."

Cliofino said, "They found you with Rael the assassin. There were no reports of missing young women. Therefore the assumption is held that however you came to be there, you came on your own. No one has come searching for you. Whatever your old life was, you seem to have left it behind voluntarily, and if there were others, they let you go. I would say not to worry about the past, but act as you see the best path."

She nodded. "There seems to be no future here."

"Exactly. I can help, if you allow it."

They reached the dormitory building and slipped inside. There was no one about, and they passed through the halls without sound. When they reached Damistofia's room, and

121

liked what she had become, that at least in this there was nothing to fear. She could do it.

Luto Pternam no longer spent the evening hours lounging on his terrace, looking over the soft outlines of Symbarupol, but instead worked long hours into the night, trying to keep up with the demands put on his organization. Not only him, but Avaria as well was pressed and they seldom saw each other save in passing.

The situation was essentially simple: for cycle upon cycle, the specialized product of The Mask Factory had been paraded, displayed, threatened with use, but actually used seldom. Now they were in constant use, somewhere in Lisagor, and their use required replacements. The Pallet-Dropped Heavy Troopers, lobotomized goon squads in uniforms, were dropped into action on cargo pallets with only drogue parachutes to slow their descent down a little, and from landing alone they could expect as much as a ten percent casualty rate, never mind the numbers that fell in their suicidal disregard for their own lives. In recognition of this terrible decimation, survivors of five operations were awarded a golden bolt to wear in their free hand; those few who survived ten got a gold bolt in their heads, all installed with all due surgical nicety.

Lisagor was crawling with incidents, and no area seemed to be free of them. The Innerlands and Crule the Swale were the quietest; Clisp, the Serpentine, and Sertse Solntse the worst. And so Pternam had little time to wonder about revolutionaries, save to note that they seemed to be having great successes, which caused him to have dark thoughts indeed about the wisdom of the plan he had concocted. The operatives he had sent off to Marula had either been swallowed up in the chaos reigning there, or reported back with negative results; they were unable to get near the place where Rael-Damistofia had gone to earth.

But late one night, when Pternam and Avaria were pausing in one of their rare occasions of camaraderie, they were interrupted by a signal from the door, which Avaria went to investigate. Shortly he returned with two individuals, to Pternam's surprise, one the redoubtable Porfirio Charodei, accompanied by a heavily built individual with beetling black hair and enormous hands whom he knew to be the equally fearsome Mostro Ahaltsykh.

Ahaltsykh took up a position at the door to the study they

went in, she said, "It's late and no one is up. All are fast asleep."

"Leave the lights off. We don't want to attract attention."

"How will we see?"

"You know your way around. There's some glow from outside, the city lights in the clouds. We'll manage." Wordlessly, with her heart pounding, she went through the dark to the bath and set the shower running. After a time, she said, "At least the hot water is on tonight."

"Is it ready?"

"Yes."

"Can we do it together?"

"Yes . . . if you promise to scrub my back."

"I promise." Then he started pulling his clothes off and hanging them on a peg on the back of the door. After a moment, Damistofia did the same, saying softly, "I feel awkward; I haven't done this for a long time . . . I can't remember it."

He said, "Don't worry. Do you want to go on?"

"Yes."

"Then don't look back." Then he took her hand again and helped her into the running water.

In the hot water of the shower, in the dark, they spent the first moments washing, scrubbing, washing the sweat and fatigue away, and it was only after they were rinsing the soap off that he touched her, and brushed her face lightly with his mouth, and kissed her. It was odd only for an instant, and then it felt right, and she did what her instincts told her to.

They finished rinsing, and now shyly stepped out of the bath, where they dried each other off. He touched her, and she felt his bare nakedness against her. Cliofino led her back to the small bedroom, turned down the sheets, and gently laid her down on her stomach, kneeling over her and firmly but deftly massaging her back and shoulders. She felt hard, hairy knees gripping her hips, the pressure of his hands, and she let herself go to the feeling, and when at last she could stand it no longer, and rolled over to face him and hold him, it felt perfectly right and good and she enclosed him within herself and held him tightly to her until it was the best, and that went away slowly; and before they parted and slid beside one another to sleep, she felt indeed as if she had passed a test she had set for herself, and there was a real sense of accomplishment in that. Rael faded a great deal. And Damistofia stretched, and felt warm inside, and said to herself that she

123

met in, and Charodei joined Pternam by the occasional table. Avaria waited a respectable moment, and then joined Ahaltsykh by the door, saying nothing.

Charodei started out, waving aside the usual pleasantries. "I have come on an errand which may sound like nonsense to you, but none the less it must be done: if there is any help your organization can give us, we would be most desirous of having it."

Pternam said, "If you mean that we should contribute to the revolution, it hardly seems necessary—your people are enjoying a singular success. The fact is, word is now from the Council of Syndics that they expect to wind up from this brawling with considerably less Lisagor than they started with. And losing it all is not out of the realm of possibility, either. We are examining several escape options along those lines already."

Charodei reasserted, "To the contrary. This 'brawling,' as you call it, is not of our doing. It is apparently spontaneous, and uncontrolled. In the few cases where our people have been able to foment a rising, they can't control it and lose it. In other cases, we have been able to take advantage of a situation, but it seems that we lose control of those as well. No. The Heraclitan Society is far behind things. We know you loosed that Rael among us, but we had no idea it would lead to this. We have thought that perhaps you had something like him left over, that we could use as an antidote, or some leavening agent."

"Not so. We tried to stop him, after release, when we realized he was more powerful than we had originally imagined." Pterman choked on the lie, but after he said it, it went a little smoother. "We sent operatives to detain him, but they were too late. We also sent assassins to catch up with the remnant, the woman Azart, but they also have failed to date. At any rate, what we had here in reserve did not work out, and we have been hard-pressed since."

"We also put a man on Azart. The best. And according to reports, he's got contact."

Pternam sat up stiffly. "Contact? What is he waiting for? My permission? Kill the insect immediately!"

Charodei held up a hand. "A moment, if you will. He had to be sure before he acted, and to date he's not completely convinced. After all, Azart is still in detention, under surveillance by the police. To be sure, it's light but nonetheless there is considerable risk to our man, and we told him not to move

124

unless he's sure, because if he strikes down the wrong woman, there's a good chance he'll be caught, and we don't want him risked on a nobody."

"What does he report?"

"He has contact with a woman who meets the general specifications; there are some minor discrepancies, but none major."

"I still ask: what is he waiting for?"

"Orlioz reports that the woman Azart responds as a woman in all pertinent matters, but that her reflexes are abnormally fast. He tested her under the pretext of physical therapy. In short, he doesn't know if he can. He has arranged a sexual liaison with her at the moment, but he claims that she's quick enough still that if she divined his purpose, she could probably defend herself well enough to endanger him. He has asked for clarification instructions."

Pternam shook his head. "This is your best? No wonder you needed Rael-Damistofia. You send an assassin in there, he gets a little sugar, and now he's got cold feet."

Charodei said stiffly, "I don't think that's the case at all."

Pternam said, "Well, there isn't much we can do to help him. I mean, he's there and we're here. He has her; he will have to make the critical decision alone. We agree on this: Azart must be killed. We don't know what she is capable of."

"Orlioz said in his report that her movements under stress revealed a concealed level of control . . . a level he thought higher than his own. He said further that this ability seems to come and go, as if she were not completely sure of herself, or was half-asleep. He fears the consequences if he initiates any series of actions which would alert her completely, or awaken her to her full potential. Apparently, under the stress of changing genders, she is attempting to bury Rael and *become* Damistofia Azart in reality. In the light of what Rael has proven capable of, and that by way of a simple agreement, we are not certain we wish to see what Damistofia Azart might try to do motivated by emotions like revenge."

Pternam said, silkily, "We are not convinced that what Rael did is the proximate cause of these internal problems."

Charodei responded, "We are! We need no convincing; we know."

Pternam looked narrowly at Charodei. "How so?"

Charodei said, beginning slowly, cautiously, "There was an element in Lisagor which acted as a dampening agent on the pressures within this society—the impetus to change, and the resistance to that which was so strong here. No one imagined that this was the keystone holding Lisagor and Oerlikon together, but Reol struck at it, and through a series of coincidental events, which we believe he could somehow perceive, he neatly sliced that element out of the picture, which allowed the contending forces to come into direct contact. They will continue to work against one another until another stable amalgam is attained. The prospectus now is that of a number of semi-independant states, some hostile to others . . . the unique conditions here will not reappear; in fact, they have already gone."

Pternam commented, "There is some truth in what you say; I know for a fact that Clisp is already loose, however much they disguise the fact. Much of The Serpentine as well, and also Karshiyaka, of all places. *They* have brought the mercenaries from Tartary. But aside from all that, I find your, ah, viewpoint, as it were, a little odd. You speak almost as an outsider, with a clinical detachment I cannot manage. How is this so?"

"I have some truth to deliver, and you must take it as you will."

"Speak on—we have need of it."

Charodei said, "The element that dampened: those people were not natives, but were from the old worlds, let us conjecture."

"Go on. Why would they care?"

"Originally, let us say that they wanted to see how a change-resistant system of society would work, because elsewhere they don't. But as they stayed here longer, they gained a vested interest in keeping things as they were."

Pternam swore, "Hellation! They were filthy spies, laughing at us."

Charodei demurred gently. "No, they may seem that way, but they were not. They were in fact mere academics, students, if you will, who wanted to maintain what they found. Change was building up pressure here, as elsewhere. And so they acted to deflect the impetus for those changes, to keep Oerlikon as it was."

Pternam was still skeptical. "Why should they care?"

"They, such people, would have to train exhaustively for such a mission, learn the modes of speech, the customs, the laws, also which are most followed, and what outlets does the system allow, or encourage. In doing so, one would become used to thinking like a native; some might come to like it, af-

126

ter all, everyone on every planet sometimes remarks about the 'good old days.' We all share the fear that things will not remain as we left them, that the change of values makes us ciphers, nothings, insignificances. And frankly, I think that some of those watchers would also prefer this kind of work to other occupations they might be doing, for in a lot of ways, the mission would be a soft job, and they would want the conditions that called the Oerlikon project into existence to continue, so they would have a place, however obscure. Let us further say that the tour here would last, say, twenty-five standard years, so that one could do a trip here and go home and have a pension. Not a bad life, eh?"

Pternam said softly, "And these people from the void; they would have been here a long time, yes?"

"From the beginning. Many—indeed, the vast majority, were insignificant people who were never noticed. Some rose to high position. One or two ruled."

Pternam thought about something Rael had told him, something about a third force. And here was this Charodei describing the same thing, although it was much more fearsome than he imagined. "How would they come and go?"

"Spaceships, naturally. The locals have no incentive to travel space in the local system, and the nearest inhabited systems are too far. Also, Lisagor has no competition, hence, no enemy to watch for. And Lisagor early turned away from space—it is a powerful motive for change. Most landings took place at sea; a few in Tartary."

Pternam said, "Why sould you voice such conjectures to me?"

Charodei said mildly, "To accustom you to the idea. Most Lisaks would find the idea insupportable, but you seem receptive to ideas of this sort, and your business here involves change in a profound way. You would react the most reasonably."

Pternam glanced at Avaria, then said, "Could I make one of my own conjectures? That you might be one such person?"

Charodei hesitated, as if weighing minutiae, and said at last, "In the light of what we have said, the assumption would seem to follow."

Pternam said, not missing a fraction of the beat of the conversation, "Then one could also assume Akhaltsykh would be one as well; one would hardly reveal such a secret before a mere idealist."

"That is correct."

Pternam nodded. "I understand. This is valuable tender to reveal. We have heard, of course, of such a thing, from Femisticleo Chugun and his henchmen, lackeys, and minions. But also Monclova is taken with the idea. I had considered it nonsense. But then, you must desire something of me. You may speak of it."

It was Charodei who flinched. He had evaluated Pternam correctly, of course, but the quickness and ruthlessness of his response took him aback. He cleared his throat and said, "Rael struck during a period when we could not communicate, and our infrastructure here was destroyed by him. Those of us who survive would like to return to our home-worlds. You are high enough to have constructed a suitable apparatus so that we can arrange for pickup with our monitor ship. Then we depart."

Pternam said briskly, "Difficult that would be, especially in such times. . . ." He glanced at Charodei. "But not totally impossible. We have a certain secrecy here, and a certain tether. . . . But what can you provide in exchange? I have no irrational hatreds against your people, but I am pressed now. Lisagor is in great danger, and with it, all of us who have ruled it. I do not care to have a mob uncover all that was here, in the pits and training cribs."

Charodei said, "One of the first native casualties of the unrest was The Heraclitan Society; it disintegrated into a score of ideological and territorial factions. Certain survivors have come together, and taken over some of the larger surviving fragments. This movement is now under the effective control of a council of four persons, two of whom are here now."

"The other two?"

"Cesar Kham and Arunda Palude. Kham was acting bureau chief for Clisp and the Serpentine, Palude was central integrator."

Pternam said, "Those are not your real names, the ones you had at birth?"

"No, but what matter? I am Porfirio Charodei now. But to the point: we are trying to salvage a core here in the inland provinces; Crule the Swale, Puropaigne, Akchil, part of Grayslope. The Lisak central government will of course be discredited and will fall as a matter of course, but something will take its place. We offer our expertise in arranging things to fall your way. We will work with those people you designate."

"There are details to be worked out. . . ."

128

"Yes. This is detail-work of no great importance. What we need early on is a sign of commitment that we may proceed."

"What would you do otherwise?"

"Just vanish into the masses. We can do so."

Pternam nodded, "And who knows who else you'd make such an offer to? Doubtless there's someone somewhere who'd stand still for it, besides us here. Yes. Very well. Proceed. I will arrange to have the proper components brought here and assembled. You have an expert to coordinate this?"

"One will be provided."

"And your end?"

"We will commence immediately. The resultant state which emerges cannot be guaranteed as to physical extent, but you and such associates as you designate will be at the head of it."

"And we'll be rid of you."

"Yes."

"Very well. Our motives seem to coincide. Is there anything else we need to discuss?"

"Yes. Rael; or more properly, Damistofia. We would like to take her with us. He, she, is a unique being, and we would desire to study this creature under controlled conditions."

"Is Orlioz one of you?"

"No. He is a Lisak. A real one, if somewhat deviant. He has asked for clarification before proceeding. Capture would be simple, relatively. We would also ask for the experimental notes and records, and some person from your staff who participated in such training."

"You would take such a monster back to your own worlds? Alive? I might, were I you, take it back, a certified corpse, encased in a ton of glass. But you have no idea what you are dealing with. It is supremely dangerous, and must—I say *must*—be eliminated. I insist. Rael must die."

Charodei began, "We must look beyond revenge . . ."

Pternam interrupted, "That creature possesses an ability to disrupt entire worlds. I am not thinking revenge, but protecting my own world from further disruption. And probably yours as well."

Charodei said confidently, "We think we can isolate it suitably there—we have devices and methods. . . ."

"Yes. Devices, methods, spaceships and telephones that speak across the void. But you couldn't make a Morphodite. We did that. And I reiterate: you have no idea how dangerous that thing, that insect, really is, fully awakened. We sim-

129

ply cannot take the chance. I say have it killed, or . . . I'd reconsider."

"How much of a reconsideration?"

"Come, come, my good Charodei, let us not fall to threats and promises of dire events. Nothing is more boring than the fool who claims, 'I intend to do so-and-so,' when one can be certain that such claimers will in fact do nothing, or cannot. I prefer to speak of accomplishments, of facts, of deeds, of 'I shall.' We made Rael. We know now how dangerous he is. He must be killed."

Charodei looked at Akhaltsykh, who nodded. Charodei said, "Very well. Done. I will have Orlioz so instructed."

"Tonight. And put some backup in with him. Don't miss; it may charge if it's only wounded."

"Have no fears. Orlioz is expert."

"Does he know what he's really dealing with?"

"To my knowledge, no. He's been told what to look for—Damistofia Azart—and to verify certain things about her. As far as I know he operates under the assumption that he is to dispatch a dangerous operative."

"Make sure he understands that if he misses, he won't get a second chance."

Pternam let that admonition rest a moment, and then added, "And for a fact, we won't get one, either."

130

～ 9 ～

Marula: The Far Side of Now

Marula was a place, to Damistofia's perception of it, limited though that was, which seemed to lend to its inhabitants little or no consciousness of any aspect of nature, save perhaps the verminous life-forms which infested the docks and warehouses and as well the poorer habitats. In Marula, as Damistofia heard it, they did not speak of the sky, or of plants, or of animals, or winds; they did speak to excess to a degree she found incomprehensible, of relationships between people, for which they invariably used slang and jargon all of which carried strong overtones of envy, jealousy, and general resentment, as well as a well-loaded cargo of sexual allusions which left no doubt as to what people did in Marula to amuse themselves.

At least in this much, she was thankful of this, because it enabled her to become fractionally more invisible, against the day when she should be let out of the Palliatory.

The relationship with Cliofino continued, although it seemed with fits and starts, and odd hesitations. But as far as his skill as a lover, she had no complaints, for he was both passionate and considerate, and although she sensed that there was no permanence to the relationship she let her new emotions and pleasures take her where they would, and afterward, when they lay quietly together, saying nothing but feeling the echoes of each other's passages ring through themselves, she admitted to herself that she felt warm and good, and full of life.

Still, something eluded her, and much of that vague absence she marked down to her severance from her original past. Old Jedily; now she would have known exactly what to do, how to feel, what to suppress and what to loose, and when to cry out and make animal noises. But that was gone and Damistofia had no way to get it back. She knew that she would have to take what was worthwhile of Rael and discard the rest, and with her own experiences make her life now.

131

But something still nagged at her, which all her explanations to herself and her allowances could not complete. She knew very well what her problem was; there was something bothering Clio as well, and as time passed, it bothered her more and more.

She sensed, weakly at first, and then stronger, that he was holding something back, something he wouldn't share, no matter what their transports. And when he went with her and paced her in her exercises, which were limbering up her body into a finely balanced supple instrument that responded in its slender, graceful economy of muscle and soft flesh much better than Rael's awkward heavy lengths of limbs, she could catch him watching her closely, more so than she felt was motivated by lust or love or interest, but by something else. He was measuring her carefully; *and what he saw he feared. He feared her!* And to her knowledge he had no reason to.

Here, she was absolutely on her own. They had known this from the beginning, when her training began, when she had been Rael, but they had counted on what she seemed to be to shield her from the worst until she could get her own bearings. So even yet she had no outside source of information she could tap, to verify what Clio said he was. And as yet, she had no reason to doubt him, and yet she did, in the dark nights when he was not with her, and she had time to think about it.

This was such a night. The disturbances, which had seemed to be growing, had faded, and now one only heard distant, hushed rumors of thwarted uprisings, or else marches and protests, which sprang up and then faded away. Nothing nearby. The weather was no longer made up of the clear bright days of summer, but the rainy season of fall. Perhaps that had calmed them down. The Marula natives were long on talk, but as far as she could see, short on positive action.

But she could not sleep, and so she turned on the light, which was weak as is usually the case at night, and sat in her soft chair, which Clio had brought her, and thought, clearly.

She had been trying to forget Rael for weeks, now, months. And it was hard to try to bring back the old formulas by which Rael had plied his deadly trade, the only one he knew. The ideas swirled in her head like leaves in a street-gutter drain-mouth. It was all there, but it was fragmented and fading; the matrix of order was almost gone from it. Still, she thought that perhaps in that arcane and bizarre formulation of reality, perhaps there was insight, and so she tried harder, trying to remember, and as she did, feeling the strangeness of the female flesh that she wore now. The ideas, the very ideas, did not seem to fit well in Damistofia's head as they had in Rael's.

She had no notes, no reminders, but it worked, after all, with a specific code of logic, and there were axioms and postulates, and then developmental proofs, simple proven bases, and upon that foundation one erected Operations, which were statements about reality. She reviewed the logic, and found she could recall it; then the axioms and assumptions, each with its name and title, according to some caprice of trickery of Rael: The First Noble Truth, Godel's Refutation, Heisenberg's Trinity, Asimov's Law, and then, for no reason, Number Five. There were a score of others, and, one by one, they fell back into place. Then the basic exercises in manipulating the symbols, which at first felt clumsy and often threw her into errors, but she began to make them work properly for her, and the symbols for the Arbitrary Exercise Answers began to come in proper order.

She warmed up to it, feeling the same thrill as had Rael when he had first built this system: it was neither mystical nor mysterious but clear and logical and scientific. It did not reveal the future, but only extremely narrow sections, as related to specific problems. The more specific the inputs were, the narrower and brighter became the Searchlight. Yes. That was a good way to look at it: a searchlight beam, illuminating something, or showing you that nothing was there. In the manipulations she could also choose the angle of illumination.

And so, one datum at a time, she began substituting elements she knew into the progress of the formulas, turning them back onto themselves, building resonances, harmonic derivatives, orders of probability. It went like music, only music always stopped too soon, and this, abstract, alive on its own, did not, but kept on building to the final phrase. She exhausted the small sheaf of papers she had hurriedly grabbed, and absentmindedly got some more, and continued, and the Answer came, with difficulty, dim, and somewhat blurred, but it came, and she knew it was Truth: *Cliofino is an assassin and you are his target.*

There was a verification subroutine, and she ran it without hesitation, suspecting the Answer, yet feeling no emotion but a sense of achievement and triumph, and it was clear: *Cliofino is an assassin and you are his target.* Hard as dia-

133

mond, adamantine and poised, it hung in her mind in the dance of symbols and formulae and was itself. Damistofia was so far into the routine that she hardly paused, muttering aloud only, "Thought something wasn't right," and continued, now using this formulation as a base, and building it into a more difficult phase, now asking "why?"

And in a shorter time, now, she also had the answer: *Because he knows what you are, and those who order him have so directed, and he will obey.*

Now she sat back, feeling clammy sweat on her body, and noticing that her palms were damp. All this time, working out together in the gym, wrestling with one another, bodies conjoined, interpenetrated, one, in the throes of love and desire; he had had a thousand opportunities, and had not tried. Why? She didn't need the system of Rael to tell her that: because he senses or comprehends that her reactions may be faster and to try would be deadly peril—to him, and he might not succeed. She could defend, merely, or defend-attack. What was the course? Here was a problem Rael's system could easily handle. She thought, and then began coding in the symbols and sequences to derive the answer she sought. The first thing that came clearly was the element of Time. *Soon.* As she would have explained it to someone who had no knowledge of the system, "at the far side of Now." And what was the correct action for her? Again she bent to the pencil and paper, again she frowned in concentration, and the answer came almost too easily: *You must kill him when he tries it. That is the only course open.*

The rest of it was anticlimactic, and tiring, and she felt sleepy. But she remembered from Rael that it was only right and only correct to carry the operation out to the last place, to derive the whole answer, for only in that way could one sense the awful chasms that lay on either side, even if they were not described. And at last she finished, knowing what she had to do, and feeling the correctness of it, however painful it was to think of it. And after she had torn the paper into shreds and flushed them down the commode, and went back to bed, she thought long on it: *And I asked, I did, if I could save him, because he is so good, so young, and so nice a lover, so pretty, so muscular and graceful, and it said there was no way.* And then, looking at the light beginning to bleed wanly into her single window toward the east, she allowed her heart to ache and a small tear formed at the outer corners of her eyes, and she sniffled once, and went to sleep at last.

The Far Side of Now. It came late the next day, toward evening, a gray and cheerless day, of damp, cold winds off the invisible estuary, but at least the rain had stopped. Cliofino appeared, quite out of nowhere, and announced that he had at last obtained a work-release for her and had secured a small place in a habitat far enough away from the Palliatory for her to forget it.

He added, "And we'll wait a bit, and then just not report back, and they'll forget about you entirely, among the much more alarming problems they have here."

"And I'll be free, with correct papers, and everything . . ."

"Everything. It's all taken care of. All it has to do is unwind."

"How did you do it?"

"Ah, some persuasion here, some chicanery here, and in a couple of cases, outright bribery." He handed Damistofia a thin wallet, which contained her new identity papers.

She took them, and said, "This is what you have been working on all along?"

"Well, in a manner of speaking, yes."

"Tell me the real reason. You, of course, are not one of these people."

Cliofino did not hesitate. "You have been recruited. We have need for operatives who are both agile and mentally alert . . . and who can be extracted from the matrix of the people with the minimum of disturbance."

"I see. All of it was that?"

"No, not all. Sometimes extra things happen . . . sometimes they don't, or perhaps you wouldn't want them to. No, that which went between us was real enough, and I hope it might continue."

She nodded, as if overwhelmed by the information, but smiled, and begin gathering up her things, which were very few. She thought, *I travel light now.*

They walked through the grounds and out the main gate, and no one seemed to care, or make any gesture toward them. This surprised Damistofia, and she asked Cliofino, as they stepped outside the wall into the street and began walking down it, "They didn't even care! How did you do that?"

"I convinced them I was a deep cover agent of Femisticleo Chugun, the head of the, ah, secret state police. Of course, I

135

have help in maintaining this disguise, but in these times, as long as one seems on the side of order, few questions are asked. I have recruited here before, and they are a little relaxed in their vigilance, and so. . . ."

"But you are not that."

"Not for Chugun. We hope to see him over a slow fire."

They walked along for a while, beside the wall still, which seemed to go on and on, and at last she saw the end of it. "I suppose you'll tell me more when we get where we're going."

"Yes, more."

"And I don't really have much choice in this, do I?"

He looked at her sidelong, with an engaging smile. "Choice? Of course you'll have choice. We are not like those who have held it so long here. I'll tell you how things are, and then you make up your own mind."

"Should I not want to work with your . . . group?"

"Read your papers. Go on, open them."

Damistofia removed the wallet from her bundle while she walked, and opened the wallet. There was, inside, a standard Lisak Identification card, listing name, residence, province and the like, and at the bottom, in the block marked "Occupation," it said, "*Landscaping Inspector, Beautification Section, Not Restricted.*" She shook her head, and said, "I don't understand this at all. I know little or nothing about plants or landscaping."

Clio laughed. "Neither do the inspectors, as a rule. It's a fat patronage job. All you have to do is travel around and fill out forms. Nothing is ever done wrong, of course, unless it's by someone you don't like. So I'll tell you what we want you to do, and if you don't want to, then go and inspect; I'll arrange an appointment with your new boss. Your initial assignment will be the South Coast sector, which is to say, in Sertse Solntse, Zolotane, and Priboy. If you are nice to the Head Inspector here in Marula, he'll post you off to the Pilontaries where you can really vanish."

"You are serious?"

"Absolutely. Although . . . I'd hate to see you go. I have to stay here in the Marula area."

They were beyond the wall, now, but there seemed to be nothing in particular near the Palliatory. A few deserted buildings, vacant lots, old warehouses. The street was broad and straight, and veered off toward the west where, farther down, there seemed to be something, an untidy jumble of buildings she could not identify. Overhead, the sky was overcast, but in the far west there was an immense pearly flare of clouds, backlit by the westering sun, now setting somewhere out to sea beyond Clisp. She walked, and stared at the bright western sky until her eyes grew weary and blurred, and then she looked back to the thoroughfares of Marula. She saw around her empty, uninhabited and unused spaces, abandoned, rusting machinery and odd parts of old buildings left behind, and trash blowing in the vacant lots. It was the most desolate and forbidding thing she could remember seeing in that part of her life she could remember, and it filled her with an aching longing to be elsewhere, now, immediately, somewhere . . .

Damistofia turned to Cliofino and said, "Why is there nothing here, next to the Palliatory?"

"Cleared it off a while back. No reason, that I know of. They were going to build something else, and then they never got around to it, and so it stayed the same."

"The smoke and . . . all that; where did that come from?"

Cliofino pointed vaguely southwest. "Over there was the nearest one. That's what you probably smelled. South Mernancio District."

"There were others?"

"Oh, yes . . . many more. Three in Marula so far." He paused and added, "We've not seen the end of it yet. There'll be more before it's over."

"There must be a better way for people to live together."

"You will hear our ideas." He took her hand shyly and they walked on into the dusk.

The untidy jumble of buildings came nearer as they walked, and the light grew more uncertain. Damistofia thought they had walked about half an hour, or less. Not very far. She felt no fatigue. As they came near the first buildings, they saw motion in an open field, behind an untidy fence long since gone to ruin, vandals, and wood-stealers. Soft, low, melodious calls, running, quick, darting shadows in the failing light.

Cliofino gestured toward the dim figures. "In the midst of chaos, they still find time to have a round of Dragon."

"Can we watch? I often heard them talking about Dragon, back there."

"I suppose so. We have nothing to do tonight, except find a place to eat, and find your new place."

137

Damistofia squeezed his hand, "And of course we'll have to try it out?"

"Oh, yes. Mind, I've already been there, and it's in a quiet corner."

"Good." While they walked up to the fence, a few late-arrivals approached on velocipedes, pedaling madly in the uncertain light, swerving and stopping and recklessly throwing themselves off their machines, to slip through the fence, and pausing for a moment to size things up, leap immediately into the action, which was at a high peak.

The newcomers quickly found places of concealment in what appeared to be an abandoned junkyard. Hardly had they vanished into the shadows when the current reigning Dragon returned from another part of the field, trotting effortlessly, glaring here and there, and carrying the Scorpion meaningfully limp, ready for instant use. Here he stopped, and called out, "Latecomers, show yourselves! Skulk not in the shadows like Bezards and Wisants. Come forth, come forth! I am somewhat tired from overexertion, and will lay my friend on your shoulder as a comrade." The spectators tittered among themselves, and glanced at one another.

Cliofino leaned close and whispered, "Judging by the crowd, this one's a famous liar. He'll wait for one to show and then pound him down. Just you watch!"

All remained quiet, however, From distant parts of the field came, at intervals, odd half-calls, subvocalized and unintelligible—Obviously, the other players taunting the Dragon. Damistofia thought she could sense movement back there, players risking little swift lunges and darts. They did not like a waiting game.

The Dragon walked about, as if uncertain, peering here and there like a stage villain, an act which seemed to fool no one. At last he stopped, and mopped his brow with his sleeve. He called out, "Come, my children, bear my heavy burden."

One of the shadows erupted into a running form that seemed to reach his top speed instantly, as if shot from a gun. He passed directly in front of the Dragon, hooting as he ran, wildly, almost like the cry of a Bosel. The Dragon was not caught off-guard. When the runner had emerged, the Dragon had been slightly out of position, but in an astonishing display of virtuosity, shifted the Scorpion to the other hand and neatly, almost effortlessly, backhanded the runner between the shoulder blades, a motion that seemed light, almost easy, until one saw the runner pitched over headfirst by the force of the blow, landing rolling awkwardly, while the former Dragon now dusted his hands off, and began walking off the field. He said, to no one in particular, "Told you I was tired. Now take up the Scorpion and demonstrate excellence to the laggards by the fence." And with that, he joined the spectators there, but made no further move to leave. He passed near Damistofia and Cliofino, and she heard him breathing hard. He was an older man, and overweight. Yet he had entered this anarchic Game and plunged into the action, chasing younger sprites.

The new Dragon, somewhat shaken, now got to his feet, and returned for the Scorpion; picking it up, he waved it about to get the feel of it, for there was no standard model. This one seemed heavy, weighted, a vicious weapon, and it moved in his hands like some live thing, wriggling, twisting. It was his privilege to give a short address if he wished, and this one chose to do so. Gathering his breath, he said, "I will now speak. Night creatures, make your moves; The demon avenger is upon you! True, we came late to this gathering of nobles, we rushed, we fretted. Would we be on time? But now we are here, and the waiting is over."

Those along the fence made fretful motions, moving slightly into positions of better advantage. They were in fact not immune to the Dragon, should he decide to attack them. Everyone was fair game.

The Dragon now swaggered, feeling the sense of power come to him. He strolled closer to Damistofia and Cliofino, still orating, "But where would we start? The far fields, where they hide in security? Or here along the fence, where they think to watch others sweat, as they stand in immunity. No immunity, I assure you. All are equal on the field."

Damistofia watched the Dragon, and Cliofino, who watched with glittering attention. The Dragon paraded back and forth, and suddenly stopped, right in front of them, and gallantly handed the Scorpion to Damistofia, saying as he did, "Here's a switch in the Game of surprises! I hand it off without mayhem or malice aforethought. I say, here's a young lady with her bravo, walking along to an evening rendezvous! Wonder what she'd really do? Will she clout him over the head like Thelonia* and her rolling pin?"

Damistofia took the instrument, numbly. Now had become NOW. This Scorpion was of a soft, stiff leather, rather heavy

* A famous character of Lisak folklore, an immense fat woman always waylaying unlucky men with a rolling pin and a venomous tongue.

toward the large end, a bit longer than her forearm. She swung it, experimentally, as if trying to make up her mind. As a newcomer who had just walked up, she could hand it back to him if she wished.

As if trying to read her mind, Cliofino hissed, "You don't have to take it! Hand it back!"

She stiffened, and said, "No, I will take it." She stepped out onto the field, through the ruinous fence, and looked back at the crowd in the dusk. She said, "People! I have not played before, but I know what to do!" The erstwhile Dragon smiled broadly, winked at her, and sidled off into the shadows, to find a place to hide. Damistofia continued. "I am small and a poor imitation for Thelonia, so I will try to attain hard-headed Caldonia, who cannot be dissuaded once her mind is made up." The crowd of idlers murmured their approval. Caldonia was another mythical woman who was notorious for being hard-headed and suspicious, and a shrew to boot. She went on, "Today is a day when I celebrate my new liberty, and what better way than to play here, to know choice and cunning, fierce pride and the thrill of the chase." This was good stuff, the crowd thought, and out on the field, many of the players made hand signs to each other, also approving. She was small, they thought, and not so dangerous. There would be action.

Without further hesitation, Damistofia turned and loped out onto the field, opening her eyes wide to take in as much as she could. For a moment, Cliofino hesitated, uncertain, and then also stepped through the fence, watching her carefully. She called out, in the manner of Dragons from time immemorial, "Come, my pretties, my bulls, my Bosel Bucks! Who will dare the arm and aim of a small woman? I will tempt you further—he whom I strike, I will sleep with . . . if he's able!"

Hoarse hoots greeted this announcement from various parts of the field, voices in the dusk, heedless that they would give their position away. One called, "Take me!" Another said, "Try me! Then you'll really get a thrashing!" One said, "I'm a credit to my gender!" Another sung, simply, "Forget the Scorpion and sit on my face!"

Cliofino followed uncertainly, not sure which way to turn. This had suddenly taken a radical turn for the worse. What the hell was she doing, egging them on like that? Could she have seen him? And if she had, what would she do? Attack him with the Scorpion? Nonsense. He had played Dragon since he had been a mere lad, and he was fairly certain she knew little about the evasions an experienced player could make. He could run her ragged. He thought he knew: she would try to escape in the dim light and confusion of the game. Well, he had an answer for that, too . . . Dimness and confusion abetted many things, and here was as good a place as any. Yes. Here. He looked for Damistofia, and suddenly she wasn't there. Damn. He loped off onto the field, senses alert, watching for the sudden motion out of the corner of his eye.

Ahead, where he thought she went, he heard running feet, harsh panting. A voice called out, "Not there, over here! Celebrate with me. I didn't see your face, but we've a sack for that!" Another voice added, "Maybe you'll need two bags—one for you if hers comes off." He heard Damistofia reply, "Come and see for yourself!" She was somewhere not far ahead; he thought he saw her slight figure, moving by a dark place, checking if anyone was in it. She had worn soft gray clothing, a loose tunic top and pants, and he thought that the lightness of her clothing would have made her show up better, but apparently it didn't, but instead, in the failing light, it made her fade in and out of visibility like a ghost.

Those who never played Dragon saw the play as a lot of waiting, broken by sudden noise and alarms, quick scuffles, rare, random violence, but now Cliofino, an old player of the game, knew this to be an illusion. Quiet? The dimness was electric and alive with the eyes of hidden watchers; currents of anticipation flowed over it like night in the wildest jungles. All his senses were alert, as he pressed further into the back reaches of this field, alert for the flickering gray shadow, which now seemed to have disappeared. No matter. She'd have to show herself—she had the Scorpion, and she had to get rid of it. Ahead, he noted an obstruction, which seemed too small and insignificant to offer concealment, nevertheless, he made a detour around it, watching ahead. And aha! There was the soft pad of running feet to his left, a little behind him. He turned to look, and caught a tremendous blow on the right temple that knocked him completely off his feet. He twisted with the force of it, technicolor sparkles flashing in checkerboard patterns before his eyes and fell heavily on his face, and he tasted dry dirt and blood where he had split his lip.

He tried to get up, but fell back, fearing he'd lose consciousness completely. He felt nauseated, disoriented. Had

141

that been Damistofia? He couldn't imagine her getting enough force behind the Scorpion to deliver a blow like that. He sat up and looked around, still dazed, and now feeling a fine, hard and hot anger rising in him, a delayed chain reaction. Groping about, he found the Scorpion nearby, dropped in contempt. And around him, the players called out the timeless insult and invective of the anarchic game:

"Off your dead arse and on your dying feet!"

"Up and claim your prize, lunker! She said she'd sleep with you!"

"He thinks she will anyway. Not likely, after taking him down like that!"

A woman's voice, not Damistofia's said, from nearby, "You had it coming, you roach, or else she would have come after us!"

"What is this, a rest-station on the Symbar pilgrimage? Up and demonstrate your excellence, else we'll take it from you."

This last was cruel, for Dragons who were considered slack in their action were often ganged up on, beaten, and the Scorpion taken from them. No more ignominious fate could be imagined. Cliofino, still somewhat dazed, felt he could handle himself well enough, one-on-one, but against the onslaught of half a dozen local bullies, with their women on the field to egg them on, that would be questionable. He stood up and glared about, swinging the Scorpion meaningfully, and saying, in a low growl, "Come and take it, if you're able!" The hoots and catcalls faded, and he noted small flickering motions out of the corners of his eyes, as the new round started and the players took up strategic positions, or made themselves secure in their old ones.

The anger he had felt before was now rising like an ancient god from the bottom of the sea. He had hesitated to do his duty, though he knew what he had to do. It would have been quick; it would have had to be. But he would have done it with compassion and mercy. A monster, they had said. Kill it. And so he would. Here. Now. No one would question a casualty of a game that produced them regularly. And then he'd vanish into the night, and make the connections to the trip to Marisol, in Clisp, that they'd promised him. No more Marula.

Cliofino made a quick tour of the area he was in, looking swiftly, sure she wouldn't be close by. His swift and methodical search flushed several, who would burst out of concealment like birds and race off, legs pumping mightily. Those he

142

left, to the amusement of those farther off, who continued to hoot at him:

"Revenge! That's the stuff!"

But they kept their distance, knowing that in his mood, he could easily injure someone else before he found her. So they all knew he was looking for her. It didn't matter.

He went back toward the street a little, hoping to catch sight of her in the brighter lighting from the streets, and ahead he thought he saw her; she stepped out from behind a rusty hulk, as if waiting for him, joined by others, who seemed to grow out of the earth like phantoms. Cliofino shook his head, wondering if he was hallucinating, seeing double. Ahead, not a dozen paces, there were four, no, six, all in gray, although they looked different, moving nervously, but staying more or less in place, as if waiting for him, dancing, inviting. Which one was Damistofia? One he selected, and he made a rush at that one, but he or she scampered off, and he saw that it was an adolescent, hardly more than a child, trying the field out a little, and a soft voice said beside him, "No, not that one. Here!"

And she stood still, long enough for him to recognize it was truly her. He checked, a little unsteadily, and turned after her, but now she ran, close in among the obstacles and dumps and hiding-places, running with incredible agility, more than he had seen her display yet. But he was catching up: he switched the Scorpion to the position of readiness. First he'd knock her off her feet, and then . . . She ducked under a low beam, and he plunged in behind her almost close enough to touch her, close, too close to swing the Scorpion for the felling blow, and he ran into an upright post that stunned him, knocking the breath out of him, as he fell back, gasping for air. No one was around. They were completely hidden. Frustration rose in his throat like a burning gall, rage, he thought, "I'll tear her apart . . ." but something moved in the close darkness, and he felt a tremendous blow on his throat, which cut off his air. He choked, panicked, struggled, but all that would come were distant gargling noises, and as his sight dimmed and he fought the darkness rising around him like a wave, he felt soft fingers moving over his face, a lover's intimacy, over his ears, under them, and there was a pressure, and time stopped.

Damistofia sat back on her haunches, still holding her fingers tightly pressed on Cliofino's carotid arteries, until the

143

jumping, leaping pulse in them slowed, became irregular, and stopped. And she still waited, counting her own loud heartbeats, until she was certain. Even then, after she released her pressure, she went back and felt for it again. Nothing. She felt over the body, felt carefully for other places, felt there for a pulse. There was none. No breathing. It was done.

She sat back in the cool darkness, feeling the heat radiate off her face, breathing deeply, trying to fill her lungs, not just pant. *In the end*, she thought, *he betrayed himself and was a fool, after all*. He could have waited and done it his way, no doubt while they were lying abed, but he had to follow her onto the field. The idiot. Dragon had been part of Rael's education, too, and the computation had showed her that was the way to do it. And now that link was cut. No one here knew her.

She stepped out into the night, now, feeling the cold of the air, the sea-damp. Around her, voices were calling out, nervously, bantering, vulgar. She answered, calling out, "Here, over here. The fellow who was Dragon. He ran into a post and hurt himself. He won't get up." In the dark, on the field, no one would examine the body closely. They'd see the bruises and scrapes from the Scorpion and the post, and that would be that. And as soon as they left her alone, she'd *change*, and there would, after a day of terror and pain, be nothing left. No Cliofino, no Damistofia.

Soon, hesitantly at first, and then with greater resolve, they came, to find Damistofia sitting by one who would not rise, still grasping the Scorpion tightly. One of them pried his fingers loose.

That one said softly, "Miss, I think he's dead."

Another asked, "What happened?"

She answered, forcing her voice, slowly, "He was pursuing me, here, and went in there and ran into that post, and fell back."

"Were you bonded?"

"We were just friends, you know. Not especially close. Just friends. This was insane. . . ."

Another said, "It's no matter. It happens: part of the game. He played like one who knew what he was about—we could see that. He knew the risks. And tonight was omened badly—Abelio was hurt earlier, and they carried him off. By the way, has anyone gone to see what became of him?" There was muttering and discussion in hushed tones in the back of the crowd that had gathered, and someone said that

144

Abelio was at home, resting, and had sworn off Dragon for the duration.

Several men volunteered to carry the body down to the Palliatory, for the night-clerk to settle, and she told them that his name had been, or so he said, Alonzo Durak, and they nodded solemnly, exchanging knowing glances. Uh-huh. He gave her a false name. Happens all the time; well, Alonzo Durak or Jaime Kirk, it was all one—they had a body to move, and so to it, lift, here, and off they went.

Damistofia remained where she was, and after a time, the spokesman for the group pronounced the Game closed, and suggested that they all repair to a tavern they knew of, not too far away, and they would there pause and consider their losses of the night, although someone ventured that, shocking as it was, at the least the accident had not happened to one of their own, and no one commented on this seeming cruelty, for that was the way of Dragon, and would the young lady come with them, and she said shakily that she would, and so, in a crowd, Damistofia left the field and walked with the others off toward the west, toward a certain tavern they knew of. She thought that she was free of the threat of Cliofino, but she was not out of danger yet, nor could she initiate *Change* in the midst of a crowd. But they would soon drink, and tell yarns, and grow sleepy, and somewhere there'd be a place she could hide, and change.

⌇ 10 ⌇

Deserted Cries of the Heart

The crowd marched along the deserted streets in clusters, all talking among themselves, discussing the events of the evening: a well-known Dragon player injured, and another, who seemed to know what he was doing, was dead, seemingly, from carelessness. And the times were odd and perilous as well. Who could know such things? At any event, what was now needed was a tavern with plenty of the rank beer of Sertse Solntse to guzzle, and all of this could then be arranged in its place. That was the way things went, and the way they sorted out. Beer. What they did not speak of, and did not consider, was how much their group, a crowd from a Dragon Game, resembled a mob on their way to a mischief.

Lisagor was in truth coming apart, the uneasy amalgam unraveling under the stresses brought into conflict by the removal of the neutralizing agent, the leaven that had kept it stable. In parts of the continent, in fact, there was no more Lisagor, although these people could not know that and did not know it. And, more importantly, to the segment of Lisagor-the-Entity that survived, it did not know it, by choice. And that entity had sensors, ordinary eyes of informers, and electronic devices, and those sensors and eyes saw an irregular band of people moving with seeming purpose toward a more populous part of the city, and that entity responded with the measures that had worked for it in the past, the threat-become-real: A Pallet-Dropped Trooper force was launched without delay, reacting. A mob simply could not be allowed to reach the city proper and ignite the hysteria which waited there.

Damistofia walked along with the crowd, with them, in their midst, and yet now mostly ignored by them. Perhaps they sensed her agitation, and thought it a kind of grief, and wished to leave her alone with it. Some of the women walked beside her, saying nothing, but providing a presence. But she felt acute danger; some sixth sense was still working. But it

146

was odd, that. Rael was almost gone, despite the exercise she had forced herself to recall. Now, after everything, she felt *herself*. Right as what she was. The walk felt natural, and the ebb of the excitement of the game in the crowd, and the sensations she knew. She was Damistofia, completely. As if Cliofino had freed her.

Nevertheless, danger. Very close. She rationalized it—it would have to be that the ones who sent Cliofino would have backup behind him, someone she could not see. And that would mean that this crowd was only an apparent safety, that somewhere the reserve was moving into active position, and so she would have to find a place to start Change soon. Odd, but as she thought it, it seemed correct, but not with that absolute certainty she had known about the formulations she could perform from Rael's science. *I was correct, but not yet correct enough.*

Another thought also worked in her mind, and that had to do with the consequences of the killing of Cliofino. With the first one, that she remembered well, there were consequencs to that, and she had known them, as Rael. But now, she had not worked the figures that way, so that part of it had been blind to her. *She didn't know anything at all about the results of killing Cliofino.* And there was here neither time nor place to sit down and perform the long calculations necessary to work the answer out. No way to know. She reflected as she walked that it did not really matter: she had taken the path she had to for survival, and that was sufficient. She doubted if Cliofino had the Power-That-Supported. He was much too ordinary, too much the climber, to fit into that schema. *She had probably rid the world of one who had, for all his motion and activity, no measurable effect on the world. It was not the people who were replaceable at will, but the politicians and climbers.*

Slowly, she let the crowd pass her, as she imperceptibly drifted to the rear of the formation by simply slowing down a little. Some of those who walked with her stayed for a while, but then speeded up to the crowd's pace and left her behind. Now she began looking for a place to hide, some dark corner. Another thought crossed her mind, a dark thought indeed: *This time I'm jumping blind. I don't know what I'll be, as Rael knew he'd become me. That's one of the longest operations in the system. And I shouldn't initiate so soon, either, because this body's still not ready for that yet—it's not*

147

completed, the old Change. But so much I know: I'll be male, I'll remember, and I'll be younger. Another odd thought crossed her mind: *I don't know what I'll call myself, then.* The answer came, as if a personal demon had entered her mind and placed the answer there: *Phaedrus. Very well, Phaedrus it is.*

She stopped and sat down on a curb, as the last part of the crowd from the game passed her by, some casually calling out to her to hurry along and catch up, that surely there would be a tavern open not far down the thoroughfare, closer in to the city; while others passed without noticing her at all. She sat, as if weary beyond endurance, folded her arms on her knees and lowered her head to the arms as if resting. She was seeking the state of consciousness within herself, the odd combination of self-hypnosis and yogi trance in which she could initiate Change. The street faded, and the noises of the crowd died away, although they were only just past her, a lonely figure resting on the curb for a moment. No matter, she'd catch up. And it came surprisingly easy to her, much easier than she remembered it from when she had been Rael. She reached the state of darkness, and the outside world was gone, and there, in the center, was the bright wormlike coiling of the threads, black-and-yellow checkerboard color washing over them, moving impossibly fast, impalpable, inconceivable, and she aligned something in herself to them, and they slowed, and slowed, and stopped, in an uneasy stasis, and she reached into that network and changed a thread, the one that controlled this process, and quickly let go and began falling out of the trancelike state, as fast as possible. The structure resumed its frantic writhing motions, and began fading to bright fog, and was gone, and after a moment her senses began filtering back to her.

Wrong, wrong. She heard the sounds of running feet, and cries, and the droning roar of motors overhead. She opened her eyes, still dazed by the aftereffects of the trance state she had just gone into so quickly, and she could not at first make sense of it. Before, the Dragon crowd had been moving south; now they were running north in disorder, while overhead motors roared and bright flares fell in slow-acting arcs too bright to look at. What had happened?

One of the running figures passed her, stopped, came back, and dragged her to her feet. One of the men she had been walking with before, when they had just started here. He was out of breath, but pulled her to her feet, shouting over the

148

noise and confusion, "Come on, girl, you can't rest here, run!"

Damistofia stood up, feeling normal, and hypersensually alert, but also knowing what dread timer was running inside her now, that it would probably be only moments before she had the preliminary attack.

She stammered, "I . . . don't understand! What's happening?"

The man shouted back, "Pallet drop! Thought we were a riot about to happen, I guess. No matter now, run, save yourself! They go after everyone standing once they ground!" He took her hand and pulled her roughly, and she started out with him, running, her heart pounding. And she thought, *What is this exertion going to do to Change?* But she couldn't complete the thought, because there was a powerful roaring drone low overhead, a rattling, a pause and then a hard crash behind her, not too far. She heard staccato sounds, then, and another odd sound, a piercing hissing. A voice, choked with running, cried, "Now leg it good, the first wave's down, and most made it!"

She wanted to see what they were running from, but others urged her on. "No! No looking. Run!" Behind her she heard a dull explosion, and something rattled around her on the street and buildings, and some around her fell. The hissing sound increased, drawing into a deeper timbre, and there was a yellow light back there now making dancing shadows ahead of them. A voice cried in terror, "plasma cutters!" And behind her she heard heavy steps, and a mechanical snarling, and there was another explosion, with more immediate peppery rattling around her, and some more fell, and she increased the pace, hearing another voice, strangling, gargling, "Chainsaws and flamethrowers and sawed-off shotgun pistols in this bunch!" And she ran on. There was another droning overhead, and another crash not far behind her, and the sounds started up again. Now ahead there were lights in the sky suddenly, blinding searchlights, and where they pointed, sudden rivers of fire lanced down in brief bursts, and where the fire went, runners went down like grass. And there were crashes to the side as well, now. Dimly, she sensed they were being surrounded, by the lobotomized troopers on three sides, and ahead, slow-moving aircraft armed. It was at that moment that she felt the first presence of Change. A sudden pain cramped her abdomen, and she doubled over, grasping her stomach, and the man who had taken her hand tugged at her. "Come on, you can't stop now!"

She fell over, coughing, and managed to gasp out, "Can't run, I'm hit. Go on!"

She saw him hesitate a moment, glancing at her, and at those advancing behind them, and then he turned and ran off, with the others who were still on their feet, and behind her she heard, with monstrous clarity, the sounds of chainsaws and flamethrowers, and an occasional boom of a shotgun pistol, fired into the crowd at random. And then she didn't hear any more, because a terrific constriction took her and firmly and irresistibly tried to bend her in two, and her consciousness faded. She sank into darkness, thinking, *I have failed, they will carve me up now with the others*. But after that she did not think anymore. Change commenced, and it was far more drastic than the first time. She had been right in one thing: this body had not been ready for the ordeal of Change—it had not yet completed all phases of its own Change.

Cliofino had been undoubtedly correct about one aspect of life in Marula, that being that the police had things on their minds vastly more important than worrying about exactly who Damistofia Azart was, or had been. For one thing, they were used by the distant authorities as a cleanup force after the depredations of the Pallet-Dropped Troopers, a task they did not relish, but one which occupied much of their time now.

Achilio Yaderny surveyed the street in the bright light of a clear morning, and shook his head wearily. Bad, bad. No good would come of this, none whatsoever. He saw a street, which would now in normal circumstances be busy with folk on their errands, empty of every sign of life except the body-recovery teams. And, of course, the bodies. In this case, they were spared much of the worst; it appeared that most of the victims had fallen to gunshots, rather than the other traumas which the Troopers were capable of inflicting. Small piles of discarded clothing—that's what they looked like. And of course, the pallets. They always left them where they lay, along with the Troopers who didn't make it on the landing. There were a few of those—something near the expected ten percent. But there weren't any Trooper bodies anywhere else.

The body-recovery teams were sorting through the victims, recording the appearance of them with bulky devices on wheeled carriages, for later comparison with the identification records. Incidentally, and only incidentally, they were also searching for rare survivors of the purge, but they did not expect many; survivors of Trooper raids were usually few.

Yaderny's assistant, a wiry and energetic young man who went by the name of Dario Achaemid, came along from out of a side alley, carrying a small notebook, to which he was adding notes. Yarderny called to him, "Find anything?"

Achaemid consulted his notes, and looked up briskly, after the manner of an overly thoughtful athletic coach, and said as he approached, "Not so much; on the other hand, quite a bit that makes little or no sense."

Yaderny, who was used to these odd excursions, by which circumlocutious fits and starts Achaemid attempted to seduce reality into revealing herself, sighed and said, "You may explicate if you will."

Achaemid looked owlishly at his notes, and said, "This habitat is hard by an area in which the Bureau of Remandation has little, or no, favor. The general attitude is negative at best, and graduates up through several degrees of hostility, which I will not enumerate, as you are doubtless familiar with them all. Nevertheless," he said portentously, "Some facts emerge: this was not an assemblage of rioters, but the aftermath of a large Dragon-game, which took place somewhat to the north of here."

"A costly mistake."

"Correct. On the other hand, they were more adept at escaping because of it. Not so many casualties."

"Now that you mention it, there do seem to be fewer."

"And so there will be much fewer of the type we'd be interested in; criminals, revolutionaries, rabble-rousers and the like."

"I see. Then you do not recommend intense search."

"I could not see any particular reason for it. Let the recording teams run routine ID procedures, and catalogue the victims. The bodies can be hauled off in the usual manner, for sanitization purposes."

"Anything else?"

"We might notify Symbarupol that they are too quick on the trigger. This will not win friends here. Marula is already a very large problem."

"Your reasoning is faultless, although the tact and discretion which I have had to cultivate in my position suggest that it might be wiser to edit such remarks severely, or perhaps

151

not utter them at all. I say that not out of fear, but out of a consideration that no effect will result. They are not listening any more."

"Ah! Truth must yield to manners, as always."

"True! But what are discretions but the glue that binds us? Well, see to it, will you? I think I will return to Headquarters, and from there try to word something that will pass through. The problem here is so far out of hand that we are not dealing with ordinary criminals at all, and they are gaining entirely too much liberty. I fear much more of this and the city may go."

"I have thought the same; and heard much more alarming things."

"I have heard them as well; you understand, somewhat fainter, but yet I still hear them."

"Very well! It will be as you say. I will clean this up, and have the remains dumped. Where should these go? The last bunch overfilled the burial site."

"Are there other places?"

"Very far out, to the northwest; the Old City ruins, in fact, was what I had in mind. These should be transported far away, to lessen morbid curiosity."

"The old spaceport?"

"Yes."

"Aren't there some stragglers lurking thereabouts?"

"Renegades, tramps, thieves, and the like. The Troopers often use the area for training exercises, and so the inhabitants are scarcely in evidence. At any rate, they will issue no challenges, neither martial nor legal. The Old City is technically not there. . . ."

"Not all that good, but I suppose it will have to do."

"I'll be back in tomorrow. This will be unpleasant and extended work."

"I understand, Achaemid. Go ahead."

And so they parted company, Achilio Yaderny to return to his office and try to say something fundamentally unsayable, and Achaemid to his unpleasant task of disposing of the bodies of the fallen.

As the body-handling teams worked their way along the street, they soon fell into a routine; after they had made a desultory search for still-living persons among the fallen and scattered heaps, they would arrange the bodies to be recorded, and afterward, bring small, three-wheeled electric wagons alongside, in which the bodies would be piled, as neatly as possible to maximize the load. Then the trucks would set off on the poorly maintained road which still led to the Old City, although few went there now for any purpose.

The members of the Bureau of Remandation who were working with the teams saw little to pass on of special interest to Achaemid; dead folk were, after all, dead, and that was that. But near the end of the street, they did find one thing, which they duly reported to the assistant, but who in turn dismissed it. They had found a young man, in fact, probably a late-adolescent, who had no wounds or evidence of trauma, but who appeared to have been afflicted by a violent disease. Achaemid examined the body, which was severely emaciated and covered with filth, although he kept his distance, and the team handled the body with tongs. It seemed as cold and stiff as the rest. Achaemid said, "What about this one?"

"No marks, no injuries. Looks like some kind of plague or fever."

"Any others like that?"

"No. Not a one."

"He couldn't have walked around like that, without someone noticing him."

"We doubt it."

"Put him in the pile with the rest. I'll see what I can uncover. If there are more, we may want to come back for him later, but I don't think we'll find any more; everyone I've spoken with said nothing about disease. . . . Any identification on the body?"

"To be truthful, Ser, we haven't looked; you know. . . ."

"Understandable. Distasteful job, this. Well, be sure it's recorded with the rest. Not to worry. Everyone will be identified, sooner or later."

"There is one other thing about this one . . ."

"What's that?"

"Has on woman's clothing, or something cut for a woman, so it seems."

Achaemid chuckled, an odd note among the somber horrors of the scene, the bright morning sunlight suffusing into the cool street shadows, innocent, clean, while squads of men in disposable overalls gingerly stacked bodies into small trucks with three wheels. He said, "That is not so great a surprise, considering this crowd and what they were doing. I remember a case in South Marula, near the docks, which was my first assignment: there was a fire in one of those transient hostels, you know? One of those old firetraps. But they had

153

time, with this one, and everything was going right. Up came the fire squad and the pumpers, and the water mains were all up to pressure. Everything was going right, impossibly. And of course, all the Information Services people were there, recording like crazy. Inside the building, you could see all these people running back and forth, but they wouldn't come out, even though they could! Finally, in desperation, the Chief formed up a shock brigade of us, and we went in there and dragged them all out! Saved them all! Turned out the reason they wouldn't come out was that they were all transvestites, dressed up in women's clothing. And oh, there were some famous ones in the crowd, you can be sure. The scandal went on for weeks, but eventually quieted down. This is probably something similar. In a Dragon-Game, I wouldn't be surprised. In fact, I'm surprised you haven't turned up more."

The spokesman for the team said, laughing, "We will exercise more diligence! But how do we tell?"

"Never mind! And be careful handling that one, will you? That looks contagious, at the least!"

"No fear! We will not touch it!"

"Fine—carry on." And Achaemid strolled off to another part of the street, to supervise another team at their sad work.

The body, lying with others in the little truck, soon set out along the broken and disused concrete road to the Old City, and after a long ride, of which none of the cargo was aware, reached a ravine by the Old City, a rugged tumble of irregular blocks, and was rolled off, with the rest, where it lay quietly.

There was one peculiarity about this particular body which no one noticed at the time. That was that it seemed to lack some of the stiffness and rigidity of the others. And another odd characteristic, hard to see in the fading light among the gullies and chasms of the ravine, was that it was more limber than its associates, when rolled off onto the pile. But the drivers were not interested in looking overly much at what was already a dreary business. If they had looked closely, after the body had stopped rolling, they might have seen some movement in it: a hand clenched, spasmodically, and a leg stiffened, but they were small motions, and the light was uncertain, and they weren't looking for movement; and to an equally placed observer, there were no more motions, at any rate. At any event, none that could be seen.

154

There were a few more loads, but they hurried more, owing to the nature of the work, and they placed their cargoes somewhat off to the side of this particular body, and left hurriedly, for they heard odd sounds in the ruins, and in the distance, the hooting and calling of Bosels, and they thought it better to leave. At least, there were no more to bring.

Achaemid made meticulous notes, and from them, assembled a report, complete with cross-references and footnotes, which was complete and magnificently documented, and which reached Yaderny's desk, along with sections of the reports of others. There was a long roster from Identification, listing the positive matches they had made, along with an abbreviated resume of the person so identified. To Yaderny's general disgust, the list totally lacked known criminals or notorious deviants, although there were a few low-grade rowdies and tavern brawlers among the listings.

What did catch his attention, was a most singular fact; there were two on the list who were totally unidentifiable. One had been found at the site of the earlier Dragon-Game, and the other among the casualties in the street, apparently a victim of an odd and loathsome wasting disease. Something clicked in his detective's mind, but it took him a bit to reason it all out. A case in which he had seen something similar to the recordings ID had sent along. There had been that girl, what had been her name? Dovestonia? No. Damistofia. Azart.

Yaderny started to call the Palliatory on the Comm, but stopped in mid-action, and decided to visit the place. When he arrived, he was most disturbed to discover that the lady Azart had departed, just the night before, in the company of a fellow who was part of the Internal Security Organization, or so they felt. Yaderny produced a record of the body they had found at the Dragon-field, and that was him. But of Damistofia there was no trace. The Palliatory had a Communications Center with all the customary facilities, although they were hardly used, and these Yaderny now applied to attempt to identify the young man, by transmitting a facsimile print of the ID recording to Symbarupol, to Chugun's own office.

To his surprise, they were polite and cooperative, but they could offer no help on the young man supposed to have been one of theirs. In fact, their Chief of Personnel was definite, and stated categorically that the young man was not one of theirs, and they could not claim him. Chugun's office was so definite and so sincere, that Yaderny could not bring himself to believe otherwise: they were telling the truth, for a change and dealing directly with a minor officer in a local police department.

Yaderny made some notes, to follow this up later, because there was something peculiar about this all which disturbed his sense of rightness, an instinct he always listened to. And for a fact, he would have investigated it in depth, but on the next day, there were urgent matters to attend to, involving a section over in Southeast Marula in which a Pallet-Dropped Heavy Trooper strike was narrowly averted, and there was an increase in looting and general unrest, which took all his time, and then came some desertions among his men, and somehow or other he never quite got around to it, and Damistofia vanished from the little awareness of Lisagor which she had been a small part of.

In Symbarupol, there were those who were very interested in the whereabouts of Damistofia Azart, and her fate, as well as that of Cliofino Orlioz, and they were not happy to discover that their own assassin had been found dead, with Damistofia vanished, but some among them conjectured that she had tried to escape, and died somewhere in the uprisings of Marula, but Luto Pternam was not among these. He remembered Rael, and his nights grew more sleepless than they had been, thinking about a mutable person, a chameleon, who suddenly could no longer be seen. Something changeable vanishes: one cannot, from that date, assume termination. Only that the target can no longer be seen. And that worried Pternam, and subsequently Avaria, more than many of their other problems, because they were now sure that whatever Rael had become, he would someday, if alive, return to extract a horrible revenge for what they had done to him; and what more they had tried to do. Pternam added guards to his staff, as well as some special experimental projects from the lab, hulking lobos who were more dangerous than the Pallet Troopers, but he ruefully considered that he did not know who he was looking for. Or waiting for.

⤳ 11 ⤳
The City of the Dead

First, there was a dream about singing, which came and went in unknown intervals. This singing made no sense whatsoever, and there were no words in it, and the melody didn't register, either. That was no problem: Liζaks were not particularly fond of music and the only music ever heard was hardly more than childish jingles, monotonous and repetitive. This was different, complex $\mathbf{I}$armonies, all high sweet voices that made the heart ache. But for what? There was no knowing.

Then there was singing, and it was clearer and did not fade. There was a sense of clarity to it, and a sense of stability. A sense of ego, of being, of consciousness of being part of a body that did not drift and fade in and out of existence. There was a room with a low ceiling and large patches of light and darkness, sense of movement, presence. A lot of people, perhaps. And the self. What self? *Am I Damistofia, or . . . something else? Someone else?*

There was movement nearby, to the side, and a woman's voice spoke. It was definitely a woman's voice, but low and harsh. "Are you awake?"

"Yes." The word came easily enough, and not in the clear, high voice of Damistofia. The sounds were low, ragged, probably from disuse. There was a moment of panic while weak limbs were moved, and the outlines of a body felt out under a rough homespun blanket. *He! Am am he!* He felt the realization run through him, and for a moment his consciousness faded a little, a delicious feeling. *I lived through it.* Then solidity returned, and now full consciousness.

He was weak, and could not sit up, although he tried. He could look around. Yes, there was a room, although the shape was not quite regular. Low ceiling, apparently made of broken slabs of concrete braced with timbers. The room was really two sections joined by a short hall. This side was large, and dim, with the illumination coming from candles. The other side was brighter, and the singing came from there, although now it was stopped. There were low voices there, in the part he could not see. Squatting on her haunches beside his pallet was a tall, strongly built woman whose features were in detail concealed by the half-light. She asked again, "Well, are you going to stay with us this time?"

He waited, and then said, "I think so."

"We had a time with you. They threw you out with a body-dump from the city. We found you there. You were moving, crawling, or trying to. Krikorio said leave you, that you were gone and didn't know it, but I thought not. We cleaned you up and brought you here."

"Where am I?"

"In the dead city. Refugees live scattered in the ruins, hiding. . . . You were more dead than alive, and much of the time out of your head. We were very afraid that you had some unknown disease, but it seemed to cure itself, and at any rate none of us caught it. You talked a lot . . . about Damistofia, and Rael, and Jedily. Who were they?"

"They were some people I used to know. Gone now. Never mind them. We cannot bring them back. And for disease . . . you can't catch it. Neither can I, anymore. I think I'm cured."

"Well, that's good! What you had I wouldn't give to a bosel!" She laughed, a rich, throaty laugh. "Hah! I wouldn't even give that to a Templebolter, and I've seen plenty of them, you can bet."

"What is this place?"

"A refuge of sorts, although . . . there're some who found it not so nice."

"I don't understand."

"This is no-man's land, where they train the Troopers. They practice on us, and so one has to be well-hidden, and strong. You live alone, they sniff you out. All sorts of conditions exist here, in the ruins. I have an alliance with Krikorio, whom you will presently meet. . . ."

"You are espoused?"

"We have an alliance. I fight, he fights. We protect each other. We are not friends, nor lovers. You understand, this just works for us. Kriko follows his star, and I attempt to find one."

"Why don't you leave?"

"It has not been possible." She shook her head, implying that she wished to say no more, but after a moment, she continued, "You may not understand it . . . wait a while, before

158

you judge. At any rate, we can't leave now, with the turmoil outside, and . . . things are unfinished. Just unfinished. Krikorio hunts, and when he finds what he's looking for, then there will be a celebration, a consummation. Then, maybe, I can leave. Now I watch over his girls, and keep them safe."

"Girls? I thought I heard singing."

"They are the singers. They are also the Brides of Krikorio, whose wedding we await. I will tell you now, so you will know it: leave them alone, no matter what they do or say. You understand? Don't look, and especially don't feel. They belong to him."

"Who are you?"

"Call me Emerna. That is enough of it. How do you call yourself?"

He had to think a moment. He caught himself wanting to say "Damistofia," But it wouldn't come. After a moment, he said, "Phaedrus."

She nodded. "Fine. Phaedrus. Now you rest. Don't try too much at first. We'll feed you up a bit, and then you can help me some." She stood up now, and he could see how large she was. She towered over him like some heraldic figure out of mythology, from the forgotten worlds. Tall, heavily built, powerful, deep-breasted. She called into the other part of the shelter, "Lia! Bring some brew from the pot! He's awake!" She looked down at him. "We've had the girls taking care of you since you've been here. I guess now that'll have to stop. But this time, I'll do it for them. You can start looking after yourself."

After a few moments, there was a rustle from the other part of the shelter, and presently a girl appeared, carrying a crude bowl of something hot. He sat up, the better to take it, and saw the girl in the flickering light from the other room, the bright room. This one was slender and graceful as a reed, very young, but also nubile and beautiful, with long pale hair that reflected the highlights of the fire behind her. Her beauty was heart-stopping, impossible. She set the bowl down beside him, with a quick, burning glance at him, and then vanished quickly.

Emerna sat down beside him, folding one leg under her, and offered him a spoonful of something that smelled odd, but made his stomach rumble. She said, in a low voice, "I know. They're all like that. Pretty little things. Krikorio collects them, he does. Come the occasion, and he says he's going to take them all in one night. A real marathon! And they are not for you, although they will provoke you to madness if you let them. You must not. You understand. That is the one rule here."

Phaedrus nodded, gulping at the hot broth, which was painful to swallow, but good, despite its odd taste. "Yes. None of the girls. Do they all wear white gowns, like . . . Lia?"

"Yes. That, and they sing, and together they weave Krikorio's cloak, in which he will go out when all is done. For now, though, you eat, sleep, gather your strength. I will tell you as we go, how things are, and you can decide for yourself, allowing that, of course, Krikorio will let you decide."

He ate, but it was with apprehension. Nothing made any sense, here. He couldn't find his proper place. Something clearly wasn't right. However, some truths emerged, which while perhaps not great universals, at least seemed workable: Emerna saved him, and was keeping him; and he was to leave Krikorio's girls alone. It wasn't much, but he thought he could live with it until he knew what he had fallen into.

Outside, it was winter now. That much Phaedrus could determine by watching Emerna dress to go out, which she did, although for much shorter periods than Krikorio, who seemed to be gone all the time, making only rare appearances, and then only to sleep. Outside, winter, but in the shelter it was tolerably warm. He did not go outside; he was not invited.

What little he saw of Krikorio astounded him, for he was very much like Emerna; large, powerful, an enormous man with heavy black hair and a luxuriant beard which hid most of the contours of his face. For Krikorio's part, he avoided Phaedrus completely, although something suggested that he approved, at least tentatively. Krikorio stayed in his end of the shelter with the girls, who fussed about him like exotic birds. He seemed to treat them offhand, like children, or pets, but now and again, when his wandering gaze drifted across one of the girls, there was fire in the half-hidden eyes, a feral glint which Phaedrus understood. He had no difficulty complying with the unstated rule of the shelter, although the girls seemed to go out of their way to tease and provoke him, without ever making any gesture whatsoever which was a clear invitation. After some time of this, Phaedrus was firmly convinced that the girls, whose number he could not ever seem to ascertain exactly, were as aberrant as Krikorio and

Emerna. Nothing seemed normal, or leading toward anything, save day-to-day survival. And he could not build a coherent picture of events outside; the girls he would not talk to, Krikorio he could not, and Emerna was as opaque as obsidian. True: they had saved him, after their own fashion. But for them, he would really belong in the body dump with the rest. In the weakened condition after Change, he would have died of nothing more elaborate than exposure—loss of vital body heat.

Little by little, he regained his strength, and Emerna saw to it that he had plenty to do, working him in the household chores; which he hated, and yet exulted in, because he was moving again. And because he knew that if he could escape this place, he would be truly free of all his pursuers at last. He also took stock of his new body, which was completely new to him. It was odd, because he remembered both Rael and Damistofia clearly, but this body was lean and wiry, somewhat like Rael, but much lighter, shorter, and without Rael's sallow saturnine color. It felt like this body wasn't completely finished yet. From what he could discover about himself, he estimated that this Change had taken him almost as far as the Change from Rael to Damistofia, and that he feared very much trying it again. If it worked out as he suspected, the next Change would place him in the body of a preadolescent girl, which he rated with low survival odds in the times they were in. It was true what Pternam had told about him—that through the changes was a kind of immortality. But it was a perilous kind of immortality, one in which you had to pass through the process of death in order to live; to live forever entailed an infinite number of agonizing deaths. He could not remember the first time: that belonged to Jedily. But the other Changes he had initiated at least had clear reasons for them. Now he knew that it would become progressively harder to face each time, until he would reach the point at which he could not face it, and yet after all those lives, would not be able to face final termination, real death, either. It was as exquisite a trap as the one he was in, in the shelter.

There was, of course, another problem, which was growing: Emerna. Krikorio had his harem, even if for unknown ritual reasons he had abstained from their supple young bodies. Now Emerna was echoing that, or so Phaedrus felt. He could feel the pressure, although she did not make it apparent openly to him, as such. And of course, Emerna had no reason to wait. Phaedrus could perceive her three ways, from three views, of the egos he had known. None of the three ways seemed to build any excitement in him, although he realized by doing so how disabled and fragmented Rael had been. In fact, Rael had been only barely functional, like something pieced together. Only with Damistofia had there been any sense of integration, and that had just been a spark, a tiny flame, before it had been snuffed out. Now . . . it would be in this body that he lived, and he felt Emerna's attention on him, as well as a deep requirement of his deepest self to engage himself with her, to build a lasting persona out of the encounter. That was the only way it could be done—by becoming involved/integrated with others. He reflected that he had a poor choice to begin with.

From fragmented accounts from Emerna, he built up a slow and patchy image of the past, how they had come to be here, and the way they were. It wasn't a pretty story. Krikorio had found Emerna, a dazed survivor of some nameless atrocity, and together they had found this place. She had been a gawky, awkward adolescent, then, too tall for her age, angular and bony. Krikorio was half-crazy himself, but she didn't mind: he brought firewood, and wild meat, and other food which he stole in long treks northeastwards into the wide farmlands of Crule the Swale, and he defended her, and took no liberties. He explained his dream, which she did not understand, but helped him with it, collecting the girls, who were also fleeing, always fleeing. The first ones had come from the west—Clisp and The Serpentine and Zolotane, but of late they had come from Sertse Solntsa, and Marula. Children, running from catastrophe, from murder and mayhem, spared by chance.

What was he waiting for? He had dreamed he would contend with the white Bosel for mastery of the world, that this magic white bosel was in fact the demon of the world Oerlikon, whose intemperate and chaotic spirit ruled the planet, and he Krikorio, would triumph, and then and only then would this world be truly a human world. He would be the Emperor-High-Priest, and the girls would be his maidens, through them he would breed and raise assistants, his spawn, to spread the word throughout the world, even to far Tartary. They would tear down the derivative civilization the old men had brought from the stars, contaminated, useless, life-hating, and they would build a more natural world.

Phaedrus listened to the fragments, second-hand from

162

Emerna, as it gradually unfolded, and reflected that all in all, it wasn't entirely insane. Only a little far-fetched, and a step backward into the trackless dark forests of Original Man of legendary long ago, on the homeworld. In a normal world, people like Krikorio would be helped to rationality, or at least to art, where they could relive their dreams in some measure of sanity . . . or adjustment. Here? For a moment, Phaedrus cursed the settlers of Oerlikon and their hatred of Change, that led them to build this flawed, broken society. But, then, on second reflection, what he had seen of the product of the worlds where Change held sway without stint or let, the brainless careerists who had manipulated this world to give themselves a job and not much more than that, that did not cheer him either, or lead him to rush pell-mell into that camp. Lisagor was finished, although it would doubtless stagger on for a time. The old worlds, wherever and whatever they were, offered nothing better. He lay back on his pallet and smiled to himself. Nothing to be done but wait for the moment, and try to understand the conditions outside he would have to cope with.

The days passed; at first Phaedrus could not discern any notable difference among them, save the distant hints of weather. But he gradually became aware that there was a change evolving in the shelter, and through these things he came to understand that things were moving forward to their conclusion. He resisted the temptation to work the formulas of Rael, to see what the conclusion would be. He wanted to be free of it, of all things the most.

The first thing he noticed was that Krikorio was staying out for longer and longer periods, and when he did appear, he wore on his dark and malign face a growing expression of unspeakable triumph. The girls were becoming quieter, more solemn, and soon ceased to sing. Also, they avoided him pointedly, save Lia, who seemed to watch from an infinite distance away, observing something she neither understood nor wanted, but powerless to deflect it.

Emerna also was changing. As he felt himself gaining back his health, he felt her eyes on him more and more, and her behavior moved between a rough truculence and an embarrassing solicitude. He knew what was coming; the only question remained to answer was when it would occur.

Emerna told him that Krikorio's moment of triumph was near; the mysterious white bosel had been sighted for some

163

time, and though eluding him with its indescribable mixture of craft and irrational randomness, Krikorio was closing in on it, and she expected him to succeed soon.

"Then what? I mean, I know from what you've told me that he will then celebrate by having an orgy with the girls, but. . . ."

"I never said this before, even to myself; but that is blank; unknown; he has this idea of what he will dare to do, and I cannot find myself in those plans. Neither are you in them."

"Of course."

"I had always thought that things wouldn't come to this—that he would never achieve what he wanted. I mean, I didn't even believe in the beast he hunts with such fervor. A white Bosel! Whoever heard of such a thing? And so this would just . . . go on and on. We have a functioning life here, hazardous as it is. Many others have not done so well. Yet now; I don't know."

"You saved me from the dump; I owe you."

"This is so."

"I have seen little of this, but I think you and I should not stay here when it happens."

"I have so thought. But consider this—we could not leave before him—he is a superb tracker, and a worse foe than those who hunt us. Besides, he can't make it alone with the girls—they are hopeless outside. He has raised them that way."

"It would be a matter of timing, then—to find the right moment?"

Emerna said, without hesitation, "Yes." And Phaedrus thought that perhaps the worst part, getting her to accept that she would have to leave, was over. She added, "You are now in some danger from him. When you were ill and unconscious all the time, you weren't real to him. Sick and recovering, also you didn't matter much. But now . . . ?" She let the idea hang in the air, unfinished.

Phaedrus said, after a moment. "I'm a rival, whether I behave or not."

"Of course you are. And no matter how they sing and weave and chatter about the day to come, they are all, to a girl, terrified of Krikorio—they have no idea what he will do with them. They see more of him than you have. More than I, although I have seen many things which lead me to make alliance with him and not oppose. You understand, I would fear, too, were I one of them."

"I must leave, then."

"There is an alternative, for the time."

Phaedrus nodded, indicating that she should go on. She said, thoughtfully, "If I take you as a lover, and you sleep with me, then according to the way he sees things, you will not matter any more, and he will forget you."

It was said matter-of-factly, without a trace of emotion, even a little grudgingly, but underneath this exterior he saw the second truth of it as well as the first, which was exactly as stated. The second was that in entering into this odd relationship with Krikorio, Emerna had also walked into a trap built of Krikorio's disordered fantasies, and traded off what femininity she had for physical prowess and survival skills. He, Krikorio, saw her as a neutral partner, and in accepting that, she had blocked off anything else. Seeing this, Phaedrus could feel some real compassion for Emerna, who had become enmeshed in a trap as vile as his own, and with that realization, he felt an emotion for her he could not have approached from any other direction. He said, "We can do that, I think." And he saw the light begin to flicker, ever so slightly in her eyes, which he now noticed were a light greenish-blue, an indeterminate agate color. He added, "We have time . . . let it happen."

She nodded and got to her feet abruptly. "I will go have the girls scrub me down. Lia will bring you a basin." She smiled now, an odd little half-smile he had not seen on her face before, and her face softened a little from the hard set she habitually wore. She added, "I don't know what you were about before we found you; as for me, I have not known much of this save in the hungers for it. We will be inept, I think."

Phaedrus said, kindly, "It has been a long time; I also plead a lack of expertise with which I will take no offense."

She nodded. "Then we must manage as we may; but at the least we will warm each other." And she turned and walked into the other section of the shelter, where she began issuing orders to the girls, in a softer voice than he could remember hearing her use. And presently there were sounds of water splashing, and Lia shyly, eyes downcast, brought him a basin of hot water, and left quickly. He wanted to say something to the girl, but the words did not come. Perhaps there weren't any.

It was much later, deep in the night, that he dreamed of

singing again, and shuddering with the thought of what he had passed through the last time he heard singing, he awakened and listened carefully. Beside him, he heard Emerna's breathing change rhythm, and she grew very quiet. Glancing at her, he saw by the light from the other part of the shelter that her eyes were open. There was revelry and singing and uproarious noise, chatter, giggling. On the wall between the sections was a shapeless thing that had not been there before, something pale and furlike. They heard Krikorio's heavy laughter, drunken-sounding, and she whispered, "Not a sound, on your life."

Phaedrus turned to her and put his arm across her ribs, curling closely to the heavy, hot body next to him. She breathed deeply, and pulled the cover over them, shutting the light out, and after a few moments they no longer heard any noises.

When Phaedrus awoke, he thought something was wrong, because there was a routine in the shelter to morning, even if no daylight filtered into the deep place in which it was built. The shelter was dark and lifeless. Emerna was not beside him. He started up, and looked carefully about, listening. There was a faint odor of a fire that had gone out, and only one oil lamp was still burning. The pelt on the wall was gone.

He got up and found his clothes, and rummaged about, through all sections of the shelter: there was no one there. Krikorio, the girls, Emerna . . . all gone. He heard steps outside the door he had never gone through, and a familiar fumbling with the catch, and Emerna opened the door, wearing her heavy winter overclothing, which made her look even larger and heavier than she actually was.

He said, "Where is everybody?"

She shook her head, as if dazed. "Gone. Left before dawn, all of them. Krikorio dressed them all up in the outside clothes they had never worn, and drove them out. They didn't understand. I saw him, and he saw me watching, but I dared not speak. He was . . . completely gone. I wouldn't dare even ask. Such was the cast of his eye. Wearing his White-Bosel cloak, he was, like some savage. I went out just now to see if I could still see them. . . ."

Her face was blank, devoid of any expression. Phaedrus looked slowly along the heavy structure of her face, trying to read something in it. "What was it?"

166

Her eyes cleared, as if she had just become aware of him. "Oh? No, there isn't anything we can do. They are gone, that's all."

"Then we are free."

She nodded, absentmindedly. "Yes, free. To stay or go as we would. I suppose you will want to leave, too."

Phaedrus put his hands on her shoulders, which were as wide as a man's. "You can't stay here alone."

"I never thought about it. It's been this way so long . . . What?"

"It is time to leave this refuge and trust to our own selves. This may have worked, but it's insane to stay. You don't have to. The old world is breaking up. We can't be far from Zolotane, and from there we can get to Clisp. . . ."

He broke off and waited, sensing that this was a balanced moment. Whatever adjustment to misfortune they had made here, she was at the end of it, and was now calculating chances. If she decided to stay, and tried to hold him there, he knew he could not prevent it, at least for a while. Finally, she looked down at the floor, breathed deeply once and said, in a soft, barely audible voice, "Yes, it's time to go, now. We'll need to get some things together. It's cold now, and we've a long walk."

"Why not just straight west? It shouldn't be so far . . ."

"Closed off. Too close to the city. We'd go north, along the Hills of the Left Leg, to about the Knee, and then turn west. Two can sneak where they could not force a way."

Phaedrus said, frankly, "And you do not know what I can do."

"True . . . at least I do not know about how you handle conflict and strife. I do know something now I didn't know yesterday, and that part . . . seems to work well enough."

Phaedrus smiled, and squeezed her arm. "We seemed to manage in that. We will do as well in this."

He said, "Never mind why, but last night . . . was more a trial for me than you realize. I think I can do well enough outside."

She smiled at him, saying, "So you say! You are a city-man. I sense it. And there you may well do as you say. But we are going into the wild, now, and it's different. Besides, you didn't fare so well, there either."

Phaedrus agreed, adding, "Cruel but true. But I remember the circumstances and the odds against me, too."

"They do not seem so good, even now, for either of us."

He said, "They are better now than they ever have been. That much I know. I will take my chances with the outside and you."

Emerna gave him a quick hug, and then shifted to her old, commanding self again. "Here now! We'll need these things; bring them here and we'll sort them out as to who carries what." And she began naming things and telling him where they would be found within the shelter, and Phaedrus gathered them up, willingly, feeling a growing excitement within him at the prospect of leaving. Even though he sensed some of her disquiet about it. Not for nothing had they hid here, in the dead city, hardly venturing out, save for quick raids and adventures. Yet he felt closer to freedom than he could ever remember feeling; the pressure and the tangled webs of obligation and treachery were gone, and he was dealing with a now-world, free of the past.

~ 12 ~

The Knee Hills

Emerna made up packs for them, and they loaded each other's, turning away alternately; Phaedrus felt his own load grow heavier, and he piled the things she indicated on until she muttered, "Enough." Even with the weight of it, there wasn't much—most of it was bedding and shelter cloths against the night wind, weapons and ammunition. She thought it might take them four days to reach the Knee and turn west across that tumbled and trackless wilderness, a day or so there, and one more day to the coast of Zolotane, where they could expect no more than small fishing villages along the coast; Zolotane was a bare and empty land.

She wasted little time, and as soon as they were loaded, opened the door to the passageway and started into the darkness, with Phaedrus following. There was a narrow, lightless tunnel, full of odd turns and slants, up and down as well, barely wide enough for Emerna's broad figure to fit through with her load, but the floor was free of rubble. Like the shelter itself, the tunnel seemed to be made of odd pieces and slabs of concrete, fitted together crudely.

To Phaedrus's heightened perceptions, the way seemed to be long, extremely so for a hiding-place, and he said as much. She said back, over her shoulder, "There are many blind turns and odd corners here, as well as deadfalls, which I have disarmed as I came in before. This place is safe! They never came near it, although they tried hard enough." Then she resumed walking on, not varying the pace.

After a time, a weak light showed around a corner, and Emerna here slowed her pace, and motioned to Phaedrus for him to be silent. Together, they crept forward, making no sound, in a silence so profound he could hear his clothing rasping, and his heartbeat. There was no sound from the outside at all, that he could hear. Emerna stopped and knelt, listening carefully for a moment, and then slowly moving into the lighter part of the tunnel, which seemed to end in a ran-

169

dom pile of concrete rubble, open to the sky. She whispered, "Can you hear anything?"

He listened. Then he said, "Aircraft, maneuvering, but not getting closer. They sound far off. Also something else, but I can't make it out; maybe gunfire, or just noise."

"Your hearing is very acute. I wasn't sure."

"Do you hear anything near?"

"No. I'll have a look. Wait here." She looked again, and then went out into the pit, and climbed upward, all the time looking about nervously. Finally he heard her whisper, "Come on." And he followed, clambering over the rough and tilted blocks with difficulty, also watching, but not seeing anything but an irregular circle of sky which grew larger, opening up.

The sky was high and cold and far away, deep blue and streaked with cirrus in broad smears and filaments, the sun low on the horizon and colorfully diffused by the clouds. For a moment, he couldn't decide if it was morning or afternoon, but as the distant horizon came into view, he saw that below the sun was the wavy outline of distant hills and low mountains, and on the opposite side of the sky there was only a dark line, very far away: that would be the east, across the lower parts of Crule the Swale. All around them were tumbles of shapeless landforms, broken blocks, tilted slabs, enigmatic shapes that could not be recognized. They seemed to be on an irregular hill, whose slopes gradually descended to a plain, flattish to the east, south and north, but not far to the west, broken by more rolling terrain of ridgelines and shallow valleys.

Emerna said, "Safe for now. And so now you see the Dead City, or what's left of it. You were right about the aircraft, too—look toward Marula, south."

Far off in the south he could see specks moving in the sky, which behind them, colored by clouds, was a pale orange. They were moving in a low, slow oval, and they seemed to be moving very slowly. She said, "They won't be back today; that's something real they are working over there, although they may very well fly back this way. We had better be moving."

She stood up in the open and reached back to offer Phaedrus a hand up. When he stood beside her, he looked long over the desolate landscape. "What was here? What kind of city?"

Emerna started off toward the north, and said back, in the

wind which he now felt to have a sullen bite to it, "Was a spaceport, so I'm told. After a while, the ships stopped coming, and people moved away, save a few renegades. *They* broke it up for practice, and for the thrill of the hunt, so I would guess."

He stopped, to have a last look at the dreary landscape, all around the circle of the horizon. Something caught his eye, south, still well within the ruins; something white fluttering in the wind. He stepped a little closer, as if to see if he could make it out. There was something familiar about that white fluttering, but he couldn't quite recognize it. Something tugged at a fugitive memory. Emerna stopped and looked back, and said softly, "You don't want to see that."

Phaedrus shook his head, and glanced back at her, and then turned back to the south, walking slowly. Behind him, Emerna stopped and waited, but said no more. He walked slowly toward the white fluttering, and saw that it was not all that far, just a little ways down the gentle slope but getting there required several detours around obstructions, some pits, others blocks tilted at crazy angles. But he was able to keep the goal in sight most of the time, and finally reached it, looked at the ground for a long time, and then abruptly turned away with a sharp motion, biting his fist. He looked back once, and farther off, to where the aircraft were now circling higher, now, not maneuvering, and returned to where Emerna was waiting for him.

He stood by her and did not say anything, but the wind was cold as it blew in his face. Finally she said, "Told you not to go."

Phaedrus said, in a low, clear voice, pronouncing each word as if each one were the only word in the universe, "Lia. Somebody cut her throat. That isn't Trooper work."

Emerna nodded. "If you want revenge, look back toward Marula; that was them, there. He's getting his now, or has already had it."

"And the girls, too."

"Maybe not. When I was out, I saw signs that he'd taken some of the others around here with him . . . perhaps the girls would have run off."

Phaedrus took a deep breath, and felt a nameless horror flow through him, but he said only, "What a waste." He said nothing else, but obediently followed Emerna when she set off, after a long pause, toward the north, where the sky was a nameless dark color, and the wind blew in their face and was cold, and they did not speak for a long time, and there were cold streaks of wetness along the outside corners of his eyes, and Emerna wisely did not speak to him of it, nor make any gestures to him, but walked along steadily, picking the trail out through the broken ground until they were well out on the plain. But he fixed an image deep in his mind of the face he had seen, eyes open to the cold sky, blank and empty, a broken doll abandoned and forgotten. They had been clear, pale eyes, and her mouth soft and gentle. He walked on, and thought only of steps forward, and wind in the face.

The luminous unlight of the northern sky guided them as the day faded into bluer tones, and then violet, with a clear patch of sky that showed a glowing turquoise color, which was an open part of true sky unblemished by the swirls of clouds flowing across the high heavens. They walked on in a silence that was not broken, Emerna leading, Phaedrus following, placing one foot in front of the other, concentrating on the discipline of that.

As the cold darkness grew and spread from the well of the east, they heard around them, some far, some farther, the haunting evening cries of bosels, each one anarchic and expressing some demonic emotion known only to the individual creature. Far, far off to the east, there were a few scattered lights, and in the south they could see a faint glow from Marula; but here, going north hard against the hills of the Left Leg, there was no road and there were no settled places, and the land seemed as empty and free as when men first set foot on Oerlikon.

After a time, the distant, hallucinating cries began to bother Phaedrus, and he asked Emerna, "Is there any danger from the creatures?"

She stopped, turned, and said, "No, not from bosels, at least not in this season."

He ventured, "From men?"

"Not so much so from organized bands, such as the Arms of the Amalgam. But from wanderers . . . best be wary. We have passed several already; they sensed us, and I them, and we kept distance. No one trusts another now, not around these parts of the Swale, and, for all I know, so it is throughout the rest of Lisagor. People do things and blame 'the Troubles' for them, and every person's hand is turned against another's. I have learned that to hold power is the only way to fix this. You must lead, or find one who will, and stick by that, gathering others. Thus I came to Krikorio, and now it is just you and I."

An odd flash crossed Phaedrus's mind, listening to her, and after a few more steps, he said, "That doesn't change anything, does it? It just raises the level of violence . . . It is still one hand against another. I sense that down that road is the road to hell, in fact, we have already walked it, we Lisaks."

She thought a moment, walking on, and finally said, "Perhaps. But one must do something; try."

"It's too much trying that makes it stir. The way out is to let go. Do what one must, but stop trying to make something that won't be made. We say Krikorio was insane, do we not? Then his insanity lay in that he was divided, planning, desiring his great dream of power and force, but also doing what he knew was right: he hid and waited. Had he accepted the one, he could have seen the foolishness of the other."

"You would have wasted yourself had you said so to him."

"I see that. The evidence he left was clear."

She scoffed, "Ha! You say let go; what then? Isolated individuals who fall to the strongest hand! You'd be prey in a heartbeat. Press gangs would catch you and you'd find out what the Mask Factory is like; and you'd obey orders."

"I know. But wait . . . did you say 'press gangs'? I thought only the criminal were sent there."

"So did I. But we captured one of the troopers once, badly injured and dying, but incoherent, and we pieced it together from him. No criminals, but whoever they can catch—the young and ignorant, and those too old or slow to escape. You were there, too."

Phaedrus stopped. "Yes."

Emerna also stopped, and turned to face him, an intense watchfulness in her face, and a loose, awkward stance to her large, powerful body. She said, in a careful, measured way, "You remember it?"

Phaedrus shook his head. "Not what they did to me as I was before. I remember the latter parts, when I was whole again."

Emerna still held the same stance, and the same intense regard. Phaedrus saw and understood the signs correctly, that at this moment was great peril. She said softly, "And they sent you forth with secret instructions in mind, horrid deeds."

He sighed, and half-turned from her, knowing that relying on his recollection of Rael he stood a good chance of taking her. He said, "No. They only instructed me in some things, and let me figure the rest out, and when I had gotten deep in it, they released me to do what I wanted to do, what I thought was right. They did not understand what they created. And I have no horrid instructions: I have already done it, and am free of them, a wanderer of no more consequence than yourself." He turned away from her, making the decision then and there to turn from the path of control, and let be what would.

Emerna did not ask him what he did, but instead, "I suspected, but only now did I know. What is it you want?"

The answer came easily, although he had not thought of it so much before. "To be free of wanting; to just be, as I am now. I know there is no going back, not an inch. No, just to become, to be nobody."

"You can't forget."

"But I can refuse to act, knowing that it does no good."

With his senses sharpened, he *heard* her relax; the slight motions of her body within its clothing. She said, after a time, "Let us be moving on; this is not a good place, but I think a bit farther on there are some abandoned farms where we might find a refuge."

He nodded, readjusted his pack, and turned to follow her. She said, "I believe you would have let me kill you, just then; that was what convinced me . . . I will take you to Zolotane, and from there you can lead. As you will."

Again, he nodded silently. Then he said, "Yes, that will be soon enough." And then they set forth again, walking now a little more confidently in the cold night.

Darkness fell slowly, nevertheless it fell, and the wind increased and grew colder. They walked on into the dark, steadily, and they did not speak for a long time. At last, however, triggered by something Phaedrus did not notice, Emerna stopped, a little uncertainly, listening, looking intently into the darkness. He had been following some distance behind her, and now he approached and stood close. He ventured, after a while, "What is it?"

She whispered, "If I remember right, we should now have an old place in sight, even in the dark, but I see it not."

"Could you have navigated wrongly?"

"No. The signs are right; something isn't right. Change."

Phaedrus sniffed at the cold air, testing it. "I smell fire, ashes. Very faint. Old fire, old ash. What would we be looking for?"

174

"House, barn. They had a commune here, long ago, but they failed and went away. House remained . . . This was a place where wanderers came; there was a well. Many people know of this place. Be wary, now."

Phaedrus started to say, "I think . . ." but he stopped, hearing a sudden rustle and pounding feet. Emerna heard it also, and began wriggling out of her heavy pack. Phaedrus shed his instinctively, reaching for the first weapon that came to hand—and what met his hand was one of the odd shotgun-pistols from the Troopers. He said, grimly, "Let them come! I've got something that'll water their eyes!"

Emerna raised something metallic; there was a sharp report, and a bright streak fled to the zenith, where it blossomed in fire: a flare. The darkness faded and they could see: a band of ragged tramps, armed, so far as they could see, with a random collection of odd things which only had marginal use as weapons: scythes, pitchforks, staves and clubs. Still, there were about a score of them, and they rapidly fanned out to surround the two before they had time to seek shelter. Keeping his eye on them, Phaedrus drew close to Emerna, who, watching the band, hissed at him, "Can you use what we brought?"

Phaedrus grinned and risked a quick glance at her. "I can use it all. Call them, ask them to leave off. I want no more killing."

She hesitated, but called out, "You, there, parley!"

The leader, a slight, furtive person who remained somewhat back, called back, weakly, "No parley. No quarter asked, none given."

She called out, "We have no money!"

The answer came, "Don't want money. Want fresh meat for the pot!" The voice was neither angry nor heated, and it had a thin, reedy whine to it that was more chilling than what it said. Emerna glanced at Phaedrus, and said, "Kill or be killed."

He replied, "All of them."

The circle was almost complete, and the flare went out. Emerna took aim and fired the flare pistol again, this time at one of the figures, the slim one who had spoken. A bright light flashed across the distance between them and lodged in the speaker's midsection, burning with a bright white light, and then it went out as he apparently fell on it, but it flared up again, reaching its flare stage. Phaedrus recalled instincts he had learned as Rael, and listened, aiming by feel, and

175

pulled the trigger six times, feeling the heavy explosive canisters slam and buck as they fired, and each time one fired, another of the would-be attackers fell back, flailing the air or grasping at its head. He threw the shotgun-pistol down, now emptied and useless for this kind of work, and reached for the pack. Emerna fired two more flares, hitting with one. A third she fired at the sky. When it exploded, they could see that half the attempted circle was gone, and there were gaps in the half that remained.

She called out again, "Now it evens up! Will you stop while you can?"

They heard a strangled voice call back, "No quarter," and by the light of the flare they could see the remaining members of the band still coming on, fatalistically. Phaedrus said, "These are fools! Break free and leave them."

She said back, in a low harsh whisper, "Close your eyes and cover them, quick!"

He glanced at the band, and did as she commanded, throwing his arm up, but he was almost too late: there was a searing bright flash that shone through the flesh of his arm. Afterwards, he heard moans and pitiful calls in the dark, which had become permanent for those who had sought them. Emerna said, "Open your eyes now."

"What was that?"

"Light-bomb. These won't bother any more wayfarers, nor roast limbs for the pot—they can't kill what they can't see. Closing your eyes is no good against it—it can blind even through eyelids."

"What about the survivors?"

Emerna bent to her pack, and began rearranging things. "It would be merciful to dispatch them, cruel to leave them alone. You left injured and maimed, too."

Phaedrus felt a sudden heat, and said, "Let them grope for each other and gnaw in the dark like worms."

"Just so: you have made judgment. But now I say we should check their stronghold before we leave; there may be more of them, one or two."

"I would not have survivors tracking us; you are right. But we cannot remain here."

"No. I wouldn't stay here, now, unless we cut all their throats, and even then I wouldn't. There may be outriders, scouts. No. We would best move on. But first we will see what we can."

She withdrew a large knife from the pack and sidled up to

176

one of the blinded attackers, who was crawling about aimlessly and blinking his eyes, occasionally stopping to rub them. Phaedrus saw her kneel close beside him, and lean close, as if whispering. The man started violently, as if stuck, and grabbed at her. She pulled his head up by the hair and cut his throat, and went to the next. After he had listened, he grew still for a moment, and then rushed up with an inarticulate cry and ran blindly off into the night until a sodden thump and a last cry revealed that he had run headlong into a pit. Emerna called to Phaedrus wearily, "This is hopeless! All these folk are mad! Totally mad!"

And he thought, *by an act of mine was all this brought to pass, these vile men and their vile end, none better than the other. One cries for the power to change a world, and I had, have that power, and used it, and this is the result. This, and who knows what miseries elsewhere? Lia, staring sightless at the winter sky, her beautiful pale limbs moving gracefully no more. Cliofino, bringing no more of the incomparable release and joy that he brought to the women he casually seduced, and thought nothing of. A hundred people looking for a tavern and taken for a riot by the overreactive governors of Lisagor, and had set upon them the relentless killers.* But he said, "We will probably have to look on our own. Do you remember anything about the lay of this place?"

Emerna came back to him, and said softly, "There was a large communal house, and some barns and outbuildings. I do not see any of them left standing."

"Yet these robbers and cannibals would have some place to hide."

She said impatiently, "Just so. Come, we will look. There would be a cellar somewhere . . . Also let us be quiet."

They moved first toward the place where the leader of the band had stood, reasoning that they had issued forth from a spot near there. They found the body, burned nearly in half by the action of the flare, smelling of burned flesh and still smoking. From there, they spread out a little, going over the ground carefully, looking for something, a mark, that would show a concealed entrance. Emerna found a blinded sentry some distance beyond the leader's body, moaning on the ground. He would have been close to the entrance, watching what he could see of the action.

The burned-out timbers of a barn loomed behind the groping figure, and close by the foundations was a low, slanted door, one of its leaves still open. Inside, there was no sound.

177

Emerna shed her pack, and gripping the knife, peered into the dark opening, and then quickly stepped over the sill and into the darkness. Phaedrus half expected to see some struggle, but in another moment, she reappeared and motioned for him to follow her. He followed, carefully setting his pack on the ground beside the door.

Inside it was pitch-dark and musty-smelling, flavored with a rancid fatty odor that cut through the lingering stench of burned wood from the barn. Emerna whispered, "It goes on under the old barn. They'll have dug a place out, and made light-baffles. They'd have to, for that big a band."

She turned and began moving slowly along the tunnel, which was low enough so that they had to stoop in places, and in others gave a suggestion of large open space. After what seemed a long walk, they saw a dim glimmer of light ahead and a bit to the left. And as Emerna went forward to draw closer to the light, Phaedrus heard a sudden scrape from behind him and above and felt a weight about his shoulders, grasping and feeling for his chin. He stumbled forward under the weight, and bent over and ran hard, for he had seen Emerna duck, silhouetted against the light. He felt an impact, cushioned by whatever had fallen on him, and the struggles stopped for a moment. He fell flat onto the floor, and then stood upright with all his strength, feeling the impact of the roof again. Stunned, his attacker went limp, and Phaedrus threw him off and knelt by him for a moment, feeling along the unkempt head for the right place, and then he sent this one into the darkness to join the others they had killed. After a moment, there was no surge of pulse.

He looked up and sensed the bulk of Emerna close beside him. She said, "Clever, that. You look innocent, but you act like a man who knows woman, and you kill with precision, like one who knows what he is doing."

He said, "Seeming other than I have been has saved my life, has it not."

"So far."

"Then observe that there is much else you have not seen, and allow things to pass as if they were just as they seem, save that I guard your flank well."

"Is that all you want?"

"No, but what I want you cannot give me."

"Hah! Fame, fortune, power, beauty?"

"No. Leave it, and let us see within. Others may lurk."

She turned abruptly and set off toward the light. After a

178

short traverse through a zigzag part of the tunnel, they emerged into a large room with a series of corridors radiating from it. In this room were lanterns, burning a greasy oil which bubbled and smoked, and a pit in the center, which was used for a roasting fire, but which now was very low. Along the walls were various devices, whose purpose did not seem clear until Phaedrus reflected that here, with such a large crowd to feed, they would shackle one victim close to hand while they were working on the other—no point in having to carry them any distance, and in addition, their lamentations would doubtless provide a macabre entertainment. A shiver rippled across his spine, and a hot fluid rose in his throat, a gall of disgust.

Emerna called out, "Is anyone left in here? Throw down your arms and come out and walk away free." That was what she said, but she stood alertly and held the knife at readiness.

No one responded, at least not anyone of the band, but from one of the corridors, they heard a voice call out weakly, "Release us! There are prisoners!"

Emerna looked at Phaedrus, and then grasped a lamp from its wall bracket, and entered one of the corridors. Not far down it, they found a large pen, or cell, in which were kept women, about half a dozen of them, mostly unkempt and filthy, and most withdrawn, with much horror on their faces. They stared blankly as Emerna and Phaedrus approached their cell, and manipulated the crude latch that secured it, and stepped inside. Phaedrus looked over the group with wonder and horror alike; most looked as if they had once, not long ago, been young and pretty, or at least plain. Now, they looked otherwise. Only two responded with any animation. One, a ragged young girl who was very dirty and skinny, but who had retained some kind of animal sense of survival. The other looked familiar, somehow, but Phaedrus couldn't quite place the girl's face, although it seemed that he should.

The ragged waif's name was Janea, and she was telling Emerna a tale of horror and abuse, about why they had kept a pit of women inside, although they could have guessed as much by themselves. What interested him, in hearing the tale, was that Janea told them that the familiar girl had resisted them long, and in fact had proven so obstinate and uncooperative that they were planning to roast her the next day. Emerna moved, so that the weak light of the lamp shone on

179

the girl's face somewhat better. It was a dirty face, to be sure, but it looked more familiar yet, and it came to Phaedrus who this girl was: Meliosme, the wandering gatherer, whom he had met as Rael, long ago. Phaedrus wanted to grasp her, for she had been kind to him, as an old friend, but he dared not, because here, in his present body, he was no more than a stranger to her.

⌐ 13 ⌐
Meliosme

They did not waste any time lingering over the possessions of the robbers; those were scant loot from poor travelers. Nor did they attempt to find or use any food they might have found. There were some cured pieces, but they would have none of it. And last, there was nothing like a place to clean the survivors, so they gathered them up, one by one; some they had to work with more than others, and guided them back through the tunnels and corridors to the night outside, by the slanted door, by which the blinded guard was still moaning and making scrabbling motions with his hands at the dirt and ashes. As they emerged into the night, which had more light than the reeking tunnel, one of the women who had been passive and withdrawn suddenly came alive, and spoke earnestly with Emerna, who presently gave her a small knife from her pack, and then went back to the others and began guiding them off, away from the place. The woman who had taken the knife dropped down on her hands and knees, and crawled to where the moaning guard lay. The rest of them moved off, Emerna motioning them in agitation, Phaedrus bringing up the rear, looking about warily. Presently they were well away from the barn, and still the woman did not join them. But they heard a sudden sharp cry, followed from the same throat by more hoarse calls, entreaties, remonstrances, confessions, and finally, sounds that bore no resemblance to a human voice at all. These sounds were still going on as they trudged away, and never quite ended, but merely faded from the distance increasing between them.

Phaedrus joined Emerna, at whom he questioned, "What did you let her do?"

Janea, who was walking nearby, volunteered, in her bratty voice, "The one who was guard was a favorite with us, and especially Lefthera; she has some instruction for him, and for those others who survive and grope as well."

181

As if to bear her words out, they noted that the distant sounds were silent, indeed. But in a moment, behind them, they could hear another start up, at first sounding manlike, but rapidly rising in pitch and frenzy and finally reaching extremes even bosels did not often attain.

Emerna added, "She told me she would rather settle with them than be sheltered, and that her home was not far, in any event. She would return when she had done what she had to do. She told me what they did and I gave her the knife: she has the right, if she does nothing else. It is fitting for them, although they seem to be protesting more than their former victims."

Janea said, "They aren't taking their medicine as well as they handed it out: how they laughed and joked! For just a little I'd go back and help her, but for the fact that she's selfish and wouldn't share one, not even one."

Phaedrus asked, "Are there any more like that around here?"

Janea answered, "No. Not one band. This one either killed or ate them all. I hear it's clear up north all the way to Akchil Sunslope, or so they bragged."

Nevertheless, they all fell silent, and waited for the next series of screams to begin, and they did not have to wait very long: it was short, hoarse, and ended abruptly. For a time they stood in the empty dark spaces and listened for something else—perhaps approaching footsteps—but there were no more sounds, save that of the wind, and Emerna turned to the north and started walking, and the rest, after hesitating a little, drifted off, following her, more or less. Phaedrus let the survivors string out into an irregular line and brought up the rear, listening into the dark warily, but he heard no more sounds, not even those of bosels.

Apparently, Emerna had decided to walk on through the darkness; either she knew some place farther on, or decided to leave the immediate area. As they walked, he noticed a curious thing happening; each time he looked up at the band, the number of people in it seemed to dwindle. He did not see the women leave, or wander off, but somehow they did, drifting off silently into the darkness, one by one, presumably starting back for wherever they had come from, or resuming their journey. The only one he watched closely was Meliosme, and she did not waver, but trudged on, tiredly but steadily. By the time light was coming up from the east, they

182

were well into the hill country between Crule the Swale and Zolotane, and there were only four of them left: Emerna, Janea, Meliosme and Phaedrus.

This was dry country, but their way crossed and recrossed water courses, at first as dry as the land around them and marked only by gravel beds and brushy tangles along the sides, but soon showing some water in them as they went higher up.

In the shadow of a steep bank, Emerna stopped uncertainly, looking about her wearily. Meliosme joined her, and Phaedrus came up to them in a moment. Emerna wanted to stop and rest, but was uncertain about the place; she was now well out of the area she knew well and additionally had turned into the hills too soon, and admitted she did not know the area. Meliosme glanced about, almost off-handedly, and told her that the place was safe enough, and sat down against a large rock over which a bare and scraggly tree hung, and closed her eyes. Emerna found another place not too far off, and Janea followed her, and they settled down together. Phaedrus watched this, and did not interfere; presently he decided to stay awake as long as he could, to watch over the group while the others slept. He looked about in the brightening daylight, and saw bare, rocky hills, sand-colored, dun brown, pale violet, pocked with clumps of vegetation, an occasional gaunt tree festooned with ragged strips. To the west, more hills against the dark sky; to the east, there were hills, too, but there was only light behind them, the morning, running across the long grasslands of Crule the Swale.

In the tumults of the times, many things had been brought to light by the ministrations of Femisticleo Chugun's Secret Police, but odd as it might be, much more had remained undiscovered, owing to the organization of the Offworld Watch on Oerlikon, which severely limited what the lower orders knew. This limitation of essential knowledge, coupled with the troubles the central government was having to cope with throughout Lisagor, effectively limited the penetration Chugun's people were able to effect into the offworld organization, with the immensely practical result that Arunda Palude was able to return to her concealed communications site and broadcast an emergency recall signal, under which conditions the main support ship was to return and retrieve as many as it could, depending on conditions available. This support ship was not armed, and could not carry out operations in a hostile environment, nevertheless they would try to pick up as many as they could. She reported back to Charodei, now with Cesar Kham, the active head of what mission survived. But Charodei did not convey this information to Luto Pternam.

Pternam clearly had his own hands full, and devoted most of his time alternating between hiding in the deepest recesses of the Mask Factory, expecting the return of Tiresio Rael any moment, and working at a manic pace in stints which might carry him across two full days before he collapsed from exhaustion. Despite the heroic measures, however, Lisagor was melting like a cake of ice placed in the hot sunlight: North Tilanque had joined Karshiyaka, as had Severovost and even the extreme easternmost part of Akchil. South Tilanque and Priboy had gone over to the rebels of Zamor, which left Lisagor with only a small strip to the coast in the central parts of the seaboard province, and this was uncertain and full of rival factions contending. In the north, Zefaa and Greyslope were nominally still under control, but this condition clearly existed solely because the inhabitants had nothing better to do, and could change quickly, in a matter of days. The West was long gone: Clisp, The Serpentine, and what passed for population centers in sparsely-inhabited Zolotane had been among the first to break off, and the new borders remained closed. Rumors were widespread that the new rulers of Marisol were assembling an army to invade Zefaa, and there were companion rumors running with those which suggested that the locals there would surrender immediately were such an invasion to take place. In the south, Sertse Solntsa was still holding, but it was clearly by force alone that the province was being held. In fact, so much of the city had been damaged that it was already useless as a port.

So far, Central Lisagor was holding together, partly from fear of change, fear of the surviving cadres of Pallet-Dropped Heavy Troopers, and partly because no one had yet tried to invade it. Oerlikon had no tradition of war, and so when an area rebelled, their chief concern was to be left alone, repulsing attacks and being content with that. Moreover, it did not seem likely that the central government could invade the rebel provinces, either, as they lacked the numbers of troopers necessary for the task, and the loyalty of their remaining population hinged on an inlanders traditional distaste for the sea-province outlanders. They would not join them, neither would they fight them, and so the one thing that enabled them to hold the inland provinces prevented them from raising an army to recapture any of the outlying provinces.

Charodei was clearly having his own problems as well, chiefly with Pternam, who seemed to be less and less interested in arranging for the Offworlders to find suitable transceiver equipment, and more interested in holding on to what he already had. Hints and suggestions seemed to have little effect on this eroding situation, and so Charodei called for a meeting on the subject. They met at the Mask Factory, this time in broad daylight. Nobody seemed to mind that Pternam had collected some odd associates lately.

Charodei did not waste words; "You know, Pternam, it's already an open secret that you have allies."

Pternam shivered and said, "So many of you popped out of the woodwork I'm not surprised people talk."

"They don't seem to mind."

"You know us well, and we know nothing of you—nevertheless there is much you miss; no matter your loyalties, there is a bad flavor to this, which we Lisaks try to ignore." He thought a moment, and then added, "We express ourselves in a few selected areas, and elsewhere restrain our plunging lusts—thereby is change thwarted; by operating openly, more or less, you poison things."

Charodei blinked once, owlishly. "You aver that our assistance is counterproductive to your plans?"

Pternam laughed hollowly, a madman's chuckle at something no one else would find humorous. "Ha-ha! Counterproductive, indeed. Perhaps, were there plan left, but I have given that up long ago!"

"You don't think we can deliver, then."

"Of course you can't deliver. You never could."

"No so; we could, and can. Of course, there are measures of the quality of appropriateness . . . the time is soon approaching when in our estimation, the situation will have gone too far to argue for a reorganization of the central provinces under controllable conditions."

"I am well aware that things are still deteriorating. Symbarupol is perilously close to the new Changeist territories; the Tilanque strip is gone, as is most of Puropagne south of here. There has been talk of moving the Center out of here, to a more protected location out in Crule. Additionally, we do not seem to have the resources to continue at the level we

185

have tried to maintain. Something more is needed, but Crule and Akchil are unwilling to supply it."

"You need troops. . . ."

"Yes." For a moment, a shred of hope arose in Pternam. "We even made some contacts with the Freeholders of Tartary, but to little use; they have come to terms with Change in a way that does not accord with the old way we defend here. Likewise, with loyalists in the rebel areas, who claim to want the old way, but who will send no fighting men to enforce it."

"You can't make up enough Heavy Troopers?"

"It takes time. We never worried about time before. The people, you see, they got used to the troopers, to their transports. Now they ambush them as they land, take their weapons, and turn them on the following waves. That was all we ever needed . . . now it isn't any good anymore. When they move to Crule, the Mask Factory will close; we can't move everything we need to continue."

Charodei could see where things were leading. Pternam was in a funk, burned out, he had already given up. Useless, useless. He had clearly no intention of helping them—he had no idea of how to help himself. "What do you imagine you will do?"

"Survive, that's what. We are already turning out some of the lower orders who were associates here. Some have left, others have run off to the sea provinces. . . ."

After a moment, Charodei said, "Then you are not going to be able to get us access to suitable components to contact the ship?"

Pternam looked away, and then back. He said, "Can you take me with you?"

Charodei felt a surge of anger, and contemptuous mirth with it. The very idea, that this ignorant savage would want to be taken to a world like Heliarcos, which would be incomprehensible to him, even though Charodei knew it in truth to be a backwater world itself. This went through his mind almost instantly, and he let none of it show. He said, instead, ". . . It's never been done. This was supposed to be a no-contact mission, here on Oerlikon, and so no provisions were made for such a contingency. . . ."

"But humans, they move around freely, they travel from world to world, back in the place where you come from?"

"Yes, of course. . . . One has to pay fares, and sometimes there are small restrictions, but in general, that is the nature of things: people more or less move about as they feel the urge."

"You have authority among your group; you could arrange such a novelty."

"Perhaps. Perhaps not. I would have to work with others, who still recall the original doctrine of this operation."

Pternam said, "No contact."

"Exactly."

"But you have violated that principle by contacting me."

"True, we did bend things some."

"Well, I will be brief. My operation is to close down, and there is little else for me to do. Additionally, I have enemies. Here, I have some security against random assassinations, but away. . . . Take me with you and you can have the Mask Factory; there are enough components here presumably for your experts to fabricate something that will work."

"Otherwise . . . ?"

"Otherwise, I will have everything destroyed. I can't afford to leave records of what we did. Doubtless there will be those who would like to redress their grievances, even though we have tried to eliminate that negative attitude . . ."

"What could you do for us?"

"I could make you another Morphodite, and all that goes with that; the conscious control of the hormone system." And he thought, deep in his mind, *Yes, I'll make another one for them, and this time I'll loose it early on, and it can savage their worlds like they savaged mine.* He forgot something crucial to reality, that it was he, and not the Offworlders, who had savaged Oerlikon and Lisagor.

Charodei saw the repressed excitement in Pternam, the rat-like hope, and read it correctly: *And when we get him there, he'll turn one loose on us, or so he thinks. Well, we can always jettison him in deep space.* He said, "There might be some use in that, after all—if for nothing else than explaining events here—how they came to be. You'd have to make do with a smaller sample of experimental subjects; we can't drag them off the streets like you could here."

Pternam saw that Charodei did not refuse outright, and therefore still wanted something from him—if nothing else, access within the labyrinthine recesses of the Mask Factory to build a transceiver.

Charodei said, "I cannot promise what will transpire; you understand that I cannot speak for those who may come. At any rate, I will do what I can."

It seemed little, but enough, considering the circumstances. Pternam said, "Very well. I will have Avaria show you where things are; there should be enough left in the Computorium to do the job."

"Excellent! Rest assured that we will leave your equipment in operating condition."

Pternam turned to go. "Oh no. That won't be necessary at all; in fact, I prefer that your people leave it inoperable. And illegible."

"Are things *that* close?"

"Close enough. You can use this building to transmit from. I will give the orders that you not be molested."

"I will put Palude on it immediately."

"The sooner the better. . . . Do you think they will come?"

"Depends on what we can put together, where they are, how far. A lot of variables. Remember, we never expected to have to recall the support ship."

Pternam laughed aloud. "What were you planning to do? Stay here forever?"

Charodei felt an odd spasm of irritation, and he suppressed it with difficulty. "A lot of people did; many more supposed that things would remain changeless on the world that lived for changelessness."

"You mean when their duty was over, some elected to stay here?"

Charodei explained, "Why not? Their own world was twenty standard years behind them. Lisagor was all they knew."

"That's amazing! And what would these people do for a living?"

"They would have some funds supplied through suitable covers, but to avoid drawing attention to themselves they would usually take obscure positions . . . it was policy that we did not keep up with those who were retired and had gone native. Needless to say, they were all model citizens . . . by definition. As far as I know, that is."

Pternam laughed, an erratic, plunging chuckle that sounded more than a little out of control. "Sa-ha! So when we were making the Morphodite, we might well have started with one of your retirees."

Charodei felt a chill along his backbone. "Yes, I suppose that would have been possible . . . we would have no way to ascertain if this was the case or not." Charodei suppressed his feelings again. Changelessness had been maintained by many

188

things, but the Mask Factory had played a larger part than they had suspected, performing experiments and transformations outlawed everywhere else, absolutely prohibited. And this Pternam thought it was humorous that he might have made up his weapon out of material that had come from some far world. And if it were true, what a fate to undergo: drugs, shock, electronic stimulation, the artificial attainment of extreme trance states. Yes, as he reflected on it, he could be certain that some of his people had been processed by Pternam. It strengthened his resolve, and he thought, clearly and consciously, *Yes, we'll jettison the son-of-a-bitch; indeed, I'll do it personally. It's a duty, a responsibility. We cannot let this monster walk about on our own worlds, free to hatch more of his plots.*

As if reading his mind, and agreeing with some internal argument, Pternam nodded, and said, "Well, that's a fine set of circumstances, were it true. I agree we'd have no way to know . . . but just imagine: we preyed upon you just as you were preying upon us, and neither of us knew of the symbiosis . . . Well, that chapter is over."

"Yes. Remember whose side we were on."

"Indeed: the side of orthodoxy, of Manclova and Chugun, and Primitivo Mercador and Odisio Chang, lifers all. But in the end it did us all no good, eh? Their orthodoxy, your support, my schemes. There were too many plotters, too many throne-upholders, and so we all pushed it over in the press. . . . Well, tell your people they will doubtless be able to come openly after a time. We will probably need the help after these tumults."

"You think they would welcome us again?"

Pternam shrugged. "You would always be welcome in Clisp. You doubtless have the tools to rebuild the Old Port as well."

Charodei said, in a low voice, "I hope you don't assume omnipotence on our part; we, too, have our limits."

Pternam chuckled again, that erratic little laugh: "Ho-ha! Yes, that's always the way it is—you're the miracle workers until we really need you, and then you're only human."

"If I may say, you have an odd perspective."

"You reminded me what you supported; I remind you that this was my world, better or worse, and that it sits unevenly now that we know that one of the things that allowed us to be changeless was the covert support of people we detested and left, back in the beginning days here. We might have

189

done better to accept some change; some of the advice of
Clisp and The Serpentine. . . . Nobody likes to be revealed a
fool."

"The Morphodite ended our mission here; if you wish revenge, you have already had it."

~ 14 ~

Morning in Zolotane

Phaedrus had been dreaming; he awoke instantly, and knew he had dreamed, but he could not remember what. And he saw, head clear, that it was already late on in the morning, and that Meliosme was sitting close by, watching him intently, her regard did not change when she saw that he was awake.

He said, "You look as if you knew me."

She nodded, solemnly. "Yes. You remind me of someone I once met, knew for a short time—a short time indeed; I am from the outlands, the wild places, and so to me all townsmen seem alike, weighted by the inertia of their destiny, pressed into a fixed course. Not so you, or the other. You and he share a mannerism, of being live, quick, unweighted. I never knew townsmen before who were like that."

"And others? Not townsmen?"

Meliosme mused for a moment, as if savoring something rather than remembering it, looking off into the distance. "I am a fleischbaum harvester, and I meet little save solitaries like me, and do you know there are few men to it? True, though. You, and the other one—you have no weight behind you, no massiness. You can go as you will."

He listened to her, and looked deeply at the plain, sturdy figure, the face that was not masculine or feminine but human, illuminated from within by a sense of repose and acceptance of the rhythm of the world; outwardly, Meliosme was rough and homely, but interiorly, she was as sleek as some furred and graceful riparian animal, alert, but not tensed. An odd emotion colored his perceptions, a quick shiver, a ripple, something that whispered to him to make bold, to speak openly of himself, of his identity. Well, perhaps not all of it. Some of it, until he could gauge how she would hear it. No one tells all the truth, for if they did, everyone would immediately go up in flames.

He said, "You met Tiresio Rael in a traveler's tavern, and

rode on a Beamliner with him, to Marula; you went with him to a room, where he bade you leave him for your safety."

Meliosme blinked once, but did not seem otherwise surprised that he would know this. "Yes, it was like that."

Phaedrus continued, "He felt a real emotion for the girl he met, or else he would not have sent her away."

She said, "You know much; then you will know something of what I felt."

"That is so."

She ventured after a long silence, "No spy knows such things, no watcher."

"I was Rael."

"I can see that; I don't know how, but I *see* it. You are him, but also different. You are younger."

"I changed. It was something that was done to me."

"I understand. There were always some like that wandering about; but they were unfinished, un-right, broken. You then were . . . I don't know. You were of two natures, one a spirit of peace, of wisdom; and the other, a destroying angel."

"I had not thought of myself as a sage; yet destroy I have. But I will no more, nor will I change again."

She nodded again, and smiled faintly. "Done. And what will you do?"

"I act only for myself, now. I need a quiet place, where I can perhaps dig out who I am; who I was. When they changed me, they took away that knowledge. I was not always Rael."

"I knew that."

"You could see what I was?"

Meliosme said. "No. That Rael had not always been so. You, too, have that quality of newness."

"But I remember the things I have been; the things I have done."

"You know them, you did them, you were them, but they are not your prison. You will learn from them."

"Where? Here, in this wilderness?"

"Zolotane is not far. I know these hills well, having passed along these trails many times; over the hills are open lands that slope down to the blue salt sea. There are stands of open fleischbaum groves, and sea creatures to catch, and a land of grass, golden under the sun. Few people are there."

Phaedrus glanced at the place where Emerna waited with

Janea, still asleep, although the morning was well advanced. "What about them?"

"They must go along their own path; it is not yours, now."

"I was as one dead; she saved me, or I would have been, in the ruin of Marula."

"Marula stands yet." She shrugged. "Such debts . . . one can never repay them, and so one cannot. Let her go—she is weighted, set, bound to something dark, black and red."

"She wants, I think to go to Clisp."

"We will show them the way. But remain with me or no, you will leave her, now or later. It is better now."

Then Meliosme led him away from the narrow valley, and showed him simple things they could catch or gather; small dried pomes like miniature apples, an evergreen twining vine with leathery leaves and long, stringy pods, both of which were edible. She pointed out a long, snakelike creature with four pairs of legs, and then caught it with a quick motion, killing it instantly.

Phaedrus said, "I would not have guessed there was so much here; it looks like a waste, empty."

She nodded. "It is so. There is abundance if we know how to look, and we take but what we need."

"People do not do that, but grow things of their own and worry if there will be enough."

She said, "There will never be enough to still the fear that there might not be enough. But they do not fear scarcity; they fear fear. Look—we may live on these things, but we will not grow content on them."

He said, "I understand; to become content is to fear that it will end. We are better a little hungry, I think." He gestured with his head toward the east, generally. "*They* feared change so much they made a world that slowed it to nearly zero, but in the end, a pinprick released the years of accumulated pressure, and so it burst."

"You did that."

"Yes."

"Why? Were you their enemy? Was there a revenge to be?"

He waited, and then said, "I knew them not. They were strangers to me. They saw to that in the Mask Factory, that I had no past. They . . . took me apart, and reassembled me, leaving some things out. I did not know it then, but I only knew what they wanted me to do, which was perform a simple, single act that would change the world. The reality of a world, of its people, rests on a single person, low and unknown, changing, shifting slowly, and if you remove that person, you can change the world. That was what I knew, and so I did." He sighed, deeply. "And now it seems like a dream, like some strange vision."

"But you changed . . . And see—the natural world is the same. At a given moment, it all rests on a single creature which we do not know or understand. And you could *see* this person!"

"I could . . . calculate who it was—that is the best way to say it."

"You can still do this?"

"Yes . . . They gave me enough so I would believe it, but they thought the idea nonsense."

Meliosme laughed to herself, a secretive little chuckle. "What fools they were! To launch a person on the only path he could take, and give him something to believe. Of course he would do it!"

He said, "So I learned. There are many phases to it . . ."

"You could extend it to the natural world."

He thought for a moment, and said, "Yes, but it would be . . . different. I would have to use other symbols, use different manipulations. But then after that . . . it would be . . . simpler."

"Then you will use your art, and understand, and you will tell us . . . and we will listen. They made you for a weapon, but you will be a gentle hand bringing water to a thirsty land." Then she said, "You found the person, and sent him to the darkness, and the world changed. Then what happened? Who has it set upon now?"

"When you take the base away, it flickers for instants among others, but not long enough for stability to be attained. Later, the center slows and settles on another, as obscure as the first. I have not looked hard since then, and the only operation I have done suggested that things were still in flux. It feels that way now to me, but it's trying to find a place."

"Then you can do it without the symbols, the paper, the figures—in your head. You can feel it directly."

"I was Rael, I was Damistofia, I am Phaedrus, and through all of those I wished to forget it."

"But you cannot; you will turn the evil they set upon you to a good—a worthy thing."

"I fear the use of it again."

"I understand. But you have changed yourself, and you may not return to what you were, but you will have to learn to live with what you are. I can help."

He wanted then to ask why, but felt the air between them growing delicate, and he did not wish to have the issue resolved just then; it felt right as it was, and so he remained silent, and let it be. She said, "Come along, we'll share with the others, and set them on their way, to Clisp."

Together, they climbed back down into the sheltered little valley, really more a dry wash, to the place where they had been the night before. Then they had done nothing, but coming back from the uplands, he felt an odd sense of immediate past intimacy with Meliosme, as if she had shared something with him; like the sharing of sex, but more intimate in a way that the sweet muscular anodyne of coupling could not reach.

They looked for Emerna and Janea, and found them cowering under a bush with nodding circular leaves, hiding. Not far away stood a solitary bosel, observing, so it appeared, its head crooked comically to the side. This was the first time Phaedrus could remember seeing one, and at first he had to force himself to *see* it, so odd were its outlines, suggestive of parts of animals he could recall, although he did not know where he knew them from. It stood upright on two legs, a bulbous, birdlike body, small, apparently fragile arms, and a gangling long neck supporting a comical head, round at the back, crowned with expandable, flexible ears, two eyes overshadowed not by brows but feathery appendages that looked like rubbery moth antennae. The snout was long and tubular, with one large orifice and two small ones. The upper body was furred, but the legs were bare and fluted with muscle.

He said quietly, "It is dangerous?"

Meliosme walked out into the open, casually, answering over her shoulder, "This one, no. A young buck, only curious." She made a ducking motion and then turned gracefully about, as if dancing, ending by repeatedly crossing her forearms. To Phaedrus's amazement, the bosel responded with a little hop which took it erratically to one side, where it turned its snout to the sky and vented a soft breathy whistling, which suggested amusement, or whimsy. Then, with one last sidelong glance toward the two hiding women, it abruptly turned and loped off up the wash somewhere to the north, vanishing among the rocks.

195

Meliosme said, "When they're young, they find humans fascinating. They watch them all the time in the wild like this. I don't know what they find so interesting. Later, they become more erratic, unpredictable, although it seems to me that it makes sense to them, somehow, that it is I who don't understand the web here we have trespassed into. That one will wander off, although he will keep us in sight for a while, or within scent."

"There won't be others?"

"They're solitaries—scroungers and scavengers who don't tolerate company very well. They maintain contact at night, when they are active, by sounds which you have doubtless heard. I do not know the import of the sounds, if there is any. They seem to communicate by gesture, and some of the basic motions I have learned."

"You told it something. . . ."

"I told it to go away. It laughed and sent back that it didn't matter."

"That sounds easy."

"It's not. The key motions are short and easy to do wrongly, so that you send a garble, which makes them hostile, or worse, you send something which offends them individually. Even that young one could be dangerous if provoked. They are nowhere near as fragile as they look, or as awkward. They can move fast, and they can . . . anticipate things. It accepted me as its superior immediately, but it also knew I had other interests: you, them. It might have moved on you. Myself I can protect, but I have never tried to defend another—that is an awkward situation."

They walked toward the bush from which Emerna and Janea were now emerging and Phaedrus said, "They sound almost intelligent. Have others tried to contact them?"

"Only such as I, gatherers, and others of the wild places. And I cannot say whether they have minds."

They shared the food they had brought, and rested, saying little among themselves. Phaedrus saw that Emerna had assumed a kind of responsibility for the ragged Janea, and had dismissed him in her mind, and he did not wish to change that. On the other hand, he could see that she saw and resented his easy relationship with Meliosme, who with a night's rest had changed from a haggard prisoner expecting to be tormented and eaten to an alert and confident person at home in the wilds. He thought he caught a reluctance in

196

Emerna to stay at this place, overlaid by a burning desire to get away from it.

They spoke of the bosel, and Emerna admitted that she was terrified of them. Janea claimed that Meliosme could have called bosels to save them had she wished.

Meliosme shook her head and smiled softly. "That's why people have never tried to learn about them; you can't get them to do things for you. They don't seem to understand doing for something else. Besides, one would have done us no good, even if I could have called one, which I can't—they have never answered my imitations of their calls—they don't do anything together except procreate."

The sun was shining and soon reached the zenith, and the light began to fall in the slanting rays of early afternoon. Janea seemed agitated, eager to be on the way.

Phaedrus said, "You will, then, want to go on to Clisp?"

Emerna answered, "At least the Serpentine." To Meliosme she said, "Do you know the way?"

Meliosme said, "Yes. But I do not wish to go there, so I will tell you how to go. I will stay—" here she gestured westwards—"there in Zolotane."

"What about you?" Emerna directed this at Phaedrus.

"Clisp is too far for me. I have things to unravel for which I need an emptier land."

"There are still empty places in Clisp."

"It needs doing now."

"Very well." Emerna gathered herself and got to her feet with what seemed to Phaedrus to be an attitude of anger, but nothing came of it. She turned and offered her hand to Janea, who took it and got up, too, eager to be on the way. Emerna said, "I suppose the sooner we start. . . ." And with no more formality than that, they started out northward again, following the creekbed as it followed the course of the defile it had cut.

As the slanting light changed slowly to twilight, and then evening, they followed the watercourse ever upward and to the northwest. Soon damp patches appeared in the riverbed sand, and then small stretches of standing water, and by evening proper they were walking along the edges of a small creek. The vegetation changed, too; as they went up, the bare ground and vines gave way to a tussocky ground cover, and there began to be trees, with short, barrellike trunks, supporting gnarled and twisted wide-spreading branches. It was quiet, peaceful country, the aisles in the forest filled with golden light falling on the tussocks that covered the ground between the trees. There was no sign of inhabitants, either native or Oerlikon or alien, a fact which Phaedrus noted and commented on. Meliosme pronounced the open forest a notorious haunt of bosels, and was anxious to be past it before nightfall, for that reason, and Emerna and Janea agreed. As if to underline her words, they began to hear some calls from the east, exhausted, tenuous wailing sounds that seemed to have no great import to them. Phaedrus listened carefully and thought to identify at least four separate callers, but they all seemed far away.

"Not so!" Meliosme asserted with some confidence. "They are great deceivers, standing within arm's-length and pretending to be miles away. But those you hear are of no matter, near or far; if they were interested in us, you would hear calls from all around. Those kinds of sounds soon end—the ones you hear—and no more is seen or heard of them."

What she had said seemed to be borne out a little later on, when the calls, after a rough, rhythmic association, faded out, not suddenly, but as if the callers were finished and had no more to say. But despite Meliosme's arguments to the contrary, Phaedrus thought he had heard distinct repeating patterns among the odd, diverse calls, which had at first seemed alike only in tone and type of utterance.

They were still down in a valley, following the creek north and west, but the sky to the west of them was open and expansive, full of light instead of shadows, and there was a warm lightness to the air that promised a different terrain. Meliosme called them to a halt.

"Here is the place where the paths diverge. Follow the creek north, and you will come to an open hilltop, with a circle worn into it. Bosels use this in midsummer, but none will approach the place now. Follow the rivulet down, on the other side, and you will come to the marshes, which is in Zolotane, but is near to the Serpentine. About a day's walk, I should think, if you're up to moving along smartly. We will turn here and go down into lower Zolotane, where there are few."

Emerna looked north, up the creek, and hesitated. "Could we not follow you to the coast? Then we could go north."

"This part of Zolotane is empty, and the coast is rough." She shrugged. "It is your choice. You saved us from the tramps; who am I to tell you where you can go and not go? I only say that where we go is empty country, and no easy way out of it."

Janea the waif tugged at Emerna's arm. She clearly did not wish to stay in the wilds. For a minute longer, she stood, uncertain, looking at the light fading in the west, and the empty creek bottom north. At last, she said, "So be the throw," and turned up the creek, neither saying farewells nor waiting for any.

After the pair had walked around a bend, Phaedrus said, "An odd and capable creature, that one. I am sorry to see her go, the times being what they are."

Meliosme said, "Surely you could see that she wasn't whole, but was damaged and broken, long before you set the world on edge. And as you were not whole yourself, so she could serve you, but as you grew in knowledge of self, you would threaten her, and in the end, she would be your enemy. She is dangerous. Better we send her back to the world, where the presence of many others may heal her. She needs those others. You know what you need."

He nodded. "Yes. At least for a time. Well, let us go. I think you know the way."

Meliosme smiled, and Phaedrus saw with pleasure that although she was not pretty, when she smiled there was a warmth in her face that was genuine. "Yes, so I do, or at least so much as I remember." She looked shyly at the ground for a moment. "There is an abandoned cabin down there, and a little creek that flows down from the hills and falls into the sea at the cliffs. The land is covered with grassopant, and the sun shines on the land and the water. A nice place. Of course, there is no food, but we can manage. You are, for the time, a gatherer. I will show you."

Phaedrus asked, "Is there more?"

"There is a matter I would take up where it left off, when you were another."

Meliosme led them up a steep path, that wound upward, and farther upward, until at last it emerged on a ridgeline where there was nothing higher to the west. The sun was sinking, near the horizon, which was a ruled line of darkness, straight, upon which there was a golden trail shimmering.

Phaedrus stopped and looked long across the openness that lay before him. At the distant horizon was the sea, and somewhere beyond that, the harsh and bare mountains of southern and eastern Clisp, that faced this bay. But here were rolling hills and ridges slanting down gently to the sea. He turned to

Meliosme and asked, "Where shall I go when you have finished?"

To which she said, "I will not be finished." And took his hand. Hers was hardened and tough from years in the wild, but it felt right, and he took what was offered, and together they walked down the first of the slopes that led down to the sea. They had not gone very far when they began to hear bosel calls, liquid, trembling wails, first from behind them, seemingly in the very place they had paused, but also down the slope in front of them, and some more to the north and south, Phaedrus listened carefully, and said that he thought there were six. Meliosme listened and agreed, and also pronounced them not dangerous.

"When they call like that, they're just curious. Actually, it's a good sign that we picked up some like that."

"Why?"

"Because it means that they haven't seen anyone like us for a long time coming this way. We're odd, and new, to them. Or so it seems to me."

"You know them as well as anyone I have known."

"You are kind. But no one knows bosels well, and after we live here for a time, you will know them as well as I—maybe better."

"Why do you say that?"

"The young one we saw before—he is with this group. And it was you he was interested in. They are following you, not me. At least, I have never heard them make that sound while watching me or following."

"Is this group dangerous?"

"I don't think so. Let us go straight ahead, and mind our own affairs; when they can anticipate what we are going to do, they will form a looser group, and move off. If the calls change otherwise . . . well, we will worry about that, then."

∽ 15 ∽

Final Focus

There was a small building, far down the long slope, which was much longer than it seemed when they had seen it from the top of the ridge that properly divided Zolotane from Crule the Swale. A long walk, which totally sapped their endurance. And the building; that wasn't much either. Abandoned for years to the airs of the coast, come whatever would, one could not tell now whether it had been a house, or a shed, or a small barn, or none of these. And it was the only place in sight, more, the only one Meliosme had ever known along this part of the coast.

They had walked all of one night and all of the following day to get there, and in the late afternoon light, the wind came off the sea and made a whispering among the grass-plants and the old ruins.

Phaedrus asked, after drinking long and deep at the shallow stream that watered the place, "Do you know who was here, who built, and why, here?"

"No. I never knew. I never came to this place before. I saw it from afar. And I heard there was an abandoned place here, the only one down this far. This is only Zolotane if you make natural borders; actually, it is no one's. Its style seems to me to be more Crule, but an old Crule not seen in our lives, mine or yours."

Phaedrus chuckled. "We do not know how long mine is; I was born only a little ago."

She made a face at him. "Even that much, however long it is. This is an old place, and the owners long gone. They came for something, and did not get it, and left, or got so much of it they wanted nothing else and so became one with it."

Phaedrus looked around for a long time, saying nothing. He took in the empty sweep of the coast, the expanse of grass-plant that tossed to the coast wind and gave it fleeting suggestion of shape; he saw the open sweep of the sky, the dark water westward of them. He inhaled deeply and tasted the world-ocean. Finally, he said, "Can we live here? Is there enough for us?"

Meliosme had been squatting, looking at the ground as if studying it. Now she stood, and also looked about, slowly. "Yes. A lot of searching and scrabbling, but it will be possible. In time . . ."

He looked at her directly. "I remember you. You have not changed."

She said, "In you there is something which did not change, that I remember."

"Well . . . let us make of this ruin a house of sorts."

She laughed easily. "I do not need one."

"Your wandering days seem to be over."

"For now. But who knows? I may someday wish to take them up again."

"Can you see this time?"

She paused, as if deep in thought. Finally: "No. I cannot. We will rebuild."

"And make some new things."

She added, "Some new things are actually older than humankind on Oerlikon."

"Some are older than humankind itself."

As the light fell, they went into the building and moved a few things around and also searched for whatever they could find. Among their finds were a few plain, worn, and much-rusted tools such as one would have about a home in an empty land. But by then the light was almost gone, and so they did not do more than make a shelter for themselves against the wind, which was still cold, and some protection from bosels, should any approach, although for once the dark seemed curiously free of them. As they became quiet, they could hear short calls, but from very far away, and there was no urgency in those. Phaedrus and Meliosme lay close together for warmth, and presently they became closer, and very warm, and afterward they lay together, wrapped in their collection of odd pieces and scraps, and slept soundly, untroubled by dreams or desires.

The next morning they awoke late and were very hungry. Meliosme led him down to the sea and along the shore, pointing out what was edible, what was not, and what was endurable should the occasion arise. She said, "We have water, we have the sea, and there is grassplant, and farther back, fleischbaum."

"Everything except clothes."

She laughed, a soft chuckle. "If it will hurry up and get a bit warmer, we will not need those. There is no flow into the great bay from the north, and so the water will be warm."

He said, "And then winter again."

She answered, "We will rest here for the while, and then go forth, to get some things. We can always take a load of fleischbaum with us. I think people will be hungry, and will trade with ragamuffins, when their values have changed somewhat."

Phaedrus looked out across the water, now more at ease, that Meliosme had caught a few things for them. During the night, the wind had shifted some, and although waves were coming in onto the narrow beach, on the brown sand, the wind from the land was lifting their crests back gracefully. He said, "Yes. But I do not want to leave this place any longer than I have to."

"We won't."

And they returned to the little creek, climbed back up to the golden plain, and set to rebuilding the house. During the afternoon, Meliosme set off on an exploring trip, back into the higher country back of them, for fleischbaum and groundnut which had survived the winter, and returned near evening with her skirts full of things. As she neared the house, which was even now looking more like a house and less like a ruin, she saw Phaedrus's slender figure climbing about on the roof he was rebuilding. Not so far away from the house, south of it, in the slanting, marvelous light of the west, stood quietly three large bosels, of the appearance of elder bucks of great age and sagacity, who stood and watched, without comment, without gesture, hoot or grumble. Phaedrus, although she could see by his actions that he was aware of them, ignored them and went on with his work. When they saw her approaching, they turned and stared solemnly at her, and moved off, a little farther south, but they still stayed and waited for a long time, until darkness fell. After that, in the night, lying together in their shelter inside the walls, the couple heard the flow of boselcall rippling about them, intermittently, like distant summer lightning.

Their life now flowed much like the sea winds that flowed over the golden shoals of grass which covered the flat lands between the seaside cliffs and the hills in the east. The long days of Oerlikon drifted slowly past them, and with more days, the imperceptible change of the seasons, always subtle and delicate. Phaedrus did not question Meliosme closely about her recent past, but he noticed a change in his own life which was immediate and demonstrable. He could not remember any period save the present when he had not measured events around himself (or herself) by devastating, calamitous events, either things he knew were to come, or those which had passed. Now was different. There was no measure. They slept at dark and arose at light, and in between, without haste, rebuilt the house and made up their stores. It was a simple, life of survival thousands of years in tradition, and soon he stopped considering who he had been and worried little over who he might become. It was enough to be as he was at the moment.

In between times when they were working, Meliosme spoke of the things she knew of the world Oerlikon: the texture of sky, the feel and smell of the wind, the quarter it came from. She spoke of the colors of the sky, and the meaning of each; of bosels, and rarer creatures native to the planet. Of plants, harmful, beneficial, medicinal, toxic, and consumable. She added, "It's silly, but this really is a good, easy world. No one need starve, or live badly. But like anything else, you have to understand it. Most of our people who came here brought rigid ideas from elsewhere, and applied them against the wind with great resolve."

He said, "You sound as if you approve of what Rael did."

"It was wrong here, and getting no better. Sometimes cures are not pleasant. Rael, or someone else; it needed doing— something, to break them loose. We who wander knew that the folk inside the cities were all closed in in their minds; they hadn't an enemy on the whole planet, but they were exiles in their minds."

"Do you think they will be any better, now? They could well be worse: doubtless terrible deeds have been done, and back there are the survivors, who are now sharpening their knives and saying under their breath, 'Never forget! Never forgive!' There is no end to revenge."

For a long time, they were alone and untroubled by visitors, but they knew that someday some would come, and after a time which seemed short to them both, wanderers and refugees began to appear, footsore and bedraggled, generally walking northwest out of Serets Solntsa and the torment of Marula, or otherwise out of the southern parts of Crule the Swale. The most of these were dispirited and broken, blown by the wind, and after some kind words, would work a little for some rest and some food, after which they would go on their way. Some of the children stayed, the orphaned ones who knew nothing and who told plain tales in simple language that chilled the soul. Others also came, looking in the confusions of the times to carve out a little place and secure it. Some of these they reasoned with; others they threatened. The most desperate and hostile ones were, in a matter-of-fact manner, either run off or killed, either by Phaedrus, or Meliosme, or, by them all together.

Phaedrus told Meliosme that the changes wrought upon him in the bowels of the Mask Factory had removed his ability to sire children, but she had shrugged, as if it were no matter, and gestured at the collection of children of all sizes which sat at the table with them, and said, "We can have as many of these as we want." And that was all was said of the subject.

Phaedrus and Meliosme did not inquire of the world they had left behind, nor of the people in it; nevertheless they heard tales, and from them they could make up a picture of what things were happening across the hills. In general, it could be said that anarchy reigned, with early alliances fissioning down to the village level, save in the area dominated by Clisp, and what was left of Lisagor, which was now effectively limited to a strip along the great river and the northern parts of Marula. Symbarupol had been abandoned, sacked, vandalized, and burned, and no one seemed to have any inclination to re-inhabit the site. It was out of the way.

A year passed. Winter into spring, spring into summer, summer into fall, and winter again. The tales circulating into their small world from the east described the dissolution of what remained of Lisagor by the fanatics of Crule, for lack of doctrinal rigor, and of the recovery of Crule, at least in part. The flow of wanderers from the east over the hills stopped, and that from Marula slowed, but they now sighted crude ships on the sea, always sailing northwest. Some of these wrecked on the foreshore reefs, and sometimes only parts of boats floated in on the waves.

In the meantime, some of those who had stayed wandered off a little and built places of their own, thinking only that this place was half wild and rude, but no warlord wanted it, and so they were left alone. Others came and went between there and Zolotane proper, and there was a small trickle of trade. And of rumor. The trade was simple, things coming down they could not make for themselves, and what went north was mostly food, and people who had been stopped in their fall into despair. And the tale began circulating, first in settled Zolotane, then along The Serpentine, and in Clisp, and in the provinces facing the grey-green northern seas, that in the far south of Zolotane sojourned a wise woman and an enigmatic wise man, who claimed no authority except over what was properly theirs, but who helped those who came to them, in quiet and unassuming ways, and sent them on, ready to rebuild their lives. And some little bit of what really passed there actually reached those settled places, but what little bit it was, it did some little good, and in the west of the continent Karshiyaka, a semblance of order began to come back into shape, and people breathed a little easier.

One day, in the summer, Phaedrus was teaching some children by the edge of the cliffs, when he looked up and saw offshore a sleek and splendid gray ship approaching, moving south down the coast, and now angling closer to the shore. This was, he observed, no refugee sailboat, patched together of packing cases, but a ship of metal, and powered, for a low droning noise came from it as it slowed, and stopped, and anchored, not far offshore. Presently, a small boat was lowered, and people could be seen embarking for the shore. Phaedrus sent the children back inland, more for precaution than anything else, but as the boat approached, he could discern no hostile gesture, and so he waited, watching the people make their way across the water to the shore, and when they drew near, he went down to the beach to meet them.

The men in the longboat, operating some kind of motor, guided the craft to the shore, where they drew it up on the beach a little, so their leader could step out. This was an individual who was dressed neatly and impressively in pants, a stiff gray tunic with a roman collar, and a soft cape which waved in the wind. He alighted on the sand, placing his feet carefully so as not to wet his boots, and observed Phaedrus.

The stranger announced, "I am Casio Salkim, Acting Viceroy of the Southern Expeditionary Flotilla."

A reply seemed proper, so Phaedrus said, "I am Phaedrus. I live here."

Salkim shook his head, as if to clear cobwebs away, and said, "You are the one they call Fedro, or Feydro?"

Phaedrus nodded. "Probably the same." Phaedrus had to admit that the visitor was impressive. A relatively young man, with clean hands and trimmed hair and beard, he set an elegant contrast to Phaedrus, who was clean and healthy, but more than a little ragged. He added, "What hospitality may we offer you?"

Salkim chuckled. "Offer me? No, no, my man, it is I who offer you."

"How so?"

"We are from the principality of Clisp. Marisol, in fact," he added, for emphasis. "In a short and I trust not rude way, let me say that we have come along this empty and barbarous coast looking for you. In Marisol there is little talk of anything else. A place on the south coast in Far Zolotane where people get their heads screwed on right again. Again, to be short about it, Pompeo is and has been prince, and rules and reigns with the common good in mind, and seeks to heal the wounds the land and its people have sustained. To this end, he has done the usual things princes do, but my prince also understands that a peace of swords and guns is not complete without the peace of the heart, and the tales have it that this is only to be reliably found here, and so I was commissioned to come out, seek this 'Fedro' out, and invite him and his family and friends to come to Marisol, in Clisp, and thereby take up employment and assignment as Worthy Advisor to Pompeo IV." It was a long speech, but he added, sagaciously, "It is not a bad thing, especially if you've been living close to the edge."

Phaedrus sat down abruptly on the sand, laughing so hard the tears came to his eyes. After a moment, he came back to his senses, and regained his feet, and, chuckling, explained to the mystified Salkim: "Your pardon. In the wild lands we have no manners. We have quite forgotten them. Listen: Here is not the place to make decisions, but here, I say, we here neither fear nor hate Clisp, nor its Prince, and we welcome his rule as an alternative to chaos and warlords and random bandits. A fine idea, that the west recovers. In fact, the sooner the better. But I have had little to do with it."

Salkim was not visibly moved, and he continued, "No, to the contrary! There is much you have done here. We do not know what doctrines or orthodoxies you espouse, but however they are they seem to work."

Phaedrus said, seriously and intently, "You do not know how little I have done that I think you speak of. On the other hand, there has been too much, that others know little of indeed. But this is a simple place, and I and my friend, Meliosme, do not rule, nor reign. We maintain a holding where the peaceable are free to come and go, and gather their wits, after having their worlds turned upside down."

Salkim stroked his elegant chain. "I see. Then you claim no lordship."

"None."

"I would imagine that equally you acknowledge none?"

"So far, that is an accurate representation."

"Hm. Well, now consider: This part of the mainland was always one of the worst places; most uncivilized, even in the times before. This area was most stringently watched and guarded against. Not against armies, or sorties, but against bandits and anarchists. And then the tales change. People began coming to the new world with no longer broken spirits, but ready to . . . do things, set things right. This is no mean accomplishment. But it affects the progress of another work—which is the consolidation of the west. We no longer have to watch this area, and so the Prince finds his task easy. He is grateful, but being a prince, he also wonders what sort of person could do this?"

Phaedrus interjected, "I make no claim to ambition—least of all to rule."

"You have none?"

"None. I do not wish to affect events. I wish solitude, obscurity, I desire only to . . . uncover who and what I am."

Salkim observed, "Many never answer that riddle, and many more never learn to ask the question, more's the pity."

"You see far; I understand why you represent Pompeo IV."

"Yes. Thank you." Salkim inclined his head, a slight bow, and an acknowledgment. "And so, I am commissioned to find out what is here, in the wilds of Zolotane, and you cannot imagine what kinds of men have passed through my imagination."

"I can. I know that way well. I do not seek it now."

". . . And I find someone who only wants to be left alone. Well, *that* won't be completely possible, as I'm sure you understand, but that does put a different cast on things. We shall not have difficulties after all."

"I have none in mind."

"Nor do I."

"You may remain with us if you wish."

"For a little time."

"A little time. All are welcome; so long as they do not rob and murder."

"None of that. The people have come to us for peace and order, and we feel honor-bound to lead them to it, not more of what they have left behind."

Phaedrus said, "I fear you will learn little of use to princes; we are trying to let go of things, not gather them. Also, this is not the city. There are only a few comforts here, and one had to grow accustomed to them."

"No matter! I will endure it. And while I am here, I will try to persuade you to come with us, despite your modesty."

Phaedrus looked at the splendid Salkim sidelong. "How much of this 'persuasion' is to be words and discourse, and how much . . . another kind of speech, however politely dressed?"

Salkim waved his arms airily. "All reasoning. Why refer to force when one can use it first and be done with arguments over 'who shot Janno first?' No, and no again. Understand me. I did not come to carry you off: you would then be worthless for the position offered, and also that would remove a valuable source of stability here on the southeast flank of Clisp."

They climbed up the steep bank fronting the now gentle waves of the ocean and laboriously reached the top, where Salkim saw the settlement spread out before him. Not impressive, not even a proper town, but a random collation of shanties, lean-tos, sheds made from scraps of broken ships that had been something else before that. Smoke from cooking fires rose in the air, and in the now-late afternoon, a soft golden light was falling slantwise out of the west. He looked again, and shook his head in disbelief.

Someone volunteered to carry some food down to the sailors waiting on the beach, and a few gathered up things, seemingly without instruction or orders, and departed shyly to perform their errand.

Dark fell, a meal was served, and Salkim was made to feel an honored guest. Meliosme observed, as they sat around a fire after eating, "You are the first visitor we have had bearing any sort of order from the civilized world."

Salkim nodded. "I am not surprised. True, there was little

209

conflict in Clisp, but there were hard times, refugees, tense moments along the frontiers." He breathed ~~deeply~~. "We long chafed under the yoke of The Rectification. Clisp was settled not by The Changeless, but by those who fled from them. And so when things started falling apart on the mainland, we were slow to react. And with good reason, for many of our finest had gone to feed the ranks of the Troopers." He looked bitter for a moment, and then brightened. "But we had no great war, at home. Everyone seemed to feel at one time that the will was gone out of it, and so there was a rising in Marisol, some scuffles, and suddenly it was over. But of course, we are just now starting to reach out."

Phaedrus asked, "Is it the intent of this new-resurgent land to unite the land again?"

"No. At least, not for the moment. Some say we should, but I think they have not thought of the costs of such a venture. No, we do not fear difference."

Phaedrus said, "You spoke of persuasion . . . but you need to know that we are only holding this together here until those who have come can hold it themselves."

"I saw that. I understood. That is why I have said no more. I see that you are encouraging here what we hoped to save in Clisp—that people would do for themselves, left alone. We prefer a prince, that all can see, but I can see your way too. Fine. But it seems a shame. . . ."

"No shame. I repay a debt, in the part that I can repay."

"Are you done?"

"No . . . Meliosme tells me I will never be done, and so that is so; but I have neared the point where I can let go. We will do so."

"To say I wished you well would be an excess, nevertheless have it so."

"It is well that you say it. Thank you."

Salkim gathered himself to his feet. "Time to return."

Meliosme said, "You will not stay?"

"No. This is tempting, but it is not for me. I have another life to follow. And of course, orders. We have other business along the coasts. . . ." He trailed the words off mysteriously.

Meliosme asked, "Marula?"

"Farther."

She said, "The Pilontaries?"

"So far. We want to make contacts with the outlying new regimes, to find out . . . Crule is an inland place with inland thinking, and they will be slow to realize, although they are trying to hold Marula."

"Can they hold it?"

Salkim said thoughtfully, "They are destroying it in order to save it, if you can make sense out of that. It is already useless as a port. But we will go by there, and lob a few bombs onto them, and see if we can make it more difficult for them. Pompeo wants them kept defensive. Besides, there's a rumor afoot about other things. . . ."

Phaedrus said, "Something from Tartary?"

"By the gods, no. They are still fighting each other out there, and welcome them to it, bust hell loose! No, it's from farther off: there's talk from the innerlands that one of the ships is coming back."

Phaedrus felt an odd feeling, a presentiment. He asked, "Someone has . . . seen?"

"Not so I hear it. No, we've not seen anything, although Pompeo has a crowd of technicians madly working on something that will work. No. This is from talk we've picked up, from traders, spies, refugees. They say 'The Ship's coming back, to pick up some people it left behind.' "

Phaedrus mused, "To pick them up . . . odd. I thought they'd never risk it."

"Odd to me, too. We heard there were offworlders here, spying and the like."

Phaedrus grimaced. "More than that. But their time is over, and we need not waste words or deeds on them. I would urge Pompeo to let them go."

Salkim agreed. "Such are my thoughts as well. But all the same, we'd like to keep an eye on things, although I don't know what we'd do if they wanted to fight."

"Believe me. That is the last thing they want. Although they will undoubtedly have weapons if some hothead shoots at them."

Salkim chuckled. "Have no fears on that score! We probably don't have anything strong enough to even reach them. Well, Good night to you all."

Meliosme said, "We can send someone. . . ."

"No matter. I can find the way. And have no fears from us." He strode to the edge of the darkness, near the banks, and waved once at them, and then disappeared into the night. After a time, they heard some small sounds of a boat moving off the beach, strange calls over the water, and after that, a

211

distant throbbing from the ship, and then all was quiet again for a time, until the bosels of the south coast began commenting on the events of the day, their calls echoing back and forth up and down the coast, and also from far inland.

Pternam had been sleeping, and now he was awake. He had to stop for a minute and consider where he was . . . Corytinupol, was it, in the center of Crule the Swale, which was now calling itself Lisagor? Yes. Corytinupol. A dreadful back-country barrack-town, without beauty or flavor, peopled by fanatics, doctrine-quoting idiots and hairsplitters whose existence he had been mercifully shielded from in Symbarupol. Yes. They had been much on the move, first this place, then that one, sometimes uneasy guests who were not entirely sure they were not hostages.

Before they had left Symbarupol, Arunda Palude had gotten contact with the ship that was coming for whomever it could salvage, but they had soon lost that contact, with the abandonment of the city to the barbarians. All over, all dignity lost, thrown away. He understood with an old skill at perception of the situation which had not left him, that his own situation had changed to something new and terrible: he was in fact completely dependent on the mercy or charity of these offworld spies, who either now ignored him (rightly so: Pternam now had no more influence than a sack of meal) or condescended to issue orders to him, none too politely. Avaria had vanished long ago, making his escape, trusting to his own wit rather than to the offworlders, who were now showing their true character, an immiscible blend of professional academic competence and the grimiest sort of treasonous espionage.

Well, give them credit, he thought. They recklessly bartered offworld technology to the stern and unbending fanatics of Crule, to buy time, and this had in fact saved the situation from total disaster. Crule managed to survive, and to hold off further disintegration. In fact, they had even made gains, mostly eastward into Puropaigne, The Innerlands. What was left of Symbarupol they had recovered, but it wasn't worth returning to. Nothing was in this world that he wanted to return to, unless he could personally wring Rael's neck, which was doubtful, even if he could have found him, which the offworlders refused even to bother with.

A squat, totally bald man thrust his head into Pternam's

cubicle and glanced about for a moment with a look of icy contempt. He growled, "Pternam? You awake?"

"Yes. I heard some noise outside, I think."

"Right. Get your things. It's time to go."

"We're moving again?"

"The last time. We're the last pickup. We'll have to walk it for a bit, out of town, you know; the elders don't want their people contaminated by seeing a spaceship, even if it's only an exploratory lighter." This was the brutal and effective Cesar Kham, who had gradually taken control of the offworlders from the temporary leadership of Porfirio Charodei.

Kham chuckled to himself. "They would just as soon shoot us as not, but in the final step, they'd rather be rid of us, as if being rid of us could stem what your own people set in motion here."

Pternam got up and began gathering a few things. "I don't imagine I'll need much."

"No."

"You are taking me with you?"

"Are you worried we'd sell you to Crule? No chance. You've seen too much now. You have to go, like it or not. Leaving you here would upset things more than the revolution did. Without you, it's just a bad dream for them. . . . They'll wake up in a year or so and find out the reality's worse, but never mind that. . . ."

"You don't think they can win here?"

"No." That was the way with Kham. Cutting, direct. No. No qualifiers, no modifiers. "No." Kham explained, "I can't fault their theology; they have that down pat; but there's no future in the economics. They can't hold Marula, and without it they have no access to the ocean. They have the center of the continent, but everyone can just sail around them—that's the trouble with living on an island, however big it is. The lords of Tartary are encouraging that, of course."

"You foresee a two-continent world united against Crule?"

"No. Nothing like that. You're in for a long period of contending states and mini-states, but you'll have more world trade. Crule itself isn't worth the trouble. They'll wither in time, and go out."

Pternam rubbed his eyes, and unsteadily walked to the door. The corridor outside was almost empty, now. Pternam mused, aloud, "I often wonder why you stuck with Symbarupol and Crule to the end."

213

"How so?"

"I am certain from what I know of you that a state such as Clisp would be more to your liking."

"As a place to live and work? Of course! But then you have to understand also that however attractive it may be, it is of course terribly backward. I have a colleague who has made a life's work of studying the principalities of the Renaissance on Old Earth; an expert, one may say, I think the best in his field. But you can bet you wouldn't find him in fourteenth-century Florence, or anything like it. One is always a historian at a distance. Remember that. They would make short work of us in Clisp, you may be sure. In fact, that prince who is running things there openly has posted a reward for any one of us, unharmed. . . . None have taken him up on it. All the people who have decided to go native here have already gone, and you may be certain they'll stay that way."

"I heard some talk. Did you lose many people here?"

"Some." Kham did not elaborate on the single word, which led Pternam to believe that their losses had been severe. He imagined this was so, ironically enough, since the offworlders had not brought down Lisagor, but had supported it, in fact, they had been its strongest pillar. But all of that was gone, now, and hardly mattered.

Kham conducted him outside, where the party was assembling, some afoot, some piling a few things onto draywagons, with the elders of Crule looking on from the sidelines, displaying no emotions. Pternam glanced around the windy darkness and asked, "What wagon do I go on?"

Kham started off on some errand, and looked back, at Pternam's question, and barked, "You walk. Get going." It was rude, especially if one recalled Pternam's former status, but again, now that did not matter greatly either.

Pternam had gradually learned the habit of blanking his mind during the unpleasant parts; of fading out in doing mindlessly, and the dull routines were soon over. This was such an instance. He set out walking into the darkness and concentrated only on keeping up with the rest of the party. He did not look around, or try to see anything of what he was passing through. Only walking, and the dark. Soon the onlookers grew less, and then the lights of the town, and then the buildings, and they were in the open, out in the open and naked grasslands of Crule the Swale, trudging along a pale dirt road that arrowed off into the darkness.

He tried to listen for scraps of what the others might be saying, but they said little that he could hear, although a low and continuous murmur floated above the line of walkers and drays. Nothing in the speech of Lisagor, at any rate. All foreign gibberish. Of course, they would now have no pretense to speak as if they were natives here. He listened to the fragments of the speech: short, clipped, terse, all the words seeming to end on consonants, and all those short and crisp. The vowels were short and rather high in tone. He listened to the whispers and low murmurs about him and he thought that it would be a language he would not speak well, nor would he feel comfortable with such speech, no matter how familiar he became with it. It was not a speech of ceremony and tradition and reassuring identity and place, but a speech of contention, of strife, however well-mannered and controlled, and above all of ceaseless change. But of course that was the way of wherever they had come from.

He often thought of that: Neither Charodei nor Kham had deigned to tell him anything about the world they were going to. When he had asked, the answers had been vague generalities which were completely devoid of informational content. He had not managed to determine if the planet where they were going had a name or not. Or if they were going to a single place; or if they were even going to a planet at all, but perhaps to some unimaginable construction in the void between the worlds, an artificial world. He had heard fleeting allusions to such places, which seemed to have been made for special purposes.

Nor did he know much more about the ship, except that it was too large to land on a planetary surface. Smaller craft, called "lighters" were carried inside it, and served as the landing craft. This was what they were walking out to board, apparently, although again, he was not sure what he was looking for. He belonged to a country of people who had not wanted space flight, and who had rapidly forgotten as fast as they could. Aircraft they had and understood, although their use was severely controlled, and little or no experimental work was done. Somehow, he could not equate spacecraft with aircraft.

Now they were far from the town, and somewhere ahead on the dim, almost-invisible plain ahead, there was a weak light glowing, a pale yellow light that did not waver. The group apparently also saw this light, for the speed and amount of conversation increased, as well as the pace. Pternam noticed that some of the people were now casting things aside as they went, pieces of clothing, odds and ends, mementoes which suddenly seemed less valuable, books and papers they would never need again, as if the actual sight of the lighter reminded them that their time here was over, that they were refugees who would soon be returned to their own. He was one with the group, and yet he felt the alienness of the thought. He was not particularly anxious to leave, and yet in the crowd, he caught the overlay of it from them.

Presently they drew near to something which he assumed was the lighter, a vague structure bulking large in the dark, mysterious, amorphous. He sensed an immense mass, squat and unlovely, resting on a forest of metallic pillars. As they walked under it, he could feel heat from the body poised above him, odd, pungent mechanical odors he did not recognize assaulted his nose. There were sounds of mechanical movements, odd snatches of voices, harsh commands being given and acknowledged.

The group slowed, and Pternam, looking around, saw a rough line forming at the foot of something that looked like a metal stair extending out of the center of the ship. People walked up to a booth alongside the foot of the stair, spoke somewhat, and proceeded up the stairs, most throwing a few more things away as they went. He felt like shouting at them, *Fools! You are throwing away the life-fragments of a whole world!*

The line proceeded at a good pace. No one was excluded, or so it appeared, even questioned much. A short conversation, and then up the stair. Now it bothered him what he might say to whatever was in the booth, whether man, alien, or machine. What speech did it use? He began looking about in concern for someone he knew, and after a moment, caught sight of the bald and shiny cranium of Cesar Kham, who stepped up to the booth smartly, spoke somewhat, and bounded up the steps, taking them two at a time. Pternam looked around in dismay, looking for anyone else he knew, Charodei, Palude, some of the others he had met. None. He was now in the midst of strangers.

Much too soon, he stood at the foot of the stair, which he saw to be indeed metal although it was finished a uniform

216

dull black. The booth contained a single opening whose nature was not apparent, as the opening did not seem to open to anything. Inside, there was simply a formless darkness from which a voice, clipped and peremptory, presently inquired, "Teilisk gak?"

Pternam answered, "I am Luto Pternam, invited guest of men who called themselves here Porfirio Charodei and Cesar Kham. Also Arunda Palude. They brought me here, so I assume to enter."

There was a long pause, during which Pternam could feel the intent stares of those behind him yet in line. He dared not look around, but somehow he felt a prickly sensation along his lower back that he had committed some dreadful breach. After a moment, something inside the darkness of the booth said, "Dilik. Mek Angren." Pause. Then, in his own language, it said, "Wait to the side for the others to pass. Then enter."

It was then, as he stood aside, that he seriously questioned the wisdom of continuing on this course, which he now realized had been as fixed as the course of the stars in the heavens. Now, something shyly whispered to the darkness of his soul, *"You can walk away from here a free man, with no enemies and no obligations."*

The old Pternam asked the new, *"Everything I have burned behind me. Where would I go?"*

The new answered, *"Away, somewhere else. Walk off. No one will stop you. These folk don't care and they don't want you. The elders of Crule think you went in the ship, and so they will say. Get dirty and ragged, and walk into a settled place, and you can get off free."*

Several people passed through the line in rapid succession, and the line of those waiting grew visibly shorter. Pternam answered the questioner inside himself, *"A bargain has been made. They will give me honor; at least they will have a native of this world to speak with. I have value. I was somebody, and I can be so again."*

The voice replied, *"You were a minor functionary with a criminal ambition and your acts loosed Change on this world. Besides, they have had years to bore into Oerlikon like worms. They manifestly do not need you."* The last few people waiting to speak into the booth passed, and Pternam was alone.

He looked around. There were dim lights under the ship,

217

and shadows around the many legs of the craft. Somewhere, something vented off, releasing a soft plume of steam. Overhead, the bulk of the craft was quiet. Waiting.

The booth chirruped to itself, a sound impossible to interpret, and then said, plainly, "Enter the ship without delay. We are holding departure for you."

Pternam looked around once more, and all he could see were the landing-legs, the booth, and the metal stairs going up into some dark orifice. Beyond the circle of dim light there was nothing but the endless night of Crule the Swale, a nothingness. He gripped the rail and mounted the stairs.

At the top of the stairs was a dim cubicle, apparently a landing, which he stepped into, and as he did he heard mechanical noises from behind him, motion. The stairs were lifting up, pivoting back into a recess in the hull. A panel slid shut behind him. Ahead was another corridor, ascending ramplike to some other part of the ship. There was a faint metallic odor in the air. He walked up this ramp until he came to another chamber, which he entered without hesitating. Here, too, a panel slid shut behind him. He felt a motion, a small surge of acceleration, and then nothing more.

He wondered what this room was for. Was he being examined by the unknowable medical sciences of the star-folk? Presumably they would not wish him to mingle with the others just yet. He waited for what seemed like a long time. Nothing happened. The air did not seem stale, although he could hear no sound of ventilation. There was another motion, as if of metal sliding on metal, although he could not say exactly how the motion was being done, or in what direction. After a time, this too stopped. Then, for a longer time, again, nothing happened. Finally, he spoke. "Let me speak with Porfirio Charodei! With Cesar Kham! I am Luto Pternam! I made this escape possible!"

There was a sharp grating sound, and instantly Pternam was flung *outside* by a convusion of the chamber, into naked space. His eyes bulged, a band of iron seized his chest, and his blood boiled, and before him he saw the dark nightside bulk of an immense round object, spattered with points of light. He rotated, and saw, not understanding, a smaller bulk moving away from him, visibly getting smaller. Then the darkness.

The community which had grown around Phaedrus and

Meliosme did not have a name. In a sense, it was not a settlement, or a town, or even a camp, considering each of those things just one of many towns, settlements, camps that could be, *were*. This was unique. A single place, the only one for those who had stopped there on their flight from the furies. It was simply home.

But the visit of an emissary from the new world that was growing somehow upset a delicate balance that had existed for them. It was true, and none disputed it, that Salkim's visit had implied no threats; indeed, he had gone out of his way to insure there were none given, and none taken. Yet it made them aware, and awareness was loss of a kind of innocence they all had thought they had regained. And so not long after the visit, there began to be talk about seeing to things, and having a little more of a sense of organization. Factions, weak and tentative, began to emerge. Some desired alliance with Clisp. Others argued for independence, so long as it might last. Still others, just to cover all possibilities, wanted to at least send an emissary to Crule to see what was going on.

Late at night, Phaedrus and Meliosme sat on the packed earthen floor on grass mats and spoke of the change. Meliosme let one of the smaller urchins use her lap for a pillow, and after stroking the child's head and gazing into the fire, she said, "Politics has caught up with us, so I hear."

"Yes. I have heard, too."

"Our original intent was to find a place of solitude and leave all that."

"For a time we had it. But it seems there is little enough of the wild left on this planet."

"The gatherers will not be able yet to wander over the face of the world the way we used to."

"True. I would not wish to go back into the east."

"What do you have in mind to do with this?"

"Little or nothing. I do not wish to rule these people; they manage well enough on their own, once they had a place where they could stop and think."

"But you could still keep this place as it was."

"By rule? Never. Circumstances change, so it seems to me; it can never be the way it was again. They would like it at first—I know that. But in time that model wouldn't agree with the real world, and there'd be resistance, and then the strife would start."

"Phaedrus, you could pick a line of thinking and stay with it, here. They trust you, and now you trust yourself."

"As I trust myself, so I must trust them to find their own way, whatever it is."

"What would you favor, were you deciding for them?"

"Clisp, of course; they need protection from forays from over the hills. They aren't much of a barrier. It wouldn't work the other way, allying with Crule against Clisp. That goes against everything these people ran from. No—it would be Clisp. Not that I don't have my objections to that, too, but it would have to do."

"Then say so. They will follow you."

"No. Control breeds the need for more control. And in freeing myself from power, I have freed myself from wanting power over others. I would become the slave of the force I used, worse than them. No. I know the way I go. You helped show it to me, and I will keep on that way. Less, not more. Obscurity, not fame. . . ."

She showed no sign of agreement or disagreement, but continued looking at the fire and absentmindedly stroking the child's hair. At last she said, "They are meeting tonight. They want to reward us for what we have done for them."

He nodded. "I know. Well, this place has grown, and it is time we had some sort of leader, isn't it? That is simple enough. Here we have no lord, but we need one. We will tell them, choose one among you who will lead. Not me." He got to his feet wearily. "Even this much I wish I could avoid."

Meliosme said, "I would take it, but I want it no more than you. . . . I miss the old freedoms."

"They are gone in the new world, but we still have a few left within ourselves."

"You say we could be so anywhere."

"More or less."

"And what then?"

"I think that we have done something here; but whatever it was, our part in it has faded, and now it's time to go further. I've rested, and been healed of some madnesses; and so I'd go on to find the rest of it."

"Where? You yourself said there was no wild left."

"Clisp. Would you walk with me there?"

She did not hesitate. "I have walked with you since then, a long time ago. I would not change now. What would we do there?"

"Just be, that's all. Struggle, suffer. Do what we could."

Meliosme smiled, an expression that always illuminated her

220

plain face with a warm glow. She said, "Well, I was not destined to be a great lady anyway . . . I will go with you. What about the children?"

"They are all our children, and then none. Let those who would come, come. And those who would stay, stay."

She gently disengaged herself from the child, and stood up to join him. "Very well. So it will be. And now we will tell them."

"Yes."

"You know that will be a novel idea to them. Me, too. Choosing—there's an idea."

"It won't cure the flaw we all have in us, but it cools it down a lot. It's hard to imagine yourself a savior when everybody knows you're a bosel's arse, and in fact you know it, too."

They stepped outside, into the night, which was filled up with the sound of the sea and the gentle winds in the grass, and from far off they could also hear distant calls of bosels, uninterested, remote.

They went together to the place among the huts and sheds where the others had assembled, and when Phaedrus came, they all stood up, remembering some of their manners from the older days, and already having decided in their minds that he was to be their lord, since he was here before them; but he asked that they but hear him once, and when they sat and listened, he told them what they should do. At first, they resisted the idea, but after a little time had passed, some of them understood enough of it to see what they should do, and presently, those who were so minded stood up and spoke of what they should do, and sometime later, a rough agreement was reached that a certain Olenzo, formerly of Near Priboy, seemed to have the best head for that sort of thing, and so was chosen leader, subject to recall.

But before that, Phaedrus and Meliosme had slipped away, and made their way back, through the dark, to their house, where they gathered a few simple things, as if they were leaving then, not waiting for the dawn.

She said, "You'd not wait for the morning?"

"No. Even that. I can do the most for these people by leaving now. In the morning, they will have regrets, questions, referrals."

Two of the orphans wanted to leave with them, and so

221

they took some extra things for them, too, so that in the end they wound up carrying more than they had planned, but their burdens were not heavy. Phaedrus stepped out into the night again, and looked out over the water, to the west. He sighed, deeply. And turned and said, "Yes. This is the right way."

Something moving in the sky caught at the edge of his awareness, and he looked up. In the sky was a falling star, a meteor, but not the quick little flicker of the usual meteor; this one was slow, tumbling and burning, red and orange, and at last it went out, drifting off toward the east. He continued looking at the night sky, at the few stars he could see, the unremarkable stars of the sky of Oerlikon. And he thought he saw, a little to the east, a point of light moving, dimming as it went.

Meliosme was watching, too. After a time, she said, "There was something up there."

Phaedrus nodded. "Yes. Ever seen anything moving in the night sky before?"

"A long time ago, once. Like that. I didn't know then what it was. Now I think I know."

"Lights in the sky. Ships. Something fell out of that one."

"Or something was dumped that wouldn't fit. They must have been crowded. We would never find it."

He agreed. "No. Useless to look. I suppose we won't see any more of those for awhile . . . and when we do, they'll come openly. Come on."

And so they walked quietly down to the beach, and began walking northward, and after a long time, they found some shelter in the rocks back from the water and rested for the night.

In easy stages, then, Phaedrus and Meliosme made their way northward along the coast of Zolotane, and after many days they came to a shallow river, in a flat land where the hill country had receded back over the horizons. But ahead, across the river, were more rugged mountains, trailing off to the southwest. The Serpentine. There they joined a group of other pilgrims, as ragged and undistinguished as they were, and with them, they went across the river on a causeway which had been built, so Meliosme informed him, since the Troubles.

Their way down the length of the Serpentine was even slower. They would stop. Work for a while, and drift on, slowing down as they went. And at last they reached the outskirts of the great city Marisol, that stood on a high plain with the sea to the north and mountains to the south, a place of sun and light and people rushing everywhere, and after a time Phaedrus found a place as a gardener in one of the immense public parks that they were fond of in Clisp, and they found a modest place to live, and to their surprise, no one troubled them, and their lives settled into a routine.

Marisol, being exposed to the northern winds off the ocean, had more obvious seasons that Phaedrus could remember, and he lived through two more of the rainy winters. One night, late, as the wind blustered and fussed around the corners of the stone house where they lived, and the rain runoff was brawling in the downspouts and street gutters, Meliosme asked him, quite out of nowhere, "Do you ever have regrets that you gave up the power you had?"

He looked up and at her for a long time, still surprised that for all her plain looks and wandering origins, she was still perceptive enough to awaken him to his deepest thoughts. He said, "Yes, sometimes. You can't forget, and you'd love to tamper. But you dare not. Just once, and it would start all over again. No. There has been enough suffering."

"You told me how you could find the one person, who, obscure and unknown, was the support of the world."

"Yes. I could do that. I have not done it for years. I have not wanted to know."

"Would it be safe to look now?"

Phaedrus sat back and looked at her attentively. "I suppose I could, if I can remember all the routines, the formulae, the operations. Remember it used a system of logic that doesn't agree with the usual one people steer their lives by."

"Do it. See if you can get an answer now."

There was an impish smile on her face, as if she knew something. Phaedrus got up from his chair and went looking about for a piece of paper, and a pen. After a time, he found one, and began, slowly and uncertainly at first, but with growing assurance, as the routines came back to him from their long disuse. He began building the logical framework, and then the inputs, using the symbolism they had forcefed him in another age, so it seemed, and then it began working easily, and he asked for more paper, feeling the flow smoothing, and at last he was forming the symbols in the system for the conclusion of the operation, and it was clear what the Answer was, as he filled in the last line that completed the whole. The pivotal person of this new world was himself. He looked up at Meliosme. He said, unsteadily, "It's me."

Meliosme, smiling still, nodded, and gave him a quick hug, and said, "Knew it."